Paved with Gold

Paved with Gold is the story of a love affair, set
in post-war London. Tom Stanton first sees
Carole Brockett in a dance-hall and senses
that she is out of her element. And when he
discovers that her background is very similar
to his own, and that she has transformed herself by going to university, he is even more impressed. But coincidence, in the persons of
Tom's and Carole's respective employers,
intervenes: when Thorpley, an unscrupulous
property dealer, becomes interested in the
business owned by Sir Henry, an industrialist
of the old school, the young couple's love is
put to an unexpected test.

DAVE WALLIS

Paved with Gold

HEINEMANN

LONDON MELBOURNE TORONTO

William Heinemann Ltd
LONDON MELBOURNE TORONTO
CAPE TOWN AUCKLAND
THE HAGUE

First published 1959

© by DAVE WALLIS 1960
All rights reserved

Printed in Great Britain
by The Windmill Press Ltd
Kingswood, Surrey

Contents

CHAPTER I

Blow you, Jack

It was a smashing Lovat-cloth suit from Monty's. Made to measure, or, at any rate, took in here and there as good as. The specks of red in it showed up lovely under the lights on the dance floor. It fitted Tom Stanton well. Something there to hang it on.

He had seen her once or twice during the evening, with a crowd of slightly posh types, mostly younger than herself. She was dark and her green dress flashed and vanished again all over the floor. Her gang started a jiving session of their own in the corner and then, through the smoke and the dust from the white stuff on the floor, he could see her arguing with the M.C. He caught her eye and, although she was still talking, he could tell she picked it up all right.

It got late and if he was going to dance with her he'd better start making a move. They dimmed the lights. The door to the bar swung open as the manager cajoled away the lads who were spinning out their last drinks. The smell of spilt beer mixed with the hot, sweet scent of woman sweat. Loud voices burst from the bar-room doorway. The rattle of collapsible chairs and the chatter and laughter hid the noise of the band so that you could only make out a thumping noise like tom-toms. She'd be fixed up with someone to take her home by this time. Oh well, plenty more fish in the sea. Then she swung past him and he asked to cut in. The bloke with her was some jive-hound in a polo-neck, and although he blinked a bit he just danced off by himself and soon found another girl.

No time to waste. Already the band was hotting it up,

I

getting ready for the final swirl and swing. "Can I give you a lift home? I've got the car outside." Better get it in quick about the car. You might think that the best time would be in a moment when the last dance ended in a spin and you looked at each other and grinned even if you had never met before. But with a strange girl you did not know if she might not turn away straight afterwards and go and get her coat and find her girl friend. If you went trailing after her and mumbled something about a car it was a dead cert way of getting the brush. Saying 'the car' sounded quite posh, and if it came out later about its being the firm's car it didn't matter so much, because you had not actually lied. Anyway girls never asked. One or two, as you were starting up, said something about its being a nice car and "Is it your own?" but no girl he had ever met asked straight away. It wouldn't be polite and why should she care, at least at first, anyway?

"I suppose it's your firm's, is it?" said the dark girl, leaning back lightly in his arms and looking up at him.

He was furious with himself to feel that he had reddened slightly and that his jaw had fallen a trifle. He thrust her into the next step with a trace of anger and felt her slender weight against the inside of his arm. "Yes, it's the firm's. At least it's ours. I mean I'm sort of one of the partners." He'd done it all wrong but at least he had the sense to shut up now and not go on and make it worse.

She seemed to get shot of her friends without long explanations. He couldn't place her crowd, quite. That helped to make her more interesting. He had known she had something special as soon as he'd seen her. And here she was in the car. If a girl agreed to get in the car with you it didn't mean she was a pushover, but you might get a kiss and a good feel round, or even the lot. It all depended on things you didn't know yet. If you settled for one of the dead certs there was no thrill about it all, and if one of the blokes saw you leaving with her you'd have your leg pulled the next Saturday; but if it was with some smasher that had maybe turned down one or two of the others in the past, then it was your turn to boast.

"Where to?" he asked, making it sound light and adventurous as if neither of them were sure. She told him a street he'd never heard of in Paddington.

"Get to the bottom of the Edgware Road," she said, "and I'll tell you when to turn off."

His mind went over quite a long series of deductions and estimates, and then he said, "You in digs?"

"Yes," she said. And then added, "I suppose you live at home."

Well, at least she hadn't said '*still* at home', but all the same it was scoring one on him, teasing him. Trying to make him feel like a kid, younger than she was. If he could get her going, if not tonight, then next time, and get it in, by Christ he'd show her!

This was just kidding himself. Somehow he knew this one was going to be a flop. All the same there was nothing to do but keep trying. If he didn't she would think there was something wrong with him. Perhaps he could stop somewhere down the Bayswater Road and get her to slip into the Park with him. There was not a lot you do in a car up West, not like further out where there were always quiet lanes with no houses, near some gasworks, railway sidings or allotments.

When she told him to turn off he pulled into the kerb and turned to grin at her. This was one of the most exciting times really, when you didn't know how it would end or even how it would go on. When he bent to kiss her she said, "Yes, I suppose so." The only other girl who'd ever had that attitude had never said a word and even after she was letting you go the whole way she had still kept as dead as a log. It had been like fooling around with a dress-shop dummy. It turned out, later, she'd been thinking of someone else all the time. This one wasn't a bit like that. After she'd said it she put both arms over his shoulders and twisted about in the seat.

Outside her place she answered him before he asked. "You can't come in. I've only got a room and a gas-ring. There's the landlady and people."

"See you again?"

"Perhaps there next Saturday."

"O.K.," and he drove home slowly, cooling off. Before he got in, the ache started. His mother had left a cup with some sugar in it and a saucepan of cocoa ready to be heated up on the gas. He left it and went up to bed. For some reason he was still tasting her kiss. In a strange way, not like other times, after other girls.

A busy week had followed and he had had a dodgy bit of bumping to bring off. The first time the others had trusted him with it alone, so of course he had to make a go of it.

There'd been so much chasing about that he'd hardly been able to think of her or look forward to Saturday and he'd had to leave over the insurance book round until late Saturday afternoon.

Two days a week he cycled round on his own bike collecting the premiums on the insurance book he had bought. The other days he drove round in the car, not his own, on business for the small house-agents' concern of which he was the junior salesman. The agency brought in commission and ex'es only and the book a certain amount of new business. Tom meant to get on.

Old Thorpley, the former master-builder who owned the agency, Speedy Homefinders Ltd., had given him the gen on 'bumping' a long time ago—when he was still a lad but had already shown that he had it in the noddle. He could remember the day Thorpley told him to meet him in the Lord Roberts at dinner-time. He sat on a stool at the snack-bar end of the saloon. Behind him the heavy doors of the billiard hall were open and some men in shirt-sleeves were spending their dinner-hour moving in the dark shadows close to the high, leather-covered benches and leaning out over the green baize into the light from the low-slung, shaded lamps. It made him think of the tropical fish tank he'd had as a kid.

"Mary, a drink for our young friend," said old Thorpley. The barmaid drew him a half of mild, bending over the pump so that the parting showed up dark across the tarnished brass of her hair. When she brought the drink Thorpley said, "Here, have one with me, Mary, after the bar closes." He slid over a half-crown above the price.

"Thank you, sir, I'm sure," said Mary. She went to the other end of the bar to serve.

"Now there's something else you've learnt, boy. How to tip a barmaid. If she's been looking after you well the whole evening, perhaps, and you want to tip her. Well, if you say 'Have a drink' she most likely'll have to say 'No'. Not many houses allow it now. Not like the old days. So you say, 'Have one with me later.' Then it's hers to do what she likes with, see?"

For the rest of the time he kept breaking off in his explanations to talk to Mary and to try and needle her.

Whenever another customer came near he would change the subject and then start including Mary in their conversation, even if he had to shout down the length of the bar. It was a bit embarrassing, but the feeling of being with the man who was one of the best spenders in the place, and knew the governor of it, made up for that.

"Now listen, Tom," said Thorpley, taking a bite of his ham sandwich, "and I'll explain something to you. You know this sale that's just gone through at Planetree Road? Those lousy little terrace houses shouldn't go for more than seventeen hundred." He suddenly stopped munching and slewed his huge jaw and face round close to Tom. It made you think of an excavator bucket about to take a new scoop. "How much did it go for, Tom?" he snapped. It was like mental arithmetic with Miss Brown when he was a kid. But he knew the answer,

"Nineteen hundred and the seller to meet all legal charges," said Tom.

"You've got the right answer, boy, and yet you're wrong!" He looked pleased with himself. He had raised his voice rather dramatically, and a man at the bar glanced up and then pretended to be very interested in his drink. "This lad knows all the answers, Mary. You'll have to watch him." Mary drifted up to their end of the counter again.

He started to needle her, to try and needle them both, but the girl most of all. "A fine young lad like this one'd make you just the husband you need, Mary, eh?"

"I don't want one, thank you. Listen to him!"

"I didn't say 'want' I said 'need'. Didn't I?" he appealed to Tom, who smiled, he hoped knowingly. "All girls need a husband to keep their feet warm."

"Listen to him, will you!" She gave an unreal laugh, using the technique she had for answering an angry drunk or someone who swore at the bar.

You couldn't get under her skin. She just said, "Listen to him, will you!" and laughed like the rattle of a cash-register drawer.

Thorpley gave it up for the time being. "You're both right and you're wrong, son." He snapped his excavator bucket closed and swung round until it hung a few inches from Tom's face. "Now listen, listen close," he said. "That deal was bumped. In all the docs the sale price shows as nineteen but it really went for seventeen. It's a way of getting a sale and your commission when there's not really enough lolly around. But you've got to have everything just right. You need a crook surveyor, a crook lawyer—that's difficult—and you need two of the right sort of mugs, not too sharp and not too dopey either. It's a dodgy thing, bumping, very dodgy. Look. There's a mug wanting to sell and another wanting to buy, but he only has a hundred. So you tell the seller you can get seventeen hundred for it but to leave everything to you. Then you got to find a mug as is real desperate, real desperate for somewhere to live. There's plenty like that these days but you got to find the right one. Find the wrong 'un and you might all end up on bread and marge and cocoa in the Scrubs 'stead of beer and sandwiches in here. Well, you get it surveyed and valued as worth an advance of eighteen hundred with an official selling price of nineteen. That bit's easy. One or two of these local surveyors are two-timing the big mortgage companies and building societies and doing the diddle on all us local agents as well. All the same to some of them as long as they can get their five guineas. And a bit over. Well, the building society agrees to put up eighteen hundred on the strength of the buyer's status and the surveyor's report. Then you have to square both the muggins that the real selling price is only seventeen hundred. 'Course you can't do this without a solicitor that is O.K., and what with the way the bastards are able to find work without having to go on the crook these days that's not easy; but never mind, I know one. Well, the completion date is roughly agreed but you get it fixed so that there's a week or so to play with. In comes the eighteen hundred from the building society. The seller gets his seventeen hundred and floats off, and us and the solicitor and the surveyor split the two hundred. The buyer gets his house and starts paying back the mortgage. You can even work it so that he don't really understand what the hell has been going on anyway. Just that he has got a house with only a hundred deposit to pay. That's what I meant by saying you've got to have a bloke as is not too sharp and not too stupid neither, see? Got it so far? Now I'll answer some of your questions before you've even asked them. Don't the building society know what's going on? Yes they do and they don't. You can only work it with one of the smaller ones like The Eel Pie Island Mortgage Society Ltd., or one of those that are after boosting up their business. What can go wrong? If anything goes wrong we all go to clink and they get an empty house back that they can flog or let as they please. We're guilty of defrauding them, not them us. They may even have cover against getting gypped and can claim as long as the insurance company don't rumble it. Why don't the big boys get their business that way too? Because they don't have to. You only take chances when you have to in business. Suppose a couple of these bumpings went wrong and it all come out, like I said. Well, it'd only have to happen twice and there'd be a very funny smell round Eel Pie Island, wouldn't there, boy? Wouldn't there, eh?"

He left Tom standing there, thinking it over and working it out, and shouted down to Mary, "Service, service up here. Get them lovely hands on the pumps!"

When Mary drifted down to their end of the bar he didn't order anything up from the beer pumps for himself but asked for another gin and tonic. He turned to Tom. "Have another half of mild while you're thinkin'," he said. "Go on, have one. It's weak as gnat's water these days anyway." He turned to Mary—"I'd've said 'maiden's water,' but there's a lady present."

"Pity there's not a gentleman present as well, then," said Mary and tinkled the cash-register in her throat.

She went down the bar length again to get the drinks and Thorpley swung his whole body around on the stool, inching first one thigh and then the other forward until he was facing Tom and could switch the caterpillar treads off and hang his great bucket-scoop forward again towards him. "Thought it over? Then tell me, who loses out, eh? Who loses over the deal?"

Sudden questions in those days still made Tom blush and fumble and he did so now. Old Thorpley never budged nor took his eyes off him. He was waiting for an answer. Tom couldn't think what to say. In the end he had come out with, "Nobody, that I can see."

"Right, boy, right enough. Nobody. We've got a bloke that can well afford it fixed up with a house and got ourselves a bit of beer money and none's the wiser. We run all the risks, and all for a miserable fifty quid or so. It's a cruel world, boy, a cruel world."

He asked Tom one or two other questions and seemed satisfied, for he edged himself round again on the stool and left Tom standing at his side like a dummy while he went on to try and tease Mary. It was getting on for closing and she had time to stand down their end of the bar.

"Like I said before, Mary. This young chap knows the answers. He'll be making real money by the time he's forty. Just the sort of young chap as'd make you a good husband. He'd keep your feet warm and you could tickle his ears."

"Will you listen to him!" Mary said. "Just listen to him! What do I want with a husband?"

"Painting your toe-nails red won't keep your feet warm," said Thorpley. He took a good swig at his fourth gin and tonic. He made a slight turn of the head as if he were really speaking to Tom and not to her. "Never liked painted toe-nails on a woman myself. Always makes me think you might get your ears scratched." He gave a laugh which was really more like a grunt and looked at Mary. You had to hand it to her. She never even turned a hair. "Listen to him, will you?" she asked the empty air in front of her. "Listen to him," she said, as if the shirt-sleeved men in the green, shadowed depths of the billiard-room behind Tom and Thorpley could hear and answer. She was a tough biddy, that one, all right.

It seemed to be narking Thorpley that he couldn't needle her somehow. He kept pegging away, just as he did at a deal or at one of the salesmen when they'd mucked something up. He kept getting on to her about marriage. Tom was embarrassed but didn't want to show it. What with drinking with the boss and being let in on bumping he was feeling very old and blasé. Thorpley still kept on at her and, although there seemed no reason why she should stay, she did not go and get on with her glass-washing down the other end of the bar. "Just don't leave

it too late, Mary, Mary, quite contrary," said Thorpley.
"Know what's a sadder sight than an old spinster? An old
spinster barmaid. Don't tell me you wouldn't like a nice
young man like this one to call your own and light the fires for
you. You could bring him in here and show him off to the
other girls. It'd be ten years before he was wide-o to what he'd
married and then it wouldn't matter, would it, dearie?" He
thrust out his bucket jaw over the counter at her. "Would
it?" he repeated. Tom was a bit surprised. If he couldn't get a
rise out of her by talking dirty in front of her, what did he think
all this about marriage was going to do? Even as he thought it
he glanced at Mary and was surprised to see a faint but un-
concealable blush reddening her neck and the underside of her
jaw, below the make-up line, and her expression, too, showed
that something had gone home. Thorpley grunted and without another word slid his bulk off the stool. He swayed a little
on his feet and took another look at Mary as if he were sipping a
drink. He grunted again but you could not tell whether it was
really with satisfaction or from the effort of standing up after
so long on the stool. He ambled away towards the Gents to
relieve himself further.

Tom stayed staring at the girl. He felt a bit queer, as if he'd
seen something he wasn't supposed to, something he didn't
understand. Mary seemed not to know that he was still there.
This annoyed him and he wanted to bully her too. He
couldn't think what to say. He knew if he waited too long he
would miss his chance or lose his nerve. He took a quick sip of
his stale, warm beer. "Goin' to marry me, then?" he said,
trying to make it sound tough.

Mary looked at him for a moment and then through him to
the billiard hall. "Speak to me like that when your voice has
broke, kid," she said. It had been his turn to blush and
Thorpley noticed when he came back. The boss never
started on Mary any more, though, that day. Seemed as if
he'd got what he wanted, whatever that could be.

All that was long ago and now he was handling his first bit of bumping on his own. Queer thing, though, sometimes when he couldn't get off to sleep or when something had gone a bit wrong and he was going over it in his mind, the whole memory of that day would come back to him and he would hear Mary's tired, hard voice saying, "Speak to me like that when your voice has broke, kid." And in the dark he could feel his cheeks flushing up red just as they had done that dinner-time years before.

Dodging around on the deal and taking some other clients around to see property kept him very busy that week. Then he had to fit in a couple of visits to some of his people on the insurance book round. The idea of keeping the round on in spite of the little it brought in was so that he could build it up a bit and then have something to fall back on if Speedy Home-finders ever folded or gave him the push.

CHAPTER 2

Sagittarians Find Evening Best
for Romance—Enter a Stranger

CAROLE BROCKETT glanced through the glass partition of her office. Mr. Dentham, the chief accountant, had just been to the lavatory and come back and filled his pipe and stretched his back before starting on his summaries again. It must be four o'clock.

"An up and coming right-hand woman," Sir Henry had called her last month. No doubt she was bright enough, with a B.Sc. Econ. and a salaried job at twenty-five. All the same there were times when she felt as Mr. Dentham must feel. No, as Mr. Dentham stopped himself from feeling. He'd been years with the firm, and in the war only a part-time warden or something, because of his heart or his liver or his lights. He came in each morning, sat down at his desk and set out his paraphernalia for the day: a tin of tobacco, a large silver lighter which had been a wedding present fifteen years before, and various instruments for cleaning his pipe. Every now and then he would rearrange these objects, shuffling them slightly with the backs of his fingers. He filled and smoked one pipe in the mornings and two in the afternoon, straight after lunch and again at four. This third one generally lasted him until it was time to go and catch his train. He wore coloured shirts with a separate white collar which he changed every day. If you had to see him about any query he was always very helpful and polite and made a great business of it, welcoming the interruption and the human contact. If you bent close, to look at the ledger, there was a dry smell of stale tobacco and dandruff, and by Friday it was time for the coloured shirt to be changed as well as the white collar.

He broke up his working hours by fiddling with his pipe and smoking it and his leisure with cosy pleasures such as taking the dog for a walk, doing a job about the house, or some gardening. Busy getting his little bit of living over with.

Sometimes she felt as if it would be nice to jog along like that, dodging all the real problems. It was, of course, already far too late for her to put the clock back, change her nature or otherwise bitch herself up. This fact about herself, however, was not apparent. The nearest it came to formulation in her mind was: 'The equivalent, for a woman, of being a Dentham would be to marry a Dentham and lose oneself completely in children, gossip and the housework.' Every time she reached this point in her cogitations she would set her teeth and say, "No." Sometimes she spoke this word aloud, once, even, standing by old Dentham. Then he had made some sly crack about it being the first word a girl should know. That had been before her promotion. Nowadays he never stepped beyond the limits of a decorous, "Yes, Miss Brockett. No, Miss Brockett." Except that when you walked away from him you could sometimes feel on your back the creepiness of one of those sly, slimy glances married men give you and then pretend that they haven't. 'No,' she thought, 'no.'

She took some important queries in to Sir Henry for his decision and made a note on the appropriate papers ready for the morning. Her memory could have made this unnecessary, but the gesture went with the whole character of being Senior Secretary, Investment Policy.

It was a Thursday and the shops stayed open late. She planned to catch the Central Line from the City to Oxford Circus. Mooning about the shops took her back a long way, to the year in between getting her State Scholarship and being admitted to U. of L.—all that bother about the grant and how much Dad earned. During that time she had gone up to town every day, leaving the stinking 'Poets' just after seven-thirty, to a commercial college. Other girls had taken jobs in Woolworth's or in the offices of friends of their fathers, but her mother had found the money from somewhere to send her to that dreary shorthand and bookkeeping factory. The whole place was nothing but a vast plant for turning out clerks and typists from every type of adolescent. The factory took the dull and the brilliant in its stride. They never received any kudos from the subsequent careers of their successes, so why should they feel at all downcast over their failures? There was no attempt there at any great regimentation, no 'character-building' or 'personality-training' for the future prisoners of commercialism. It wasn't a bit like school. Bells rang and classes changed up and down iron-tipped stairways. Attendances were recorded and progress charts made up. It was assumed that time and life would break the leggy colts to conformity without any efforts on the part of the staff. This casual, underlying assumption was more terrible and demoralising than the harshest discipline might have been. There had been nothing there to resist. Suppose you walked out? It would only save your dad and mum the money and move the college waiting-list up one place, and you would be left with finding a job. Your only qualification being that you had not completed a course in commercial subjects.

In that uneasy year, with all the other worries of sixteen, she had sometimes gone on a Thursday to the big stores. She would drift about and then buy some little thing, in shocking taste, a scarf with cocktail glasses and violet wine bottles printed on it or some cheap costume jewellery. Then she used to travel back in the rush hour, buying an evening paper and flipping it open with a casual movement of the wrist, just like any other bored City worker, and standing in the train and the bus queue looking at it. Often when she reached the Tube station at the far end she used to give the bus queue a miss and hurry into the

Ladies and there unwrap her new purchase and admire it, try
it on and bundle it away again anyhow. The fun had then
gone until it came to the first time for wearing it. Those had
been the great days, too, for having rows with her father. It
had been her religious time as well. Her mother had kept
firmly out of both these phases, seeming to know that they
would pass. She used to come home, hungry, and there would
be her father slumped in his armchair. It's true he'd been
working all day, but then who hadn't? She'd dash out to the
kitchen to show her mother what she'd bought, ignoring her
father's "Close the door, can't you!" Then she would go up to
her bedroom, tiny and icy and only her own for the last three
years, and kneel in front of the little home-made *prie-dieu* with
its two brass candlesticks and the confirmation Bible Miss
Tillyard had given her in last year voluntary sixth-form
R.I. Here she would pray for guidance to withstand the trials
of life and for strength to forgive and show understanding
towards her father, 'even as Thou showeth—or is it
showethest?'—and so on. Then she would go back downstairs and find her supper ready and her father asleep in his
chair. Seeing the old head bowed and the gnarled hand hanging limp, she would be filled with a tenderness and pity
beyond her capacity to bear. Relief would always come in the
form of her, then, favourite day-dream. "You see," she would
say to her husband, the millionaire film director, "you see,
when I don't know for sure whether ordinary people would like
it I go and ask my dad." "Darling, whatever should I do
without you and your father?" Then he would take her in his
arms and kiss her. After that it started at the beginning again.

It seemed almost impossible now that she bore the same
name as that silly girl, occupied the same body. They said that
all the cells in your body were renewed once every seven
years. Surely that meant all the cells in your head as well, up
where the memories and the personality lodged?

Mr. Dentham's pipe had burnt down to a smelly dottle.

He went out to the washrooms again and came back just in time to put on his coat as the clock twitched the last minute to five-thirty. He was starting to put his bits and pieces away. First the tobacco tin and then the pipe-cleaners and pen-knife and the fat silver lighter. All went into a neat despatch case with the folded greaseproof paper in which his sandwiches had been wrapped and a Penguin Conrad, about typhoons and gloomy battles with the man within, in the South Seas at the turn of the century.

"Good night, Mr. Dentham."

"Good night, Miss Brockett."

"Hope it's not too crowded for you tonight."

"It'll be pretty much as usual, Miss Brockett, I expect. Pretty much as usual. Never varies much, you know. Be better, of course, when the new extension line's finished. It'll take some of the crowd who live further east than I do."

"Good." She rattled the bones of small talk for a few minutes longer. For some reason she wanted to be kind to Mr. Dentham. Not that he really seemed to need it.

After Sir Henry had given all his decisions and chatted a bit they left together, passing through the deserted office and taking the lift. Then he walked off, very straight and looking like a retired general on his way to a meeting in Whitehall, instead of just a middle-grade company director on his way to London Bridge.

Going up the escalators at Oxford Circus, in the rush hour, instead of down them at that time gave you an illusion of freedom, rather like being a student again and once more free to go and see a popular foreign film at eleven in the morning or to sit up reading and making notes till four, knowing that you could miss one lecture safely and get up at twelve. It sometimes felt as if her degree and all her student past provided an ill-defined kind of emergency exit from the office and the City. When you are bored dizzy with a journey you sit and read over and over the words, "In emergency press disc and pull lever in direction of arrow," and wonder, if it came to it, if it would all really work. Might not the arrow have been painted on the wrong way up by some other bored dreamer, or the disc be rusted in position? All the same it was pretty certain it *would* work. If you got really frightened you could always try it and see.

Of course, the degree and that which seemed to be an emergency exit was really keeping her in the job. The trap-door was a fastened safety-belt.

The crowds waiting their turn to file into the Tube and lurch and sway their pressed-up way home filled the footway and over-spilled into the roadway. It was a damp evening and the pavement seemed to exude an oily scum. The shuffling feet shattered and splintered the golden circles of reflected light.

An odd by-product of living in the largest city in the world is that it is hardly possible to be unique, no matter how eccentric or erratic one's actions.

Going up West to the stores on a Thursday evening could hardly be described as eccentric. Carole found herself with allies in the fight against the stream. Several girls and one or two married couples, the man with his new week's wages in his pockets and a best suit and tie on and the woman pulling him along, roughshod and inconsiderate of the feet of others, whilst he hung back, embarrassed and married, a tamed stag led by the nose and hence not obliged to show chivalry any longer, joined with a dozen or so elderly women on their own to make up a small force, enough for a battering ram. Shoulders touched and hips jostled, feet tripped and ankles became splashed, toes scraped at the heels of others' shoes. Only the eyes never met and the tongues were never used except to murmur a vague complaint to the damp air, "Dear me. . . . Sorry, so sorry. What a crush!" Such remarks whilst addressed to no one in particular were meant to be overheard by everyone and excuse the speaker from any responsibility in the proceedings, making it as impersonal as the weather, or the as bombs had once been. It was, in short, an English crowd.

Few people stopped at the first counters of the store. Carole, with the rest, drifted further down the warmed avenues, past the bright coral reefs of the display counters and into the weedy growths of the dress racks. Up and down the girls floated, unblinking fish-eyes taking in the colour and sizes of the bright clothes which eddied and waved slightly, frondlike on their chromed steel stems. It was a quiet and calming ritual, searching, comparing and clicking the plastic hangers together to pull out a dress and try it against oneself and put it back. You never seemed to see anyone buying anything, but the cash-registers kept clattering and, if you did decide to buy a dress or a slip, there was always a little queue. At the far end a benign shark in black coat and striped trousers presided over the shoals: the only male for twenty yards around.

Carole bought a blouse and swam the glades for a bit more. She really enjoyed these odd hours spent in mooning around the shops alone. Once she had run into some of the junior typists and filing girls, arms linked and giggling together. "Oo, there's Miss Brockett!" had come out from one of them before anyone could shush her. Carole had gone around with them, dropping eight years and her education and position as quickly as the first stiffness passes at a party where everyone is in duty bound to be pleasant and enjoy themselves whatever the social distinctions. None of them had taken advantage in the office afterwards, whatever they may have said among themselves. Good girls, really, when you thought of it. She'd looked for them the next week and half expected to see them a couple of times since. Never mind. Better, really, when you thought about it.

Turning a corner of the racks she suddenly faced herself in a mirror. A slim, dark girl, looking rather tired, her shoes splashed and her coat belted unbecomingly in a careless manner. A teenager might have got away with it.

On the way to the door she looked round casually in case

the girls from the office had come that way. Then she left.

The tide of the rush hour had turned and ebbed, leaving behind pools of people about the cinema entrances and others darting in pairs across the thinning streams of traffic to the safety of the granite and asphalt islets. With the schools and shoals cleared and dispersed to their home grounds the queer fish stood out more plainly. The man with a hard face who sold soft toys on a tray swaggered out from the shadows as if he were really a gangster with a sub-machine-gun. The well-dressed man who talks to himself outside the big store's furniture display windows stood with his head cocked to one side nodding shrewdly at something said to him by his non-existent companion. The tart with the tight black dress and the silly, slack mouth sailed past her prospective customers like a duchess through a hallway of footmen. After the apoplectic spasm of the rush hour the city started on the rhythm of its night-life.

Carole caught a bus to her corner and walked down the street towards the security and shabby felicity of her bed-sitter.

The tall houses with their huge basements and area wells showed to their best at this hour. Their imperfections were softened and romanticised by the shadows. Once they had had a brightly-painted front to reflect back the clatter of the cab-horses' hoofs. Today their stucco peeled off and the edges of the stone steps crumbled and chipped and the area railings rusted away, weeping brown tears of neglect in streaks across the grey flags. They were like Edwardian impoverished gentlewomen who have at last admitted defeat and come to terms with the world, laid aside stays for good and done up their greying hair any old how, thinking nothing now of appearing at the doorway in slippers and dressing-gown to pick up a lonely milk bottle and a copy of *The Times* so that they can shuffle away to make their own tea and read the Court Circular and news of the death of friends.

The problem of the girl in the bed-sitter is supposed to be

loneliness. 'If only it were,' thought Carole, making her joke to her imaginary companion for the hundredth time. 'I don't mean boy friends when you're out of the bed-sitter but the things that happen while you are in it.' Her room was part of the honeycombed hive. First there were the actual callers. Little Miss Plumley back from her typing at the Ministry with a Peace Pledge Union petition; Mr. Hadley to ask if the wireless plug is still all right since he mended it six months before, but really to tell you about his married daughter's new house; Mrs. Lenton, the landlady to complain of having had to sign for a registered letter for her and taking a good look around while she did so. Then the noise. When these enormous old houses had been lived in by enormous families and their slaveys, butlers, cooks and bootboys, everyone shared the noises. Identifying them then must have brought a sense of security and familiarity instead of a feeling of exasperation and misanthropy. A door slammed—Mrs. Lenton's married niece was in. That board on the second floor landing creaked and a rusty plug clanked and gurgled—Mr. Bannerjee off to a meeting of the Indian Students' Union. Time to start to get something to eat.

She started to peel an onion and some potatoes at the square zinc sink behind the faded chintz curtains. It's not fair about supper, really. Another injustice to women. If a man cooks his own supper he makes a great business of it to his friends (or else, of course, hides it altogether) and bores both men and women with details of his recipes and of variations he has discovered for himself. If this is not enough for his vanity in any given social circumstances he can say, "All the best chefs are men", with a self-deprecating smirk, at once both including and excluding himself from any claim to the professional title. On the other hand, if he is fed up with it and has the money, there is nothing more natural than that he should eat at a cheap restaurant. A woman on her own cannot boast of her cooking nor even report on it without seeming to wish to sound pathetic. And if she goes to eat alone in a café a girl must make it plain by her dress and manner that she is not there to pick up a man nor to wait for the arrival of one.

Then this in itself invites even more shrewdly speculative glances from the waitress and other women. All around, as well, there will be couples eating.

She opened the top window a little, so that the rusty sashes clanked and grumbled in a muffled fashion and little pieces of dust and cobwebs and flakes of iron fell down and settled in some hidden, secret recess of the wainscoting. Damp, cold air poured down the face of the dirty glass like a waterfall taking the overspill from the polluted river of an industrial town. The blue gas-ring flickered and the smell of onions cooking seemed to solidify in the cooler air. Carole felt the magic hour of rest and food creeping upon her and all the industrial, commercial city around her. Her back ached slightly and she was calendar-edgy. It had been a busy day. She had had to get out a lot of figures in a rush for the special board meeting and still not forget to keep well abreast of her share movements analysis. You had to keep ready for any board meeting which might come along in eighteen months' time. Scattered over the City and in the offices of the big insurance companies further west were all her year at college except those who had gone into the Civil Service and one who had gassed himself. Carole had been too busy escaping, first from her home to grammar school and next from the paternalism of the groves of Academe, to think much of the future. Now her job was largely 'futures'.

The draught from the window was pushing the gas jets over and bending them so that they became less sprightly and thermatic and more wobbly, vague and will-o'-the-wisp. The cold air from the streets outside seemed to be pressing the onions down in the pan and stopping them from cooking properly. She turned the gas up a little. A dusty wire looped its way down from the high centre point and hung inconveniently on the corner of her dressing-table mirror so that a lamp-shade had scorched in a brown, black-centred crater against the faded pink. She paused there for a moment and then set about odd jobs. The bed needed making and she stripped one sheet off, ready for the visit to the launderette on tomorrow evening. It looked as if it would be a quieter day on Friday and then there was Saturday to look forward to. Some of her friends from student days, who were now, mostly, young marrieds, had invited her out and they might go on to dance somewhere. On Sunday she had promised her mother to visit home. Nowadays she kept such promises. The two women had become much closer again than at any time since her childhood. Carole felt grateful to her mother for having made the effort to pinch and scrape and push her through university and now understood a bit better how much her mother must have resented the ruthless way in which she had insisted on walking out and getting a room, up town or anywhere, away from home. The baby chick is equipped with a special hard covering to his beak and this he uses to peck his way out of the shell. After this is done the covering drops off. She started to think once again of the past and of the road she had travelled and of her home. Oh well, she hadn't built such a bad life for herself, and there was plenty of time yet. A faint blue smoke blurred the shadowy corners of the room. The onions! She rushed to the gas-ring set on its chipped marble slab that had once been a wash-stand. Sure enough they were past saving, curled crisp and black at their damned edges and sending up smoke smelling like the waft of hot air from an iron grating in the pavement in the side street behind a cheap restaurant.

She spread the evening paper on the floor and scraped the onions into the middle of it. A paragraph from a twice-read City page caught her eye and she stayed kneeling and reading it for a moment with the fat soaking and yellowing the newsprint to a smudged translucency. Then she bundled the traces of the disaster into a ball and put them in a cardboard box near the door ready to be taken down to the dustbin. It seemed extravagant to go and eat out on a Thursday. In the end she boiled two eggs and opened a tin of soup.

Saturday turned out a bit of a flop. She was odd girl out with two couples because 'a nice man', to whom arch references were being made all the time, had some excuse and never turned up. Her former fellow students shared amusing stories about their respective domestic problems and children. The only common ground seemed to be the past. When they'd eaten they drove out to some dreary pub with fake tapestry hangings and a brass warming-pan hanging over the pin-table. When the men brought the first round of drinks across to their table, after some man-to-man fumbling with money at the bar, they all raised their glasses and said, "To our baby-sitters," and laughed. It was evidently a traditional observance. Carole smiled weakly and sipped her sherry.

After a time they got into the cars and went up West to a dance-hall.

Sitting in the car Carole thought, 'This part's all right.' The phrase had become a habit with her when in certain moods. It had begun some time between thirteen and sixteen. During any lesson she loathed, or when the gym hall was freezing cold and everyone seemed to be enjoying their netball or apparatus practice except her, she had found some small corner for herself, either in the game, or with a fellow sufferer on one of the lower vaulting stools. This had helped her to forget the cold and her fear of life and, glancing at the clock caged in its wire basket high on the tiled wall, seeing that there were only twenty minutes more to the lesson, she had got into the way of reassuring herself with the realisation of the tolerability of the immediate present. 'This part's all right,' Carole had thought, changing back out of her gym tunic, taking a sip of water from a fountain in the echoing entrance hall to the examination rooms or waiting to be interviewed for her first job.

Her friends were in the front seat, talking to each other from

time to time about money and shopping and plans for the next
week. Every now and then the wife, who had been a year her
junior at college, would remember to perform her duties as
hostess and turn round in the seat and say, "Not far now," or
"Not much traffic at this time. The cinemas aren't out yet."
Then the husband would enter with details of the route and of
how long it usually took him to drive up to the office. Carole
thought, 'If I marry it won't be like this and we won't live like
they do.' This made her feel slightly disloyal and rude to her
hosts. "This is a very comfortable car," she said. They
started to tell her about the car and its costs and performance
and she sat half listening and making the right noises from
time to time. Past the windows floated and swayed the shops
and pavements of South London. At this dead hour of the
evening there were not many people about. A few couples
pressed like dazed moths around the harsh, white glare from
the windows of furniture shops. Clothing dummies posed and
simpered behind plate-glass in the glow of pink strip-lighting.
From the windows of the radio shops the telly screens flickered
mauve and grey. She wondered how they got turned off.
Perhaps the shopman came down in slippers from the flat
above, rubbing his eyes and yawning from watching his own
telly, and pressed some master switch at the back of the shop.
She looked above the level of the glaring windows to the dusty
casements which reflected back the light of the street lamps.
The car swerved to pass a trolley-bus, its bright interior giving
the sudden impression, which reason stifled before it fully
emerged, that the shops had at this point suddenly projected
themselves further forward, had thrust their frontage out into
the roadway. After all loonier things had happened in the
process of unplanned proliferation of London streets. No
sooner were they past the trolley-bus than the row of shops
became one storey lower and, without straining, it was
possible to look up out of the car window and see the slates and
the chimney-pots. The unreal fluorescence from the tall

concrete posts forced the homely picture of guttering and tiles and mouldering, gap-toothed stacks into silhouette. With their front face sharply lit and their backs invisible in the darkness behind, they looked as if they were cut out of cardboard and showing their dusty surface in the artificial glare of stage lighting. Thus, there was no night sky visible behind them. They stood isolated above the slick and chic faked-up modernity of the shop fronts below and the black darkness behind. She thought, 'How did it get here and why in this particular shape? Miles and miles of little buildings, cottages really, and now turned into shops with lighted windows and trolley-buses swishing past them all day and night. What a mess! Other cities aren't like this. How did it all grow up in this way?' She knew what she was doing, but, as is said of a drunk, it didn't stop her doing it. Within moments she had induced in herself that great fear of the loneliness of human consciousness upon this small planet which falls upon people of a certain temperament at inconvenient times and places.

It was a relief to reach the dance hall and join in the search for somewhere to park by making suggestions of side turnings and cul-de-sacs which she knew better than her friends. They were near *her* home ground now.

She had always liked dancing, but a streak of English puritanism, and, perhaps, of intellectual snobbery, made her feel that time should be better spent, at the theatre or in reading. She straightened the folds of her green dance frock and joined her little group of acquaintances at the side of the hall. There was a good band and later in the evening their music was to be broadcast from this very place so that it would trickle into the steamy kitchens of the Black Country back-to-backs and seep tinnily from under the dashboards of cars taking lovers through the night. The thought that it originated from here made her feel slightly sophisticated and very much the inhabitant of the capital. If she laughed extra-loud, for example, just as she was dancing past the band's dais, all the world might hear her laugh before they went to bed.

The excitement of the dance began to reach her, fading out the bleak blackness of her cosmic fixation in the car and banishing her silly guilt to a filing cabinet whence it could be extracted and examined at some future time. 'After all,' thought Carole, 'it's probably all just a subconscious hangover from being a student, so that now I feel uneasy and guilty whenever I am doing anything with my free time but swotting.'

After the third or fourth dance she really began to enjoy herself. A gang of students from L.S.E. came in, wearing jeans, some of the boys in polo necks or T-shirts. She was dancing with one of these students and feeling ever so slightly a baby-snatcher when a tall, curly-haired young cockney asked to cut in. She hadn't seen him before anywhere, not even at one of these hops, so it was a bit startling but not worth making anything of. She didn't know the student either, come to that. But then with that sort you didn't have to. In essentials they were all the same and, for all their wild talk, would end up as liberal-minded engineers or teachers or statisticians. 'Like me,' she thought, so as to keep it fair and not be hypocritical.

She had been following her new partner and owed him no more than that. Under these circumstances her thoughts could be her own without any social demands to be fulfilled. The time must have gone very quickly—though, of course, they had got there late—because the band started to pep it up for the last number. The boy suddenly asked if he could give her a lift. Up to that time she had not really thought about getting back. She had supposed the others could give her a lift to her corner before going back to relieve their baby-sitter from her sentry-go. She'd walked further than this before now.

She took one good look at his face. He didn't seem to be anything more than she could handle. It must be his firm's car, she decided. When she asked him it put him off his stride, but he tried not to show it and started some silly business about being a partner. He tried hard to impress her and to seem confident but she could see him getting ready to make a move and ask to take her home, gathering his courage up and making her think of a little boy going in to bat.

She went and told her hostess not to worry about her getting home and there was laughter and leg-pulling about her 'mystery man'. It had been a gay evening.

Getting in the car reminded her of having had that feeling in the other car earlier on, and she played up to the boy. He was really rather nice and, besides, if *that* didn't stop the feeling coming on, then nothing would. When he began to get a bit too worked up for comfort she asked him about his job.

Men would always stop whatever they were doing to talk about themselves. Even that. Some sort of house agent and trying to show her just how smart he was with stories of this and that. An older, and really smart, man would not have tried to boast in that way. It seemed he still lived at home. What she really wanted to ask him was why he had gone out of his way to pick her up at the dance. Did he think she was easy game for some reason? Or was he trying to make someone else jealous, or what? Surely there'd been plenty of other girls there more his type? He said something about meeting again and they'd left it vaguely for next Saturday, perhaps.

'He had nice hands,' thought Carole alone in bed. 'And he was a nice, clean young man and not nearly so experienced as he pretended to be. But then am I, really, myself?' she thought, with her habitual trick of destructive self-analysis. She snuggled down further in the bed. The room still smelt faintly of onions that week. In the distance she could just make out the late-night traffic, taxis mostly and a printers' bus. What way would he drive home? Where was his car now? Perhaps he'd pick up another girl on the way? 'No, he won't,' thought Carole and fell asleep.

CHAPTER 3

You're Only Young Once

SATURDAY was busier than ever and Tom had all the worry of tying up the last few knots on the bumping job. It wasn't really his turn for the car but he persuaded the fellows to let him have it again. He told them about the girl. He laid it on a bit and made out he'd got it all right last week. "Let's meet her", they had said, "Don't keep her to yourself", and things like that. "Not likely," said Tom. "Not likely."

He got there late, but that was O.K.; it didn't do to seem too eager, they said. A lot of the hounds he knew gathered round him, pushing him into the bar. He didn't want to start the evening with a drink. It made you less quick on your pins on the floor and girls smelt your breath and wrinkled their noses. The bar was crowded three deep and the gang formed a syndicate. Not a school or a kitty, just a syndicate so that whoever could get served first put in the order for the lot. There were only a few girls in here: sitting on chairs against the walls, sipping gin and lime or cherry brandy or sherry and looking up at their boys and listening to them. For the first time he wondered what it would really be like to have a steady girl. Up to now he had just taken it that it would be horrible. He thought, 'I bet that dark one wouldn't just sit listening and making soppy eyes at you. She'd have plenty to say.' Without realising what he did he looked across the crowded room and at each girl on the chairs, though he already knew she wasn't there.

"What is it, Tom? Looking for one? There's plenty next door. Plenty of lovely crumpet, toasted and plain. Not like you to look far," said one of the lads. They weren't slow in that crowd, any of 'em. All good cockney boys on the make.

They soon went back to the dance floor. He danced first with a thin one with heavy make-up over three or four mauve spots on her cheeks and neck, then with a fat one with a waist which creaked and felt as hard as the iron side of a boiler under great pressure. The band seemed to play nothing but old numbers he was sick of hearing. He went and stood in a small stag line at the side of the hall, away from the entrance to the bar. He tried to think of a good opening remark such as, "Hello, Paddington Green" or "Hello, green dress". He would not admit to himself that he might not need any opening remark at all. It never came to him that she might make the first approach. He was sure to see her first and anyway it was up to the man. If she was to dance past him now he'd nod and not show too much pleasure. Then he'd keep his eye on her and think up some really good crack to open up with. He glimpsed a green like that of her dress but it turned out to be a girl not a bit like her.

"Hello," she said, standing right in front of him. He tried to think of one of the good wisecracks he'd had ready. There was something about green. Before he could stop himself he blurted out, "I was looking for a green dress."

"I've got more than one. In fact I've got two," she laughed, gesturing at her red skirt. He thought, 'Another girl might have taken advantage somehow when I made a clot of myself by letting out that I'd been looking for her.'

The band started one of his favourite numbers. His confidence came back. "Let's go," he said. The minute she came near him he started tasting her kiss again from a week before. She followed him perfectly. That was a funny thing: a clumsy girl who was a bad dancer or who had had a jug or two could bump against you and knock her thighs on yours and push her front against your chest and still you didn't get any real feeling of her body near your own. But with a good dancer you had the sense of her following your movements and her limbs moving and swaying and tensing even if you jived off a few steps apart at arm's length. She looked up at him, but her look didn't really say anything more than, 'You're a good dancer. I like dancing with you.'

As they danced he weighed up whether to ask her name or not. If you had just met a girl or even seen her home once, that didn't mean you exchanged names. The whole point of these big dances in the inner suburbs or up West lay in their anonymity. Once when he had just started going to them he had asked a girl her name. "Does it matter?" she had answered and he had realised that it didn't and that the queer thing seemed to be that it made you more fresh to ask a girl her name than to kiss her, or try to. He had blushed and, seeing him off balance, the girl had been kind and said, "That's how it's done here, see? Then there's no hard feelings next time, see? If you're with somebody else and might have to say, 'Hello, Jean' and the other girl'd ask, 'Who's Jean?' See? 'Course there's no harm really. Just that it makes it more serious sort of, if you've told each other your names, I mean, sort of, really."

Since then he'd once done the same for a girl, only out of blasted kindness and to pay back the debt to the fair sex, sort of. But he'd made a balls of it and the girl had left him there and then in the middle of the floor and looked as if she was going to cry. Girls are funny.

"What's your name?" she asked.

"Tom," he said. "Tom Stanton. What's yours?"

"Carole Brockett."

There must've been some sense in the rule or unwritten law or whatever you call it about names, because for the first time it got awkward between them. He couldn't think of anything to say. He looked down at her and she just kept dancing away there, looking just the same. Girls could always put on an act better than fellows. Somehow he could tell, though, that she felt just as he did. The number ended. "Care for a drink?" he asked.

Going through the door she went in front of him for a few paces and he took in her shape. Thinking about it all later, after he'd fallen good and proper, he realised that this had been the last time he had ever thought of her like that, as just a girl. Once you fell for someone it made it different. If they could see your thoughts they wouldn't like you, and anyway you just didn't think in the same way any more.

He could see some of the hounds looking at him and eyeing up the girl. Other times he had been pleased whenever this had happened. He moved in front of her.

The fellows hovered around the bar and bent over their girls, talking to them, and the girls sat with their knees pressed together, looking up and listening. He spotted an empty seat and took Carole's arm to guide her towards it.

"It's all right. I'd rather stand," she said. She only asked for a shandy. Not on the make for liqueurs or any of that muck. As if she would be. 'That's queer,' he thought. What exactly it was that was queer he could not have put into words. The real thought had been, 'Why should I feel loyal to someone I hardly know?' but loyalty in that sense did not exist for him as an abstraction.

He knew enough not to appear too interested in such questions as who had she come here with and what was that crowd she danced with. It didn't do to start asking questions of a girl straight away as if you were a copper or someone doing consumer research for an advertising agency. Let her ask the questions if she were interested. If she didn't, then at least you knew where you stood. A bleakness, so slight as to be barely noticeable, touched him. The girl was looking at him. He had just time to think, 'A posh girl'd say "What's up, darling? You look a bit harassed." And a middling sort of office one, "Well, cheers!" And a factory or shop girl, "I seen you here often. Do you come every week?" ', when he found himself

saying, "What job've you got? Have you always lived in digs?
I mean, have you any family in London?" His stomach
suddenly felt like that of an amateur toboggan enthusiast
who finds that the artificial slope he has climbed and launched
himself upon turns out to be a ski-jump. Everything depended
on her now. He had left himself wide open. She could give
him the air or keep him stringing along a bit on her own terms.
She had only to say, "Blimey, ask me another", or something
like that, and he'd look a bloomin' fool.

She looked up at him and smiled. "Tell you later," she said
and, just to make it plain that she knew he'd lost a point in the
game, added, "What about you?"

"Tell *you* later," he said, weakly enough.

After the dance it went just the same as last week and yet it
was all different. They drove to her corner and parked for a
while. And talked and the usual. Something funny had
happened. She seemed to want to kiss him more than last
time. Of course you couldn't say he exactly held back himself. But if he started to think about how far he could go and
plan to get his hands busy on the next move he'd suddenly
remember how she hadn't scored off him when he'd asked her
all those questions. Then he'd feel mean, as if he was taking
advantage of a real young kid or something like that. Better
not ask any more questions anyway.

"Been in digs long?" he asked, as if his voice belonged to a
ventriloquist's dummy and said the very things it wasn't
supposed to.

"No," she said. "Tell me about you first."

It turned out that she knew his way quite well and had a
family living in that old part of the town. She was surprised
when he was able to reel off all the names of the streets around
the Lord Roberts. Then he let on about being a house salesman and about the insurance book. She asked a lot of
questions and got him going properly. She seemed really
interested and when he said, "I'm doing all the talking. You

shouldn't keep asking me questions," she said, "I was just getting my revenge." They sat quiet and then started off again the other way. Looking back, long after, when he'd packed her up and was wondering if he hadn't made the mistake of his life, he remembered that time. Then he realised that it had been one of the little changes that had taken place between them, bringing them a bit closer. And after each of these had taken place there had always been a moment of awkwardness, of silence, until it had been ended one way or another, usually with him kissing her or something like that.

He was glad when it came out about her family living in some street in 'The Poets'. She had seemed a bit too posh for him before that. Of course it wouldn't be the first posh girl who'd fancied it with him, especially after a dance, but that wasn't what he meant.

On that second evening it seemed only a few moments before it reached the stage of talking about how they felt. He said, "I thought you were too posh to have a family in somewhere like 'The Poets'. No offence to them, I mean, of course. Just that you . . ."

"It's all right," she said. "So do they."

That marked another tiny stage. She brought him into it against her family. They went on a lot then about their families. It got a bit much, too, sitting and squirming about in the car. They got out and walked, doped with each other, up and down the long, shadowy street.

It took some putting into words but always after Carole, and even after it had all ended badly, he wasn't scared of Central London any more. Perhaps you shouldn't say 'scared'. Put it this way: the car had made the first big difference. There was a difference between going up to the City by the Tube and bus on some errand for Thorpley and driving through the streets in a car. Suppose you thought of the real posh people. Well, you never even saw them walking on the pavements or changing trains at King's Cross. At the most you got a glimpse of them as they crossed from the doors of a Daimler to the entrance to their clubs or hotels. But when they were inside the Daimlers and waiting for the lights to change or for a chance to cut in, then, if you had a car of your own, or leastways the firm's, you were their equal.

All the same it seemed as if up West and in the City they were living by the game at which you were only playing. You played marbles, and perhaps won a few, and they owned the factory where the marbles were made and didn't bother to play with them.

In a way, a bloke from the provinces, even, would feel it less. If he failed he could go back to Oldham or wherever it was and at least talk about his year among the cockneys and hint at his early return. For ever after his time in London he would be camping out in his mother's house or his father's shop waiting for things to be just right for his return to the capital. If you came from the outer suburbs, however, you could make a way for yourself going up to town every day and competing with the boys and girls from the universities, or claw your way up through buying and selling things like cars and houses and job lots of fire sale stocks, or on an insurance round, flogging it up to something worth having and then selling it to someone who thought it worth buying. As for the other thing, taking a job behind a blasted desk in an office and trying to creep your way upwards, if you did this the odds were all against you. There was the boss's son and the sub-boss's nephew and all the slick types with their G.C.E.s and their pals with degrees one step higher up and ready to put out a hand to them, standing between you and promotion.

All those streets seemed to know about this and to be looking down on dozens like you. You could walk along them if you had business there or if you'd paid your fare there and had no business. Always provided you didn't try to get in on the act.

When he kissed her and she let him and made it plain that

she wanted more, it seemed to make it even on those streets up West. That first time he couldn't help thinking, 'This is a girl who lives up in town, just west of Marble Arch.'

She told him about her job, but not about the having gone to the university and all that, until later. It was as if she were ashamed of it instead of proud.

He started on to boast a bit about his job and the car and making out he was a junior partner to Thorpley and so on. Then, as they were walking up and down, he started to tell her the truth, as near as damn it. Right to the end it was always like that. She became the one person to whom he felt he must tell the truth, without underselling himself, of course. That made it often very difficult to do.

He said, "Can I phone you at work?"

"What for?" she asked. They were still sparring about then and not wanting to admit what had happened.

"Just so as to be sure you'll be at the dance. So I don't come for nothing." What he meant was, 'I can't go the whole week not knowing whether or not I'll see you again,' but it wouldn't do to say that.

"I was hoping you'd ask," said Carole.

Driving back alone he tried to remember when he had felt like this before. The nearest had been when he was still quite a kid. In those days he had been going through a craze for never wearing a coat. Then there had been this girl he'd picked up outside the pictures. They fooled around a bit and arranged to meet the next evening. Going there to meet her he had been thinking about her shape and making up his mind to try and go as far as he could that evening. It had been a cold evening, and he'd turned up his collar and bunched his scarf and come swaggering up to her in a tough sort of way, like Victor Mature in a film about truck drivers. It was all part of screwing up his courage to have a real try at her that night. "You'll be cold," she had said. "You shouldn't've worn a coat." After that he'd felt soft about her and ashamed of having thought of her like that. It went on for a whole two weeks. Kid stuff. He'd told a close mate of his about it later when they were having a good old talking session. "She only meant you'd need it to lie down on in the woods," said his pal and that had been the end of it. Of course that time he'd only been a boy, but all the same there was something about this girl that brought on the same feeling. That time he'd felt that he both wanted her to fuss on about his coat and it, being cold, yet to admire him for being so tough he didn't need to wear one. And now, with this Carole, he liked her to think he was smart and sharp but didn't want her to think him a crook or someone without any real feelings, sort of.

He drove up through Hampstead to pick up the North Circular Road. There were still a few cars parked about the White Stone Pond and down dark side turnings. All right for some. Perhaps one day she would come out with him in the car right out into Hertfordshire or somewhere. For a long stretch he had the road to himself except for a couple of night haulage lorries. Cat's-eye studs flared down the centre of each curve, glowing a moment and vanishing as if the car headlights both sparked them off and snuffed them out a moment later.

His bedroom was cold and he was glad to get into bed. For some reason he could not sleep. It was as if something very exciting had happened or as if he were afraid. He tried to reassure himself by remembering that tomorrow was Sunday and of how he planned to amuse himself with easy, familiar things. He began to have a feeling that this Sunday would be different and that he would just moon about, restless, unable to settle or do anything but think about her and go over what they had said to each other. It turned out he was right. That is exactly what did happen. He got up late and skimmed the Sunday paper. His mother was banging about in the kitchen and, feeling guilty, he told her about the dance. Sure enough she stopped it and came and stood listening, wiping her hands on a tea-cloth. Of course he kept the girl out of it. Just made up a yarn out of bits and pieces from other evenings in the past. Once or twice, when his father had been in the room, he had boasted about some smasher he'd just met, using that half-joking, half-serious way that you could sometimes use when all the family are together. But he never did this with either of them alone. It was time to get out of it. He stood up and said, "Have to take the car round to Jack's. It was really his turn for the Saturday night as well, so I don't want to be late with it."

"Good of him to let you have it," she said and he saw his bloomer at once. She wanted to know what had been the special reason for it. He started to mumble something about, "Nice bloke, old Jack."

"One of these days you'll meet a girl at one of these dances," she said. It was certainly time to leave.

It was a nice Sunday morning, cool but bright, and men were out in shirt-sleeves digging their gardens or doing jobs to the fronts of their houses, cleaning out gutters and shouting to their neighbours about the Saturday match results and their near misses on the pools. He felt well disposed towards the world and the suburban householders caring for their property; the mugs that found the deposits and took on the mortgages. The biggest mugs of all seemed to him to be the younger men. Fancy getting yourself pinned down with kids round you and all your lolly going on repayments for furniture and the telly and all your spare time on doing up the rooms and digging the garden. Somehow it seemed to him that all the men he drove past were older than he. In fact several were the same age and a few even younger.

Along the by-pass at this point a stretch of lumpy waste ground lay on the right and on the left the line of 'desirable Tudor residences' ended in a bank of greenhouses, their glass catching the watery English sunlight.

Outside the Ploughing Team a broad gravel sweep-in extended back from the road. The pull-up area was as wide as it had been for farm-carts in the 1870s, when the first rebuilding had taken place, and as it had been after the second reconstruction in 1927. The two-tone—toothpaste and mayonnaise —cars of the men in the money slouched like thoroughbreds, ignoring the oily, unkempt donkeys of motor-bikes and three-wheelers nuzzling alongside.

You could hardly hear yourself speak in the saloon. All the blokes were in their Sunday best, shoulders, high-padded, brushing and setting crooked the oak-framed pictures of coaching scenes and beaglers in green coats on the walls cut with a pen-knife from an illustrated weekly by the first land-lord to take over the house when he'd handed in his scrambled eggs and covered his wrist with a plain blue serge instead after the '14 War had ended.

A gang of the local lads were stuck around the front of the bar. Away at the back, in the pink glow of the table lamps and the artificial candle sconces done in twisted tin sprayed to look like wrought iron, stood his pal Jack talking to the boss. This was Sunday morning, off duty as it were.

He waved to Jack, and Thorpley raised a huge, fat hand a few inches from the bar-top and winked at him. One or two fellows at the bar knew that he worked for Thorpley. That gave him a good chance to show that he didn't have to rush up to the boss as soon as he nodded, like some.

In any case Thorpley was drinking with some old men of his own age. One of them even looked quite posh. Of course you couldn't tell until you heard him speak, but his suit and his face looked like it. The boss was certainly moving up. During the week he went up to the City to lunch with big-shots two or three times a week and sometimes never bothered to look in on the office at all. Just phoned through and asked those questions of his which got right to the point. It was beginning to look as if the local Speedy Homefinders' office took a real back seat among Thorpley's interests. Maybe he might close it down. Then he'd have nothing to fall back on but the blasted insurance book, which was already becoming a bit of a bind, especially when there was a rush on at the estate office. On the other hand Speedy Homefinders might become one of those big property companies. The way the boss kept buying up interests in estates and blocks of flats and selling 'em again at a small profit made it look as if Speedy Homefinders would either pack up soon or else change its name to something more important sounding like 'Thorpley Properties Ltd.' or 'Thorpley Estates'. It'd never be 'Thorpley anything and Sons' because the boss didn't have any kids.

He saw Thorpley pushing his way off to the Gents and took his chance to dodge away and follow him. He planned to come out at the same time and so move in naturally without the school down the bar noticing too much.

"Glad you looked in, boy," said Thorpley. "Come and have a drink. I want a word with you later about a job." He grunted and stamped and sighed as if even in discharging the lower biological functions he had to be louder and more forceful, putting more animal effort into it than might a subordinate or a business opponent.

Tom followed him out and turned half-heartedly towards his earlier drinking companions. "Here, boy, here." Thorpley put an arm around his shoulders and drew him towards his own little group. "This is Mr. Stanton, one of my best and brightest boys." The other old men didn't seem too pleased. It was almost as if they suspected Thorpley of edging in a witness of his own in case something was going to be said later of importance or as if they felt that it was now up to them to produce some underling of their own.

The boss seemed to sense the atmosphere all right. That was one of the things about him. You thought he was just as tough and pushing as a bulldozer, but he felt his way quite gingerly and almost always knew when to back-track. He knew what to do now and he did it. " 'Scuse us a moment, boy," he said. "We were just talking about something important." And he half turned his back to Tom and went on talking to the others about some piece of City gossip that was not important at all. Tom stood uneasily at what had now become the outside of the group, and just then one of the crowd of fellows down the bar looked and raised an eyebrow. He smiled faintly back and nodded and shrugged at the boss's back. His acquaintance turned round and said something to the others and Tom edged about and found himself facing Thorpley's turned back, the heavy, sagged shoulders moving, as he talked and nodded, under their covering of top-quality blue serge pin-stripe.

In a little while the older men left. Two of them said, "Cheerio, Mr. Stanton," and of course he didn't know their names. In those plays on the telly or in a British picture they always had young men calling older ones 'sir', sometimes even their own fathers. But he'd never actually heard anyone say it. Not even some of the real posh people Thorpley had a drink with from time to time.

The boss never seemed to have to worry about getting back for his dinner as others did. But he was married, to a dumpy, grey-haired old dear with glasses. One of the blokes from the office had seen her.

Thorpley slid himself into his favourite position on a stool. "Well, boy, enjoy yourself last night?" he asked.

Tom said, "Yes, dancing and that."

"Plenty of nice girls there?"

"Yes." This didn't seem enough, so he added, "Some real smashers. There's more variety up West."

"Quite right, boy. Enjoy yourself while you're young."

A silence fell. Usually he enjoyed talking to the boss. He was good company and easy to talk to. He liked listening to stories about girls and of disasters which had happened to other blokes, such as not getting anything and the car breaking down in reality and their having to walk eight miles home on a rainy night, and things like that.

Then there were always stories to swap. The boss picked up all the new ones at his business lunches and in the saloon bars. Thorpley liked juicy ones, though. Almost put you off your beer at times.

"What's the matter, then, boy?" The boss had been watching him all the time he had been dreaming and trying to think of something to say. He couldn't answer. There wasn't anything wrong, it was just that he wondered what Carole would say if she were there, what she would think if she could see him here and now with the boss. 'Oh, well, it's business,' he thought. But it wasn't, not really.

"Didn't it go all right, then, last night? Didn't you get your oats? Never mind. Can't win every time."

He started off then to tell Thorpley about last night and the new girl. He made it sound like all the other times and laid it on a bit about what a smasher this one was. He started to joke about how uncomfortable it got in the car and Thorpley stopped drinking and slewed his bulky body round on the stool and listened more closely—and all at once he seemed to hear her saying, "I was hoping you'd ask . . ." He dried up suddenly and, seeing the boss looking at him in a puzzled way and waiting, said, "Her name's Carole."

"Oh, got to names, has it? Take my advice, boy, and don't go getting your emotions involved any. Otherwise before you can turn round twice you'll be spliced. I don't suppose there's a man, not a man in this bar leastways . . ."

Thorpley swayed on his stool and took a sip of his gin and tonic to steady himself up. He had become more red-faced, and made slightly embarrassingly theatrical gestures. His speech had become louder and more emphatic.

". . . Not a man in this whole bar who has been over the side oftener than what I have. But I've always kept it out of the home and never let my emotions get involved. A bit of fun and games is only natural and healthy when you're young and cheers you up a bit when you're older, but if you get your feelings into it as well as your ——— you'll regret it. You take my advice and be guided by me, boy." He started to say it all over again from the beginning.

Tom couldn't see what had started him off on that tack. Who'd said anything about his having fallen for her, about his emotions being involved? Evidently seeing his face and sensing an unease between them, Thorpley paused, swayed and sipped his drink and then said, "Sorry if I've upset you, boy. Envious, I suppose. Not but what I haven't had my moments, mind. But when you get on and have the lolly as well to buy it anywhere you like, up West or at Brighton, then it don't taste so fresh any more." He shook his head in mock sadness from side to side. A thin dribble of gin and saliva trickled from one corner of his great jaw as might an hour-glass skein of muddy water from the idle scoop of an excavator when the operator switches off and gets out his sandwiches. "Just envious, I suppose."

Tom was feeling a bit awkward. It seemed a cheek to sympathise, but that was what the boss was after, wasn't he? "I don't intend getting hitched yet," said Tom.

"Never, boy, never, if you know what's good for you." He stopped, sunk in some private reflection. As if reaching the end of an inner dialogue of which Tom was unaware he went on, "Sundays I let go a bit and have a jug too many. Where's the harm? I always drive careful, especially careful, after. Day of rest, ain't it? Envious of you, boy, that's the truth of the matter."

They chatted some more and Thorpley sloshed another couple of gin and tonics down himself. He really believed himself to be envious of Tom's youth and chances. After all those gins even a more subtle man could be forgiven a mistake in recognising his own emotions. He was not envious. He was jealous.

Thorpley seemed to have a clock in his head. He came out of his reverie with some inner, silent jerk, which showed no outward effect, and said, "Blimey, five minutes to time. 'Scuse me a moment, boy." He slid off the stool and moved with the nimbleness of large people, when they choose to do so, to the door. His shadow could be seen turning sharp right and moving past the frosted glass panels towards the off-licence. Tom was left alone at the emptying bar. He knew that he should be getting back if his mother were not to moan at him over a burnt dinner. This thought hardly fitted in with the present business-man's atmosphere and act, so he thrust it aside before it could really scramble its way to the front of his brain, and thought, instead, 'I can't walk out on the boss, can I?'

When the boss came back it was time. They said good-bye. The boss seemed to want to say something more but to decide against it. He'd bought himself a bottle of brandy with one of those screw tops that make a cup for emergencies and stuffed it in his pocket. He went and got a cheese roll wrapped in a paper napkin and pushed that down on to the flat shoulders of the bottle so that two corners of white paper stood out like the ears of a conjuror's rabbit. A few minutes later, as he was driving to Jack's, he saw Thorpley's car parked down a little side turning called Cornfield Lane, which was only used by local people who knew where it led to. There was, even today, a field on one side, full now not of corn but of householders' rusted water tanks, broken bricks and old tyre and cycles wheels. The boss had been after it for some time for a building site but there was some trouble with the council or the Town and Country Planning bods about how it should be developed. He slowed the car and glanced up the lane.

The boss was sitting slumped behind the wheel munching his roll and looking straight ahead up the empty lane. What a cushy life! No worries, just booze away your Sundays and sleep in your car or at home as you chose, your own boss all week. He wondered if Thorpley would go home when he'd finished eating or have a kip in his car. He just had

D

time to see that all the windows were shut. Must be stuffy in there.

Thorpley chewed on his crust of bread and swallowed hard so that his throat was scraped slightly. Better be careful. The booze stopped you feeling the pain. You could do yourself an injury that way. A drinking man had to keep his wits about him. Suppose a rozzer should show up now, for example, and stick his damn nose in? Well, he'd just say, "It's all right, officer. I've to take an old pal and his wife and kids out for the day to Whipsnade. I'm a bit before my time and don't want to show up in the middle of their dinner. You chaps keep the traffic moving so well. Room to pass behind, ain't there? No obstruction? You're sure? Thanks, officer, cheerio. No day of rest for you, is it? Never mind." The drink so intensified the reality of his own imaginative plannings that he glanced towards the window and moved his lips to form the opening phrases. There was no one there and his gaze fell on nothing more than the clay-heavy footings of a half-built house being slammed up by one of his smaller competitors. Crumbs fell down his waistcoat and stuck to his lips and he brushed them away and washed the feeling of them down with a pull of brandy. He started to think over his plans for the bit of ground on his left, but without slewing round to look at it, partly from the indolence of drink and partly because it was Sunday, a day of rest. If a man couldn't let go a bit and not to have to worry on Sunday, then when the hell could he?

The bread and cheese started to soak up a bit of the alcohol. He felt a drowsiness, though not a calm, settling upon him. The familiar and reassuring smell of his car was all about him. He didn't want to fall asleep here. He'd take one more nip just before he got in and then he should be able to face it.

He started up and backed and turned with the solemn deliberation of the very drunk. Nothing dangerous about it, over-cautious if anything. Two teen-age kids in shorts and bright sweaters stopped their bicycles and waited for him to swing right round again. He nodded and smiled a pleasant apology to them. The girl stood, holding her bike with one hand. She had slid off the saddle and placed her feet wide apart. Blimey, he wasn't a baby-snatcher yet! Gets worse, though, once you're past forty. He'd tell Tom that some time.

He arrived at his own villa and left the car on the gravel runway outside the garage doors. All was quiet and still in the suburban street, as families took advantage of having sent the youngest children off to Sunday school, to snooze in armchairs. He crossed to the front door and let himself in.

The smell of furniture polish and of the dry, hot air from the exhaust of the vacuum-cleaner closed around him. The house breathed its disapproval and unspoken rebuke. It was her house. He just filled it up with junk, anything she wanted. Even with getting some of it wholesale from pals it cost him hundreds in tellies, fridges, and vacs, electric-mixers and sink-disposal units. There wasn't another house in the whole street, in the whole suburb—he swayed slightly as he declaimed the point inwardly, with such a collection of home helps and junk in it. Yet she didn't even seem to bother to bring the neighbours in to admire, not even that loony bunch of hymn singers from the church. The drink had turned out, as it often did, to be an insufficient barrier after all. He needed to work up his hatred a bit before he could really face it. He turned into the blast of sound coming through the living-room door. She looked up at him from the armchair, where she sat knitting, clicking the needles together in her dumpy, brown fingers. The light from the window behind her showed up the faint, grey down around her lips and under her chin. Her greying black hair was scraped back and held by a comb. She looked like the mother of all the schoolmarms, but lacking even a schoolmarm's brisk decisiveness. Though they were the same age she looked much older than he. 'But it's me that has had all the worry,' he thought to, give the edge to his courage to meet her

gaze. "It's in the oven, dear, if you want it." She knew he
didn't. The sixth sense developed by twenty years of pro-
pinquity told her exactly how drunk he was. She only meant
that every wifely function and duty would continue to be performed, that the fault for the impasse and the failure should
always and everywhere be his and his alone. "Sorry I'm late.
Bit of business to discuss with the boys. Got to keep the wheels
turning." He gave the slightest glance towards the blaring
telly to indicate what it was that the wheels had to be kept
turning for. She got up from the armchair of the three-piece
and adjusted the clean linen back-cover. The covering of the
suite matched her person, faded to a rather indeterminate
fawn and grey. Silken tassels, each fixed to a knob like an
acorn, hung from the arms. Casting a bleak wave of martyr-
dom and virtue, she crossed to the sideboard and got out things
to lay the table. It had become a duel. If she got him his
dinner without any complaining and then he didn't eat it, he
would be in the wrong and she the brave little wife of the
drunkard. If he did eat he would be sick and she would fuss
around him and try to hold his head and take advantage of his
weakness to push him about and sit him down before he could
protest, clicking her tongue like an amateur nurse or a busy-
body interfering with the neighbour's neglected children,
meticulous but not really very helpful and without tenderness
of any sort.

"Bring it on, I'll chance it," he said with a beery, man-to-
man smile, making her an accomplice in his battle with his
condition, assuming she was sympathetic. An old dodge and it
never worked but meant that she had to change her ground
slightly and say, "I'll make you something light, an omelette,
if you like, instead." You could not blame a man for having a
bad stomach and he had to step back one pace in order to
launch his next thrust from this level. Assuming that they were
moral equals in complicity over the problem of keeping a
Sunday dinner down not only de-sexed his wife but himself as

well. Besides, the implications of such a relationship could easily extend further than a matter of sharing some digestive mishap. In making it all an act of God which had befallen them Thorpley sought to slide them both unnoticed to the point of view that his total failure as a man in marriage was a natural catastrophe to be jointly endured. His wife, setting the food before him and sighing, would not be drawn the whole way. She was doped with habit as he with drink. The duel ended in a compromise and a draw, just as every more important and decisive moment had always done. He sat and picked at the dried-up food around his plate and even swallowed a mouthful, and his wife held her silence and contented herself with clicking her knitting needles, turning down the volume control of the set so that her sighs could be heard more plainly, and filling the warm, overfurnished room with an icy and man-killing disesteem.

The man pushed his untidied plate aside and lurched over to the other armchair. He picked up the Sunday paper. There was some story about Lady Docker on an inside page, with photos. Now if a man had a wife like that! Not let herself go at all, backing up her husband in his business life, being a good pal to him as well. A day-dream of a sunny beach and a blonde wife at his side merged itself into an uneasy actual dream as he dozed off, ears closed to the babble and chatter from the telly and senses insulated by a souring film of alcohol from full consciousness of the symbol of guilt in the chair facing him.

Later she turned off the telly because it was hurting her eyes and it was time for an hour of light music on the radio. Thus Thorpley swam upwards through a blonde sea towards a golden mermaid shining in the sunlight, moving without effort, slim and young again, to the swaying tune of the Blue Danube waltz. He burst through the surface of the sea and the sunlight hurt his eyes. "Mermaid," he tried to call, "mermaid!" but the sea water had dried out all his throat. He gasped and blinked his eyes and was awake. His wife had just switched on the standard lamp. He had been asleep with his mouth open and his gorge was dust-dry. The only real bit was the waltz. He lay for a minute gulping like a great fish stranded on the beach. The lamp drooped from the top of its tall, varnished totem pole, like some rare variety of palm or monster orchid, spreading an orange glow through its dusty silk and hanging fringe. When he turned his head a bit he saw it all as nobody else in the room or walking past the windows and peeking in could do, from the inside with the twin naked bulbs lighting up the miniature bell-tent more brilliantly than a circus ring.

He felt awful. In a little while she went and banged about in the kitchen and came in with the tea things. He heaved himself up and helped to lay the table. Afterwards she cleared away and washed up and left for evening chapel. That meant it was half-past six. In thirty minutes they would be open again. Her steps faded down the empty Sunday street. Not a word had been spoken.

He had a good evening with some blokes of his own age and brought out two new stories they'd never heard, the one about the northcountryman and Dr. Fuchs and the one about the orphanage. Young Tom never looked in at the Ploughing Team. He went on to whisky. It kept you cheerful and posh bastards like these always drank it.

When he got back she was already in bed. He got undressed and into pyjamas in the bathroom so as not to wake her. The sheets chilled his whisky-heated hide. His ticker was thumping a bit. Better cut down the booze next week. Still deeply asleep, his wife had, all the same, been disturbed by his arrival and turned slightly into the sag of the bed. Her hand, quite nerveless, touched his thigh and he felt the goose-flesh pimpling out his hot, flushed skin. At once he was sober, weak and hot but sober, with nothing to be done now but lie, as it were, in the sheeted trough of his own making, here in the one place where no deception is possible between two people, the place which was for him no more than a nightly visit to the battlefield where he had suffered total defeat over the twenty years. He rolled over with his back to her. Her breath smelt of prayer-books. He tried to make the mermaid come back but you could never work it that way. All the same he was soon asleep, pressed alongside the only person in the world of whom he was truly afraid.

CHAPTER 4

"When Will You Pay Me?"
said the Bells of Old Bailey . . .

GREEN-PAINTED and hosed down dust-free, the trains of the
Southern Region rush and rattle up from the coast and the
Downs to London Bridge, falling down perhaps, but not this
year. Four solid English feet above the rocketing wheels and
the turquoise sparks, fat hams flattened the cushions and dry
fingers rustled the lead-heavy pages of the papers. Modern
metallurgy and applied electricity served a system of finance
which had already become old and unneeded in the days of the
horse tram. The top people could now live at Brighton or high
up on the edges of the downland among the clean gorse and
still leave their cars in the courtyard of some country station
and be in Moor Lane or Lothbury in time to glance at the post,
bully the clerks and think of pinching the typists' bottoms
before lunch.

Sir Henry joined the slight, well-dressed crush at the ticket
barrier, where the first-class seasons flickered white and grey
like egrets hovering around a herd of hippo. Most of the men
who did not look like sharks looked like turtles. Sir Henry,
however, was a trifle taller than average and still kept something military about his walk and moustache.

Arrived at his office, Sir Henry sat looking across a desk
through a dusty window into a well, faced with white tiles like
a swimming bath, down which filtered a thin, grey light
looking as if it were supplied grudgingly by the City Fathers in
return for the rates and in proportion to the amount levied.

Let it run over the quarter and the sky might give a warning flicker and dim itself even further until you paid up.

It looked like being a reasonable day, thought Sir Henry. He'd go over some estimates that Miss Brockett had ready for him and then toddle off to lunch with old Charlie Illstone and that awful, common chap Thorpley, all armed with the latest figures and share movement analysis, exact balance and so on, that he needed.

These were worrying times for a small to middling, sized industrialist and financier. Sir Henry held forty per cent of the shares in his own company. Twenty per cent were held by his old friend Charlie Illstone and the remaining forty by various trust funds, individual investors and members of the family. The company did not attract speculators and its dividends remained fairly steady. Charlie Illstone used his large holding as a platform from which to perform more speculative operations, though even he had been known to go bear on some of his own holdings in a difficult year. But he always came back in the long run. He really knew the company and had inside information about its workings and prospects as about no other. He was up to something now, though. And exactly what it was Sir Henry did not know. However, Charlie would never let him down really badly.

He dictated some letters and told Miss Brockett what figures he wanted her to get out and sat dreaming for a moment about himself and old Charlie. The excuse for this time-wasting activity was that he needed to think about the coming lunch. His friendship with Charlie went back a long time. Neither of them had gone to university but both had been placed in jobs in the City, in their fathers' world. They had known one another slightly at Charterhouse and became closer as their paths crossed again. Both had developed into fairly shrewd but, of course, very inexperienced speculators in their early twenties. Then had come the hot, long summer of '14. There were still horse buses then and the smell of the exhaust of one

of the old General omnibuses was still strange and exciting in
the City air. The solid tyres were full of faults. After a few
months of wear, round holes would appear and when they
pressed against the tarry wooden road-blocks would suck at
the road and let go again with a crack and a pop. The whole
great vehicle trundled and rumbled along more steadily than a
horse bus but started and stopped more quickly. Anyone with
any feeling for horse-flesh could feel a horse bus stopping as if
the collar rode up the back of his own neck. All that had been
long ago. Today there was hardly a horse in the streets and
everything was quicker, more impersonal, less easy to understand. Neither he nor Charlie had ever quite forgotten that
night. The market was closed and all kinds of rumours going
around the City. Late at night they slipped half a guinea to
that pimply little chap in the cable offices who knew the world
market prices before even the night City editors down the hill.
One or two chaps used to see him and sometimes use his information to make a bit by arbitrage—taking advantage of
slight differences of the same shares on different world
exchanges. This famous evening they had had a late supper at
the old Troc. Joey hadn't bought it up in those days. Charlie
had stared at the whitebait and said, "Don't look 'em in the
eyes, old boy, just shove 'em down." Then they had gone and
hung about, sniffing the air, as it were, trying to sift the rumours.
There had been crowds in Whitehall and around the end of
Downing Street, with black-moustached policemen keeping
them moving.

They had judged the time rightly and, sure enough, the little
white-faced, pimply chap had come out to the coffee-stall that
used to stand at the corner of St. Martin's le Grand and
Cheapside. "I'm entitled out at this time, gentlemen, quite
entitled, for a coffee and bite halfway through the shift, but
you'll be discretion itself, gents, won't you now? Discretion
itself."

When it was certain, he had taken a cab back to his father's

house in St. John's Wood. In those days the big houses had
been full of enormous families such as his own, and not
parcelled off into flats and bed-sitters crammed with tarts and
artists, as they were today. Every now and then they would
pass another cab and the two drivers would raise their whips
in salute, as they always did. There had been nothing to
distinguish this from any other warm summer dawn until he
had noticed the policemen, dark against the paling night,
gliding like ghosts on bicycles, the long overcoats hiding the
rotation of their knees, as they delivered telegrams to the
homes of Reservists and Territorials. By seven o'clock in the
morning the drill halls and assembly points had been crammed.
He had been there himself, feeling a perfect fool and trying not
to show it, with his new pips gleaming on his cuffs, where they
were then worn, watching the cooks, whose faces he knew from
summer camps at Bulford and Aldershot, brewing tea over blue
gas-rings.

It had been all going to be over by Christmas. Every now
and then Charlie and he had been on leave together and made
a night of it at *The Bing Boys* and the Troc., exchanged news of
the front, both had got married and watched every single one
of their friends killed. A lot had happened since then. They
didn't meet very often. Took their wives to dinner and a show
as a foursome once or twice a year. Sometimes they'd go six
months and never do more than nod and smile to each other
across the aisle and blackened oak pews of the Peppercorn
Lane Chop House, or raise a glass and wink in the bar of the
Royal Consort Hotel. Three or four times in the last twenty
years they had met by chance in times of crisis—1929, 1939, the
Korean War, once or twice when the Bank Rate had altered
and so on. Then they had teamed up again as in the old days.
Charlie was quicker at getting a man going by tickling his
vanity and offering some other inside information in exchange,
but Sir Henry knew slightly more important people in slightly

greater numbers, so that between them they made a good team. Of course you had to pal up with someone, but it wouldn't be quite the thing to choose someone who wasn't a gent. Besides, you might have to say something, one or the other of you, about having made, for the time being, for the day as it were, a 'gentleman's agreement' or something frightful like that. The whole thing would be simply too embarrassing for words. And then, of course, the other chap might do you in the eye after all. Even supposing he was a gent he might come all that 'love and war' stuff to himself to drown his conscience, and after a couple of stiff pegs, to douse the rest of it, he'd be all right. Only nod even if they met again.

That could never happen with old Charlie. If they were ever up against it they'd always just said so, without any damned whining, of course. Then they'd shared whatever information they had had, and, if they had needed more, had gone and looked for it together. Without any word being spoken both of them always remembered that evening in August '14 when all the world was young.

If this vulgar chap Thorpley thought he could split them up in some way he had another think coming.

Miss Brockett came in with the figures. Nobody could say he was an old stick-in-the-mud as regards admin and all that. He employed a post-war type of angry young woman to do the firm's own market analysis and investment prognostication. A girl, mind you. Not some younger son of an old friend but one of the new generation he'd picked out for himself. He took in the figures very quickly and asked one or two questions. They understood each other very well, Carole and he.

"Sit down, Miss Brockett, please."

"Thank you, Sir Henry."

"I saw Big Tom as I was coming across Cheapside this morning."

"Did you hear about the nest of kittens found under the arch on the old Velum-scrapers site?"

All over the City there were the cats. Some ran wild altogether, catching pigeons and pinching fish-heads from Billingsgate. Others allowed different people to feed them, but never a stranger. Groups of typists clubbed together and bought fish for them. A banker would open his calf-leather brief-case at half-past ten every morning as he strolled up from Cannon Street and put down the scraps which had been wrapped and set ready on the hall table and handed to him by his chauffeur. At week-ends, when the City was empty, the caretakers would clump down from their rooms among the rafters or climb up from their damp cellars and, blinking in the Sunday morning sunlight, shuffle to the pubs, which were open for them alone. Then, on the Monday morning, they would have tales to tell of the cats, how they visited at week-ends, just as people did, and how Big Tom had walked alone up the very centre of the steps of St. Paul's and let himself in the great west door for matins.

The caretakers were all old chaps, ex-Service, who knew a gentleman when they saw one. You could talk to chaps like that without their ever dreaming of stepping over the mark.

They chatted some more together and it was time for Sir Henry to go to lunch. He nodded to the sergeant of the Corps of Commissionaires at the doorway and stepped out as the heavy glass doors swung open for him. The air of the City blew damp around him. He had allowed himself time to walk comfortably to the meeting place. The pavements were not too full. The dodge was to strike the mid-point of the lunch hour, so that the clerks and typists were all either queuing or eating. A little stroll to the Royal Consort gave you an appetite.

Smoke-heavy clouds rolled downwards towards the dome of St. Paul's. Buses and taxis filled the narrow streets and lanes designed for the age of the pack-horse. The good old City still stood. Most of the great gaps of the bomb sites had been filled, but around St. Paul's they gave unexpected views of the river and of other alleys and passageways descending to the high, blackened backs of the warehouses.

The Royal Consort stood beside the terminus of the former Great Consort and Lowlands Railway Company. Dummy castellations sooted over and whitened again with pigeon-droppings topped the Victorian-Gothic frontage. Sir Henry thought, as he climbed the grey steps, 'I've been coming here for damn near forty years now.' This message to himself was meant to convey that, although everything had changed out of all knowledge, the City was still the City and that he had his sure place in it. But it also meant 'I'm getting old.' At the top of the steps he turned for a moment and looked out across the courtyard to the roadway, where the red buses swooped round the corner past the plate-glass windows and granite pillars of the Marine and General Insurance Corporation. They'd taken over and done up the whole lower floor of the old Saddle-makers Building. 'For forty years,' he thought again. That line of poetry he'd learnt as a boy at Charterhouse and for some reason never forgotten came into his heart, ". . . London, my most kindly nurse." He turned and pushed through the rotating doors. He was rather dreading this lunch.

He stuck his head into the cocktail bar with the assurance of his years but with the brisk jauntiness of a somewhat younger man. He was all ready with a gay greeting, but Charlie and Thorpley were not there yet. He strolled through to the washroom. The Royal Consort wrapped its friendly smell about him, beef-steak and mutton chops, stale cigar smoke, dusty carpets and musty hangings and the faintest tinge of coal smoke and steam, as if the ancient railway with which it had originally been associated sent ghosts of long-forgotten arrivals and departures to tenant the grill-room.

"Gooday, Harris."

"Gooday, sir."

"Fog going to hold off, eh?"

"Hope so, sir."

The washroom echoed their voices around its vast, brown marble walls, mottled and ribbed as if with rust streaks. On entering, Sir Henry caught a glimpse of Harris's cubby-hole. A faded sepia photograph of Earl Haig, torn from a copy of the *Illustrated London News*, cupped grey dust in its curled corners; a broken chair showed the peg-holes whence its back-rods had fallen, like an idle poker work; two bales of hand towels bulged over a shelf, and a chipped saucer, near the doorway, held a few coppers and one sixpence. There were not enough coins to make one think of a pavement artist or a busker or to wonder just how much the Royal Consort Hotel paid Harris, above his war disability pension. Nor were there so few coins as to seem pathetic to the sensitive and quite meaninglessly accidental to the obtuse. Nobody dreamed of reaching into Harris's doorway and dropping coins in the saucer. You tipped him and he hooked it away neatly and deferentially, nodding his head sideways, as a cockney sparrow might acknowledge a crumb, and chirped " 'Kew, sir, 'kew." Most likely the same coins had sat in the saucer for years.

Big mirrors, faintly spotted in brown and grey at the edges and corners, extended and repeated the perspective of heavy and ornate wash-bowls, rust-streaked under the brass taps and supported by pedestals encrusted with a lumpy moulding of scrolled *fleur-de-lys*.

The ceiling was a lofty one, its corners almost out of sight in the shadows high above the dark, varnished doors of the compartments. Dusty pipes climbed the walls and writhed away out of sight in the corners, hissing like snakes as the plumbing clanked and groaned to itself.

Sir Henry washed his hands and carefully smoothed his grey hair. In the mirror he could see Harris hopping and lurching about his work. He'd lost his leg on the Somme. Other things wrong with him as well. Give him half a chance and he'd tell you all about shrapnel working its way out of his elbows, chest and knees.

Like a faded jackdaw Harris jerked along, polishing a bright row of brass door handles with a long grey cloth hanging limp like a broken wing. At each step he took there came the faintest creak of leather straps. The 1918 Victory medal, the G.S. and Mons Star ribbons showed up like a single-coloured plume among an old jackdaw's dowdy feathers.

"That's all right, Harris," said Sir Henry opening the door for himself as Harris pivoted and veered with his good leg towards it.

" 'Kew, sir. 'Kew very much." As the door closed he went back to his cubby-hole to read the racing form, and Sir Henry went towards his lunch appointment.

They were sitting in the cocktail bar. It had once been called the lounge until the bar and the metal chairs had pushed out the palms and sofas in the 'twenties. A partition had gone up and a glass screen discreetly shut the bar off from the rest of the lobby. It had all been one of the 'post-war improvements' when there had been a new generation knock, knock, knocking at the door. Now the 'new' bar held its own period charm. Stained orange and black jazz stripes flaked from the wood panelling. Spaced around the walls were fading prints of bobbed-haired, tiny-mouthed, short-skirted women looking archly up from satin cushions or blowing smoke-rings from a cigarette held in a long black holder. All very chic, my dear.

Sir Henry saw them before they had noticed him. Thorpley sat with his back to the light from the huge plate-glass windows and hunched his shoulders and rolled his head from side to side to show amusement at something Charlie was saying.

Did the fellow have his back to the light from habit or accident? Well, there was nothing to worry about, really. Charlie often asked him to lunch to meet some queer fish or other and listen to a proposition or be asked to take part in some plot or plan. Sometimes there was a chance of picking up a bit, but quite often Charlie must have known from the start that he'd turn the thing down and seemed to be satisfied with just the exchange of gossip, or even, though one hardly liked to think it of a friend, with having impressed his new associate with his ability to fix up a lunch with a fairly big director.

This would be one of those lunches, no doubt. This fellow Thorpley had bought a few shares in the company and there had been rumours that he had made a packet on some property-market deals and been among the first to cash in on the Rent Act. Now he was playing the market and seemed to have some contacts in industry as well. They had met once before and Thorpley had struck him as still a trifle unsure of himself at this level. This showed itself not in any timidity nor in aggressiveness, but in his eagerness to pump one about little, unimportant things which everyone took for granted: which jobbers specialised in property and real-estate company shares and where they could be found at different times of the day and so on. Couldn't be much harm in lunching with a fellow like that. You'd be able to see what he was up to hours before he tried it. His mind would be like one of those old-fashioned ticker-tape machines that had gone out of use, showing all their works clicking away under a glass dome.

"Hullo, there. It's the man himself." Thorpley heaved himself up to his feet and shook his hand firmly, but with a damp and slightly pudgy hand.

"How do you do?" said Sir Henry. "Good day, Charlie." They settled themselves. Thorpley ordered drinks.

They'd evidently been talking about golf before he came. Charlie glanced across at him and said, "Mr. Thorpley's keen on improving his game." Sir Henry nodded. The code in use here was not technical but social. Charlie did not mean to convey any warning or message, as might have been the case if they were a pair of gamblers or con men with a new prospect.

E

He did not mean so much that Thorpley was keen on improving his fortune, for that was axiomatic with all three of them. The slight intonation given the statement meant that he had come late to the game and to the world of contacts it carried with it. He must have grubbed and scrabbled his way up via social clubs, local Conservative Association billiard-rooms or Rotary clubs, and only lately, making his health and corporation the excuse, have taken up golf.

Thorpley said, "There's too many clubs to remember. I never remember which one to use." He laughed with an open and hearty self-depreciation. He had them. You couldn't patronise a complete rabbit who made no bones about it.

Charlie took the only possible line as soon as the three of them emerged from their chuckles. "True enough, true enough," he said with the air of one who has also known a similar suffering in the not so distant past. But he demonstrated his real, his superior, knowledge in the same breath by going on, "And yet some of the American clubs are talking again of having more."

"More? Never! And it isn't as if they gave them to you for free." And Thorpley shook his head from side to side in mock sadness.

"Fact, I assure you. Sixteen, or some number like that. Seems they feel they need three sorts of pitching wedge for a start. One type for grass, another for sand and another for the hard ground they get out in the south-west. Of course the Royal and Ancient'll never wear it for a moment."

"Of course," said Sir Henry, "over there they go in for electric caddy-cars and all that nonsense."

For all of them the gin and tonic had filtered its way to the blood-stream, opening the capillaries and softening the very highest levels of consciousness so that they became more pliable to the touch of the next level below. The conversation could now slide and glide along comfortably enough until it came to grips over the coffee and cigars. They chatted some more, Thorpley keeping up his act of a buffoon for whom golf-clubs and business lunches were all too much, quite beyond such a simple chap as himself. Then they went in to eat in the grill-room.

Sir Henry led the way to his usual table. They all three began with cold consommé, but after that the differences began to appear. Charlie ordered a jugged hare and Sir Henry roast beef. Thorpley asked for a mixed grill. All three chatted about golf and mutual acquaintances. Then the first course was cleared away and golf seemed to be understood to have gone with it. Time had passed. The huge dining-room, which had not been more than half full, now cleared further of travellers with a train to catch and provincial ladies with just time to catch a taxi to a matinée, and left only groups of business-men talking in low voices at scattered tables in corners, as might lovers in an emptying night-club. The cigars were lit and the coffee cups and brandy glasses set out. As the waiters swung through the doors to the kitchens a rattle of crockery, hitherto hidden behind the murmur of conversation, swelled and dwindled again with the shutting of the doors, as if a sound-effects man toyed with the volume control.

Somebody had to start. Thorpley had lit his cigar and sat back, grunting and chuckling pleasantly from behind his smoke-screen at appropriate points in the conversation, which had been for some time carried on entirely by the others. Now he moved forward to train his guns through the camou-flage and said, "Well now, Sir Henry, has Mr. Illstone told you why I was wanting to meet you?"

"Can't say he has."

"Mr. Thorpley has an offer to make," said Charlie.

It was quite impossible to tell from Charlie's voice what was afoot. Most likely the fellow simply wanted to buy his way in and offer some vague inducement as a bait.

Thorpley sat back again and from behind a fresh puff of

cigar smoke said, "There's no sense beating about the bush. I got nothing to hide and something to offer. You're after a piece of land to extend that factory out on the Winstead by-pass?" The question had been made as if it were a statement, except for a slight rise of voice at the end, and Thorpley went straight on. "I've got interests out that way. These things get around. Now, I could help you find that land, I reckon just where you want it. I'll give you more details and you can make me an offer. Only thing is, I want part of it in shares. I see you're standing at 41/3. Now here's the proposition: I'll get you a nice slice of land adjoining that by-pass works of yours at about twenty pound a foot frontage less than you'd get it anywhere else. I heard it rumoured, heard it rumoured very reliable, that you're going to extend and maybe float a new issue or raise some money by fresh debentures. Now, I said to myself, 'Thorpley, you can do this firm a bit of good and, of course' "—he sank retiringly back behind his smoke-screen and sent through it a disarming message of openly admitted, honestly recognised weakness—" 'yourself a bit of good and all, and you need it more than what Sir Henry's firm does.' So I worked it out this way, I'll give it you straight and then we can get down to figures. I'm looking for an open-ing for a bit of my capital, something less speculative as it's called, not quite so dodgy I call it. You'll be wanting money for the land, money for the new plant and a contract with a builder who'll put it up for you and perhaps have to wait a bit for his money. So I looked around and I thought about it and I said to myself, 'Thorpley, help this firm get their land, fix up with—with a pal of mine for the building contract, and in return ask to get in on the ground floor of any new share or debenture or preference share issue they may be planning.' Just to start us off on real figures, I'll offer Mr. Illstone here 42/- for a good slice of his holdings, say a thou. I know they're going to rise to that when your development plans leak. Then when you've satisfied yourself that you can't get the land cheaper'n what I said, I'll get it for you twenty pound a foot lower."

Now that he had finished firing his first salvo, Thorpley pushed his muzzle up through the smoke and leaned both elbows on the table, hunching his shoulders so that the well-cut suit folded in an untidy yoke behind his neck.

Sir Henry was feeling relieved. Although he had no reason to suppose that Thorpley knew a lot about the affairs of the company, it was true that they had made a few, he had hoped, discreet enquiries about sites for extending the works. The board and he had both thought that even the news of this might push the share prices up a point or so and show the firm to be in a healthy position and so on. If things went well they might be able to get started and swing the rest with an over-draft. And if things went badly they could make the need to expand the new plant an excuse for cutting the dividend next year without there being too big a slump in price as a result. The rest could be accomplished by what is known as 'gearing' here and, with the customary national choice of a stronger and more picturesque word, as 'leverage' in the U.S.A. Thus Sir Henry had little real interest in Thorpley's offer but more than a curiosity in finding out just how he knew as much as he did and if he knew anything more. To some extent, too, although he was so very much the bigger fish, this very fact made him feel in slightly unfamiliar and shallower waters where he might have to give an undignified flap and twist to get off again if he were not careful. Damn it all, *he* couldn't be expected to know that leaks might occur among tuppeny-ha'penny real-estate chappies. He started to feel slightly annoyed, the vague annoyance of self-defence against a wholly imagined accusation which is so often the manifestation of a deeper, disguised unease. He decided to play for time for a bit.

"What've *you* got to say to Mr. Thorpley's offer, Charlie? It's you Mr. Thorpley's making a real offer to." This con-stituted a nicely phrased provocation as well as a delaying tactic. Thorpley, however, did not bite it, but the implications of "making a *real* offer to . . ." were plain enough.

"I'm not clear just what conditions Mr. Thorpley is making," said Illstone, who had been sitting watching the opening rounds from a neutral corner, as it were. "Is his offer entirely conditional on his getting the total number of shares he asks for? And upon his friend getting the building contract?"

Unexpectedly this drew Thorpley. His heavy jowl reddened and his voice took on a rasping, bullying tone plainly more habitual to him than his previous near-whine. "I'm not asking for the favours. I don't need no favours. I suggested this little talk because I thought it might do us both a bit of good. If you don't want, I mean if you think . . ." He checked himself by some inner process whose only outer sign was a tremor and slight whitening of the nostrils. "If there's no deal, if that's how you feel, we'll talk some more about golf and have another drink and part as friends."

Sir Henry was not ready to have matters take this turn just yet. He could not be certain, either, at the moment, whether the man was really angry or using the traditional device for cutting short an unsatisfactory interview or encounter, by taking offence where none has, in fact, been offered. If he *was* upset it meant that he had hoped to get a lot more out of it than was apparent or that he was naturally touchy and unsure of himself at this level of commerce. Most likely the latter, Sir Henry decided and said, "Come, Mr. Thorpley, we don't do things quite like that here in the City. If you want to make a large offer for some of our shares—and may I say how gratified I am at your confidence in our company?—then you must find a jobber to act for you. We don't do things quite like this here." 'If that doesn't draw the damned badger, then he was putting it on before,' thought Sir Henry.

"I'm making an offer. If you or Mr. Illstone take it up, of course it'll go through whichever of your pals you choose to name."

"That wasn't quite what I meant."

"Let me say it just once more. I want to take up quite a few of your shares and I have ways, more than all that about the land, to help the company along. That should suit all concerned. If it don't, then it don't, that's all."

Sir Henry hooked out at the indiscretion as lightly and quickly as a playful cat: "Other ways?"

Thorpley had to choose between plunging deeper or seeming to have made a silly bluff. He paled a trifle and said, "Never mind. If we can't do business it doesn't matter."

Sir Henry was not keen to have a bounder like this buy his way into the company and perhaps in a few years become a substantial shareholder. If the fellow wanted to climb, let him stick to property and leave industry and finance alone. It became quite impossible to save anything of the atmosphere of the luncheon. Thorpley lost his temper again once towards the end. Charlie glanced across at him and raised an eyebrow, which was a bit much really because it had been his doing. However, they all three shook hands on the steps of the Royal Consort.

Just before the market closed Sir Henry looked in to the Stock Exchange. He saw Charlie talking to a jobber. Most jobbers kept to a special part of the house and any broker knew where he could find one who specialised in any particular desired type of security. Sir Henry couldn't place this one, though. Oh well, it was none of his business what old Charlie was up to.

Incidents such as the lunch with Thorpley were regarded by Sir Henry much as he had once looked upon the filth of the trenches and army life when on leave. The scuffle and dust of the market place could be brushed off your clothes and washed off your hands and left behind. Once the train had taken him forty miles south-east of London another world and a changed code ruled his actions. The rules and taboos of the City were quite different from those of the home; the week from the week-end. Sir Henry held that one should never underpay or treat badly a personal servant but one might a clerk; that one could borrow a very large sum of money and delay its repayment by every known legal device but should settle one's tradesmen's bills promptly; that one might not cheat at cards but could do so in business. He would never have dreamed of bringing a mistress into his home, during his wife's absence, but saw no harm in a man's visiting one at her flat. One of the old school, in short, who believed in going to church from time to time, but not in God.

Though he never felt the slightest sense of strain in casting off one set of edicts and slipping into another, the process was generally accomplished by traditional personal rituals. If he were dining in town, the pleasures of drink and relaxation blurred the sharp edges of the day's skirmishings and skidded him home without need to bother with any transference of manner. Just a wealthy man who has dined well coming home to a lovely house and a placid wife. But if he were leaving early he would first walk across London Bridge. However harassing the day might have been, he made what he called "an effort for the sake of my blood-pressure" and assumed a calm and unhurried manner. This, and the unmistakable presence of a successful man, alone distinguished him from the neatly-dressed clerks and bowler-hatted lesser City men pressing and dodging forward with the exact speed needed to catch the 5.43. The first-class waiting-room gave on to one end of a long bar which thus discreetly hinted at its 'saloon' status. Railway officials turned a blind eye to the occasional gentleman who re-passed the swing doors and stood just inside the unlicensed waiting-room to finish his drink away from the third-class crush. This action Sir Henry performed with unfailing accuracy of social judgment. To have strode boldly over and sat down with a drink on one of the benches, upholstered in the same material as the first-class compartments, would have been too overt and brutal a challenging of the law and the regulations. At the same time it would be no good dithering nervously in the doorway all the time as if expecting the station-master to arrive with a policeman at any moment. The correct manner, that which Sir Henry carried as naturally as his umbrella, was to behave as if one were in a club of which one was an old and distinguished member, and which was undergoing some temporary alterations. As a good co-operative member one put up with a certain amount of inconvenience, drank standing in a draught and tried not to get in the way of the workmen.

The extra Pullman coach added to certain trains was quite like a club in atmosphere. Most of the men knew one another and chatted and exchanged City gossip over drinks at the small tables lit by pink, composition shaded lamps which quivered and hummed as the travelling bar sidled over the points and swung and rattled its way past the backyards and railway arches and factories of South London.

The country darkness of the station courtyard and the fresh smell marked another stage. A single high-powered bulb over the exit lit the tyre-marked gravel and left the shadows beyond as black as only a moonless country night can be. Secretly Sir Henry would have preferred to have used the estate wagon to drive the five miles to his home, but his wife liked it for the shopping, so the townish-looking black saloon had to serve instead. Even in quite cold weather he drove slowly with the window right down, letting the hedgerow smells and the momentary manure stench from a field or farm blow into the stuffy interior. The headlights flared the leaves of low-hanging boughs into a sudden, unreal green, like the decorations and hangings of a display of gardening tools at some exhibition. But this was the real thing. Moths and gnats spattered the windscreen in summer and sometimes a hare would dash across the road in terror of the great white beam.

After garaging the car he would walk across the gravel drive to the front door, smelling the damp earth of the garden. His tired shoulders would droop a trifle and his pace become much more leisurely than it ever was in the City. If it were a light night he could make out the dark shapes of cattle or horses in the distance on the two acres belonging to him which he let out to a local farmer—"my tenant farmer" as he liked to call him in casual conversation with acquaintances. He let himself into his large hall with its burnished brass gong hung from two buffalo horns and its fake Jacobean chairs, assuming now all the air of a leisured member of the landed gentry. When they could get one, there was a house-boy to take his coat. His wife, Mary, would come out of the drawing-room or down the stairs and commence local gossip and news and matters for his attention. "After dinner I wish you'd write to Mr. Fowler"— the 'tenant farmer'—"about those lorries. He's bought three Government-surplus army ones, awful-looking things, rusty and camouflaged or something, and parked them at the far end of home acre. I think he's going to sell them again soon when he's done them up or something, but they do look so awful there." Or else she would give him news of the garden in season and ask him to look at certain things before he left in the morning, remind him of local events to come in the next few days, garden fêtes in aid of the church rebuilding fund and bridge parties with others of their kind. Sir Henry would listen and give each matter his whole attention. The squire returns.

On this particular night they dined alone, waited upon by a girl from a D.P. camp. Then they watched a play on the television set and listened to the news. The servant brought in late coffee, which his wife served, and Sir Henry poured a liqueur for each of them and a second for himself. By domestic tradition his wife retired first and he was supposed then to 'work' for half an hour or so, answering letters of a purely family nature, dealing with 'estate' business. Over recent years this delay in his time of retirement had become a ritual formality. Measured by the clock, which, of course, it never was, the period was often little more than five or ten minutes. And these Sir Henry had spent only in sipping his drink and fiddling with objects on a corner escritoire. He came across odd scribbled memoranda and notes of his wife's. "W.V.S. 3.30 Wed." or "Hall windows—three yards" and snaps of their grandchildren which she had been complaining of having mislaid. 'Dear Mary,' he would think and it would be time to go to bed.

Halfway up the wide staircase a grandfather's clock fingered the hours with hands which jerked and trembled slightly from age. But its sound old heart clicked and thudded inside its oak case as strongly as it had ever done. The clock stood one step below a turn in the stairs where a small leaded window gave on to a view of the garden. Except in very bad weather Sir Henry always opened this window slightly on his way up to bed— "to give the landing an airing". Tonight he paused here and listened to the beat of the clock. It had stood in the hall of his father's house in town years ago, and even now the sound could sometimes bring back the smell of his father's cigars and the dusty, thick carpet. The stroke of the pendulum and sharp release of the ratchet made a double click, of which the second was muffled and deeper. He stayed for a moment or two after opening the tiny casement, letting the night air trickle on to his face. There was a smell of damp grass and a sudden rustle as some small animal went about its business in the darkened garden. Sir Henry washed and got into bed quietly and carefully so as not to disturb Mary. Already asleep in the short time, she sighed and put out one hand to his. It was a long time before he slept. He lay enjoying the comfort and security of his home about him in the dark. Everything was so secure and familiar it seemed a pity to waste it all in sleep. He had no sooner fallen asleep than he seemed to be awake again. A slight cramp in one leg and the last traces of some uneasy dream made him realise that he had in fact been asleep for some hours. He looked at his watch. Just after three. Better

get up now, no use putting it off. Worst of getting old, your
bladder nagged you and you couldn't tell it to go to hell and
hold on till the morning any more. Because it was further
down the hall and its plug made less racket he visited the guest
bathroom. There was a clean hand-towel and nothing else in
the room. It smelt dusty and unused and looked unfamiliar
like a hotel room. When he switched off the light he was
blinded for some seconds in the dark and made his way back
with one hand on the wall, towards the sound of the clock.

His sight slowly returned and he could make out the outlines
of the window and a triangle of starry sky. An owl hooted twice
and the clock clicked and tocked steadily. He leaned on the
banisters and looked down at nothing in the well of the stairs,
but the perfect familiarity of his surroundings enabled him to
imagine the exact appearance of the spot at which he gazed in
the hall below. It was like being the captain of a ship on a
familiar night watch on the bridge. His command was all
around him. A warm, safe machine for living floating on the
cold sea. Thinking only of his home and half pretending to be
engaged in some investigation into his powers of seeing in the
dark or of judging distances at night, he was surprised to find
the thought, 'That fellow Thorpley wouldn't know how to live
in a place like this,' suddenly come into his mind with such
force that he almost spoke the words aloud. 'But then that's
true of a lot of people,' he told himself. The sound of the clock,
of which he had been unaware for some minutes, now reached
him and he started to count its beats to distract himself. 'Must
get the mind bored or I'll never drop off again,' he insisted.
He crossed nearer to the top of the stairs and felt a chill draught
blow up from the open casement. 'Blast it,' he thought, 'I
wonder what exactly the swine is up to.'

CHAPTER 5

Family Matters

CAROLE got up at her Sunday morning time and went down in a dressing-gown to pick up her half-pint of milk and the *Observer*. She made herself a cup of tea and slice of toast and sat in bed reading the paper and studying the company reports and City Notes.

She was due to go home for a visit that day and her thoughts reached ahead, as she did her Sunday jobs—triple-folding a scorched blanket and laying it along the top of the chest of drawers, and ironing a slip and some hankies and a blouse and a towel and a sheet. Then she made the bed with the clean sheet and dusted. Her mother would be doing the same at this time, only for four beds instead of one. She had a sudden picture of the bedrooms of her old home and of her father pottering about and grumbling because someone had touched one of his tools. He'd given in to life too early and her mother had not. She started to think of her father and of how she had loved him and just accepted her mother as something in the background, a part of her environment, and then how it had changed and gone wrong. She had fought with her father and brother and suddenly found her mother an ally, not over anything silly but over anything to do with her studies. Sometimes even now she blushed to think what a little prig her mother had had to defend against the menfolk, especially after the battles had started over going to university. As if it all wasn't difficult enough, she had just discovered Freud and drove her father mad explaining the nature of the emotional patterns in the family and so on, so that her mother had to keep coming out from the kitchen and saying, "Leave her be, Alfred," and "Shut up now, Miss Madam! That'll do." It wasn't until years later that she discovered that it had been to pay for her extras and uniform the last few years at grammar school and to contribute towards her upkeep afterwards that Alfred had taken on all kinds of week-end work, helping at the green-grocer's and then going to collect glasses and fetch drinks in a pub. She glanced at the very bright and shiny alarm clock she had bought herself. In another half-hour he would be starting out. He kept it on for beer money and to get out of the house on a Sunday and, she realised, thinking about it deeply for the first time, as a kind of doubly inverted pride. He shambled off to be a part-time, odd-job man at a pub with an air of "That's all I'm fit for now", but at the same time he did not need the job desperately, as might some old-age pensioner, so he "kept his independence" and could walk out at any time. For the last few years Carole had been sending five pounds a month home to her mother. More was not yet needed.

Thinking of Alfred at his pub made her think of this new boy in her life. She hoped they wouldn't meet where her father was working. It was the sort of fantastic thing that happened in life when you didn't want it to. Besides, Tom knew her home area. He must be in and out of pubs there all the time either with clients or with this 'senior partner' that he was always talking about. Heavens! What did it matter? Hadn't she more important things to think about!

Quite ruffled with herself, as if she had been caught out in some stupid slip of memory or personal efficiency, she hurriedly got ready, picked up some presents for her younger brother and sister, and left.

"On parade, then, Alfred?" Alfred Brockett nodded, pushing his way clear of elbow-leaners and standing customers around the bar of the Lord Roberts. Though no one knew it, the 'on parade' gag was peculiar to the house, having started,

perhaps years ago, with soldiers from the barracks or blokes
having a quick one before the British Legion bar opened. At
all events it held to the public bar, passing from person to
person and generation to generation of regulars as if it were a
common cold or the name of a speciality of the house. The
two words were able to carry any number of shades of meaning. Between neighbours, meeting on the sly out of sight of
their wives, on the way back from the allotments, 'on parade'
and a wink held the bold swagger and charm of a pair of
highwaymen in top-boots and tricorns meeting at the cross-
roads. From the landlord to the customers it was a form of
familiar welcome and greeting. Alfred knew that to him it
meant the easy familiarity and comfortable superiority of a
sergeant meeting one of his platoon in a civilian bar. He
shuffled, dodged and ducked his path with a cluster of foam-
specked mugs clubbed in either hand by the sticky handles and
dumped them double-handed on the far, dark corner of the bar,
to be washed. Then he would dart and weave away for more,
under elbows and past stomachs, among friends and between
red-faced opponents in argument, with a " 'Scuse, please,
gents". Either he went as unnoticed as a Chinese scene-shifter
or met with, "On parade, then, Alfred, on parade, eh?" And
he would nod like a dusty, tropical bird in a zoo in a cold
country, feeling past its prime, but knowing whence the tit-
bits came. "Having one, then, Alfred. Having one, eh?"

"Thanks, Charlie, thanks very much. I'll have a half in
here," and he would reach up and gingerly finger down a pint
pot lodged on the corner of the curly, dark-varnished shelf
which housed the clock, set to run its regulation ten minutes
fast. A steady number, collecting glasses. It brought in a bit
extra, kept you out of the old woman's way, and then the
customers were good for a couple of pints at least.

The public bar filled on Sunday mornings with working men
in their best clothes. At the week-ends a banker likes to dress
casually and coolly with an open-neck shirt, walk around his

gardens or play golf in loose cotton and alpaca like a baker at the oven. But the baker puts on a blue suit and a stiff, winged collar and dark tie, sets a black homburg with a dirty silk ribbon around its curled brim on his grey head and goes to the pub looking like a banker. The young men came in bright and startling clothes, parti-coloured shirts and draped jackets. They grouped together with their backs to the respectable elders, telling their own jokes and bursting into sudden guffaws.

They were no good for a drink and Alfred hated them. That's how Harold'd turn out, for sure. All the same, young people today had it too soft.

When the crowd thinned there was time to stand at the corner of one of the tables and talk to some of the old regulars, who kept his glass topped up.

"How's the missus, then, Alfred?"

"Fine, worse luck." The convention was to rattle off the accepted jokes in turn, quickly but without even a smile, let alone a laugh.

"Kids all right?"

"Not earning enough to keep me yet."

"What, not even that posh daughter of yours?"

This was getting a bit near the mark. Alfred drank from his mug and turned the point to its opposite as sharply as his horny thumb could flip a coin. "Going abroad again this year. Public relations they call it, hotel people and all that." He jerked his hand off quickly but vaguely to the right and nodded his head with a faked-up shrewdness. The men at the table nodded in return, everyone showing they knew what public relations were. But obviously none could know better than Alfred, who had them in the family. The balance thus restored and honours even, patronage could start again: "Ready for one, Alfred?"

It was getting on for closing. The single men in lodgings, where they had a Sunday dinner all in, drank up and left along with the more considerate or hen-pecked of the married men.

Soon it was near time and only a few tough old boys, widowers who would go back to their empty cottages by the railway sidings and have an easy fry-up and after a good kip go and have a high tea at some married daughter's or son's home, were left, together with one or two of the wilder young men. The bare, white, scrubbed table-tops were darkened with beer-glass rings and smudged with cigarette ash. Alfred ducked under the bar flap and started to help wash glasses.

The bar turned a sharp corner into the saloon, where the draught beer was a penny more a half-pint and the walls were covered with pebble-dash pink paper and prints of green and yellow hopfields and hearty harvesters from the brewery's publicity department, all in light oak frames. If you could not afford to have the chairs and tables replaced in the new contemporary styles, at least you could brighten the place up a bit. Makes a change, when all's said.

The saloon customers, given a few more minutes' grace to finish their drinks, sat sipping and talking loudly. Now that last orders could not be taken, Alfred was set with a nod to gathering glasses.

The last customers went out and the boss shot the bolts with a rattle that echoed up among the cigarette smoke and the brown, gilt cornices of the mirrors. The Lord Roberts fell quiet, so that the chink of the glasses in the sink seemed to go on of its own accord. It was as if the whole place were still settling and shifting slightly after an avalanche. All at once everyone felt tired. The boss's wife went out to the private kitchen and turned the roast potatoes over. A greasy, opium-heavy smell of roast beef followed her back, mingling with the spilt beer and smoke. Alfred found a light ale nearly untouched and poured into it the heel-taps of three gin glasses and knocked it back. The boss was watching, but he was getting on with it, wasn't he? Habit he'd got into in the old days. Not so much need for it now, of course. He wasn't all that short. But you can't put a half glass of light ale down the bloomin' ullage surely? Might send the lot off, mixing 'em like that. Then the blasted boss'd never shift it, not even on the last knockings at ten-thirty of a Saturday night. What was the boss looking so sour about? Wanted his dinner? But then who bloody well didn't?

"No need for that, Alfred. Have one with me, if you like," and the boss put a shilling in the cash-register and rang it up as even a bishop bows to the altar, to keep the accounts straight and set an example. Alfred knew that it all really meant, "Don't make me out to be a mean old swine from whom the staff have to pinch drinks behind his back. And don't go putting me off my dinner with your down-and-out's habits. Time you forgot 'em, like me."

The boss's wife sniffed and trotted up the whole length of the bar to pick up some dirty glasses, as if to say that *someone* had to do the work. The boss ignored her. Master in his own house, that one. Even if it was only a public one.

"Ta, guv'nor. I'll have a light a bit later when we've shifted a bit more. Just before knocking off," said Alfred. The boss nodded and waved a hand behind him in Alfred's direction. He had his back turned and was counting the notes.

When the place had been cleaned up and the new crates shifted in from the yard ready for the evening, the guv'nor let Alfred out of the side door and gave him his ten bob. Alfred stood for a moment. If there had been someone with him he would have made the old crack about, "What's that funny smell? Fresh air?" But he was alone. He heard the bolts rattle home inside the door behind him and the sound both reminded him that he was outside and brought back the atmosphere of the last two hours. Now they'd all have their dinner and then sleep until it was time to get ready for the evening opening time.

The big Sunday afternoon radio and TV shows were starting. The last few kids had gone to the corner shops to buy ice-cream for afters and Tizer to drink. A few of the less popular

Sunday papers flapped limply in the damp breeze. The streets were empty.

The others were just finishing and Carole had already arrived. She stood up and gave him a duty kiss on his cheek. The old trouble-and-strife said, "You've finished up early, then? Ready for your dinner, I expect." She liked to make out that everything was fine between them with Carole there. And her saying "finished early" as if he'd come in from some business of his own or a shop or something, instead just from collecting up glasses, sweeping the floor and pearl-diving in a pub!

"Wait a minute, Dad, and we'll clear this lot for you," said Carole. If she had just done it without saying anything he might've been grateful. At home it wasn't very pleasant, was it, to have to eat your dinner with other folks' left-overs scattered all around you? At work, in a caff or a canteen somewhere, it'd be different. "Never mind, never mind," he said. "We're not at the Ritz now."

Carole ignored this and went on clearing the custard-smeared plates away to the scullery. She set the mustard, salt and pepper at his elbow. "There," she said. She sounded like a blooming sister in a hospital or one of those posh W.V.S. cows in the blitz giving you a cup of tea and a plateful of soya links and dehydrated murphies when you'd come in from scraping the bodies out of the rubble.

After he'd eaten he sat in the armchair by the fire. The kids were out of the way and the two women washing up or getting the tea or something in the scullery. He could hear their voices and the odd word. He opened the *News of the World* and started to read. There certainly were some dirty swine in the world all right. Soon he was dozing.

"He's off," said Mrs. Brockett, nodding towards Alfred. Carole met her eyes and smiled. The smile was a conspiracy of women but not of the immediate present. It went right back to the time before they had drifted apart, to the days when her mother had said things like, "Help me get this done before your dad gets in." The two girls, as it were, having the task of keeping the peace and doing the jobs, seeing that things ran smoothly and there were no rows, because, well, just because they were the girls. Later mother and daughter had fought. The mother, both proud and jealous of her daughter's studies, mocking them and at the same time fighting for her right to quiet and a room of her own to do them in. Then Carole had gone through a period of looking down on her home and complaining that she couldn't bring her friends back because of its shabbiness and the noise and the sight of her father in shirt-sleeves. Now that she had grown up and become a woman in her twenties the two were closer again.

"I wanted you to see Harold. He's growing up. Getting to be quite a handsome boy," said Mrs. Brockett. Carole knew that this really meant, 'I'm sorry he's not in. I tried to get him to stay. He's still the same, jealous of you.'

"Still dashing around on his bike?" asked Carole. "Or is it girls yet, with him?"

"Both, I reckon. But of course he never tells me anything."

The tiny scullery was hot with steam but an icy draught cut across the floor. Moisture ran down the cracked, green-painted walls. There was still nowhere to put the plates as you dried them. Each one had to be carried across to the table and stacked properly. The drawer for the knives and forks was at the opposite end, three paces away. The draining-board wobbled and leaked. Everything had been like this ever since Carole could remember.

"There's one thing I will say," the elder woman went on. "He's stuck in this last job at the factory. Must suit him. 'Course he don't give a damn for it, only for the money, though he's got one pal there. Smart lad. Brought him home once, very athletic and all that, boxing. That's a nasty sport, that is. It would have to be that for his pal. I mean, shows there's always something."

They had finished the washing-up but stayed standing in the damp scullery, leaning back on the table edge to talk. Alfred slept in the kitchen, where there were still a couple of comfortable chairs empty, but they held to an unspoken agreement to stay for a while standing, as if even Alfred's sleeping presence might inhibit them. There was an awkwardness between them, however, as if they were too close to use words and not close enough not to have to.

"How he is now I'll tell you. He don't know if he's a boy or a young man. One minute he's playing his jazz records and then begging the fare up West off me till Friday to go up to some club or other, and the next he's tearing around on his bike timing himself and all that. We had a right dust-up the other week. Over money. I'm always subbing him. Well, I said he wasn't going to get another penny until he'd paid back what he owed me already. Then he started on about his friends at the club and about his jazz, saying I didn't understand, which is true enough anyway. He started to swear at me. I slapped his face. I shouldn't've done it to a boy that age, I know, but I won't be sworn at by my men-folk. You can ask *him* that." She jerked her head to the next room. "I was pleased with him a moment later and of course that made me feel worse. He stood up straight and just said, 'I'm sorry, Ma.' He's not the sort to act it, not sharp enough. It was just how he took it. And walked out with my finger marks across his cheek. There's a lot of his grandfather in him, a lot. Anyway he went out. He came in earlier than I'd expected, panting and hot and his eyes bright. 'Ma,' he says, 'we got the rozzers to time us over the measured mile where they got the speed-trap set up and I averaged twenty-seven. Boxer was next with twenty-two.' Full of it he was and expected me to put the flags out. I thought to myself, 'Tell your jive pals and see what they say.' "

Carole said, "You're too soft with him. You always have been."

'Still jealous, at her age,' thought Mrs. Brockett. She then thought, 'Eager enough to leave home, though. More so than the boy and it'd be more natural in him. Still, she's a woman now and at least knows enough not to try and boss him or show off her book-learning in front of him. She's that much older now anyway.' She only said, "Perhaps I am. He was my first boy." She too was older now than when Carole had been a child.

The two younger children came back from Sunday school and woke up their father, who started to grumble. It was time for the women to go into the other room and keep the peace.

Later Alfred went off to his glass-collecting at the Lord Roberts. The children and the two women sat in the front room watching the Sunday night shows on the telly. Then it was bedtime and her little sister was still young enough to demand that Carole visit her in bed to say good night. Now that she no longer had the burden of shopping and housework and child-care which falls upon the eldest girls of all working-class families Carole enjoyed the cosy familiarity of these sips of family life. She could take it or leave it nowadays. Going down the narrow, creaking staircase brought the feeling of her youth around and upon her: trying to do homework with the wireless blaring, fetching ten pounds of potatoes back when she'd only just got in from a rounders match, darning and re-darning her own gym slip and ironing her own blouse at eleven at night whilst her mother was still busy doing the washing for the rest, and accepting it all without question until she was about sixteen. Then had come that day of the big rain-storm. Probably her mother could not even remember it particularly, for her it would be just one row among many that she'd had with one child among four. For Carole it had been a day of decision. All the other girls seemed to be met by indulgent fathers in cars when it rained. (Didn't *their* dads have any jobs?) Carole had got in soaked and found her mother in tears over some row with Harold, and she had been told to go out to the fish-and-chip shop to get the tea. Running home so

quickly had not given her time to drop her school personality
and she had said, "Oh, jolly dee! Now? Or shall I wait until a
cloud-burst starts?" and "Why can't dear little Harold go?
He's got his Wellingtons." She could see now that perhaps her
mother had then had a moment's guilt, which had made her all
the harder. Besides, in her world, the girls had always had to
do such things as soon as they could be trusted with the money
almost. Why should she have treated her daughter differently?
Anyway, her mother had gone off the deep end altogether. She
could still remember her exact words now, after all these years:
"Don't come your posh talk and airs in this house! Go and get
the tea and that's the end of it, madam." She had thrust the
housekeeping purse into Carole's hand and pushed her to the
door. Then had come a lot more abuse that neither Carole nor
her mother could have remembered, not the actual speech,
just the feel of the two of them standing in the narrow hall, half
sideways because of the pram, and screaming at each other.
It had been one of those terrible moments in life when one's
physical surroundings and even one's talk seem hardly to exist
in reality but only the general sense of anger and hysteria and
the sound of noisy words. Walking back later from the fish-
and-chip shop with the newspaper bundle warming her chest
under her mac, she had caught sight of herself reflected in a
shop window and had giggled to think that she looked like a
bosomy old woman. Before she had reached the end of
Coleridge Road it had stopped raining. A blackbird had sat on
a chimney-pot and sang. She had made up her mind there
and then to get out one day, and not just to another lot of
working-class digs but out of the whole set-up. Before she had
turned into her own street a little steel dagger and a tiny shield
had started to form in her mind and heart and she had known
that she could do it, no matter how hard or long the road.
'Even if it takes five years,' she had thought with a young
person's sense of what constitutes a long time. The new blade,
as it had turned out, was soon to be tempered, for hours later,

when she was in bed, her mother had come into her room with a cup of cocoa and had said something about not catching cold after having got so wet. Carole had said "Thank you" coldly and had taken *Kennedy's Eating Brimer* from under the pillow and pretended to be studying. Her mother had stayed dithering for a few moments, expecting or hoping that she might sit up in bed and sip her cocoa and that they could then have exchanged some unimportant chit-chat, to show that things were all right. But Carole had sighed and frowned over some declension she was staring at without really seeing and her mother had gone. She had had her little shield toughened, it is true, by its first use in battle and the little dagger tipped with its first heart's blood; but she had yet to learn that such instruments are precious and must not be used on each and every occasion.

For some reason, coming downstairs this time reminded her of her mother's footsteps retreating slowly, in defeat, down these same steps all those years before.

Her mother stood by the kitchen table getting some things ready for Alfred's late supper and the men's sandwiches in the morning. There was not a lot to be done about it all now. You can't bring back the past. She went and stood by her, putting one arm around the sloppy, middle-aged waist. Mrs. Brockett thought herself to be the victim of some transference of affection from the child upstairs and said, "Turning out quite nicely, she is. Not much up top, though. Can't seem to learn her tables. *You've* taken all the brains on the girls' side of the family."

The gesture had, however, loosened restraint between them and Mrs. Brockett said, "How are things with you, dear, really I mean?"

Carole started to tell her things about the job and was soon skating near the thin ice of talking down to her own mother. She gracefully swooped away on one leg with, "I was going to give up the room because I had a chance to share a flat with

Julie, a girl I knew at college. She's a marvellous cook, and you know I'm hopeless. Last week I burnt some onions again. But . . ." She saw a patch of crumbled ice and black water ahead, put down her other skate, tried to stop and fell flat on her face. "But it all fell through. She's going to get married."

Mrs. Brockett seized her chance with the brutality only possible between close relatives. "And when are you going to get married? It's ages since you told me anything or brought one of your fellows here. Of course you're still young, younger than you think you are, but all the same . . . What happened to that nice Jewish boy you brought here once, the tall one, very good-looking? He was a good boy. You could tell from the way he played with the kids. These days there's a lot of them marry outside their own religion and I know *you* haven't got any, you've told me often enough. You could do a lot worse. What was his name? Ronald something."

"Donald you mean. Yes, I've seen him lately. Mum, I—I mean, how . . ." Carole wanted to say, "How do you tell if one really loves you? How do you know if you really love him yourself? Why have all the brainy ones got weak characters and all the strong ones got no brains? Where's the one for me? Am I aiming too high all the time, expecting too much, or what? Is there something wrong with me?" But it was too late for such confidences. 'I suppose it always is too late in life,' thought Carole. 'That's one of the things about it.' So aloud she just went on, "I mean, how can I bring every possible or prospective all the way down here? Even if they've got cars, which some of them have, the traffic's so awful these days."

"I understand, dear," said Mrs. Brockett. And so she did.

The house had suddenly become very quiet now that the children were in bed and the telly switched off. They went back to the kitchen from the scullery and sat in the armchairs. The cushions were lumpy with age and under each were hidden slithery layers of old magazines, cycle catalogues of Harold's and Alfred's *British Legion Journal* and comics of the kids, knitting patterns, women's magazines folded back at recipes which her mother was always meaning, and never having time, to try.

Mrs. Brockett was plainly hoping that Harold would come in before Carole had left. It gave her pleasure to see her two handsome, grown-up children together, even though they might be rude to one another.

"Harold's late," she said. "I suppose he's off somewhere with that cycling club of his, or else at the pictures."

Carole nodded. There didn't seem to be anything she could say. She could hardly repeat, "You're too soft with him," and to reply with something like, "I'll hang on a bit. I'd like to see him," would be too plainly hypocritical.

"I mustn't miss my last train. It's Sunday," said Carole.

They talked of neutral and unimportant subjects for some time. Carole had become ever so slightly bored. Soon she stood up to go.

Her mother saw her to the gate. All around them was the haphazard district they knew so well. Mrs. Brockett would have given anything to say, "What's it like, that room of yours up town? How can I even see it? Tell me." But instead she said, "You'll catch it all right. Worth your while waiting for a bus at the corner to the Tube station." Carole gave her a brief kiss and went down Byron Road. Though neither was aware of it she walked with her mother's walk.

Mrs. Brockett turned and went in. She fetched a dust-pan and brush and swept up a dusting of plaster in the passage where the handle-bars of the men's bikes had torn the wall-paper and gouged out a scar in the plastering.

Alfred came in and she fetched him his supper of cold beef and pickles. She did a bit more ironing and then joined him in the front room for the last news on the telly. There was no room for the set in the kitchen, so the parlour had become a room to be used other than for weddings, funerals and at Christmas.

She went to bed first, Alfred following after he had shown his independence by making himself a last cup of tea. It was no use going to sleep until he was in bed. Then after that there was the worry of wondering when Harold would be in and what he was up to. If he came too late and crashed about and woke Alfred up there'd be a row.

It turned out that he was not late. She heard him lean his bike against the handle-bar-gouged wall and the rattle of a bit more plaster falling out. He climbed the stairs. One, two, three and the one that creaked, five, six. Good. Now that the boy was in she could get to sleep, she told herself, but this meant that she had already begun to admit that it was to be another of those nights when she couldn't sleep.

Now that the house was still she could hear the traffic three streets away on the by-pass, and from time to time the sound of the fire settling and smouldering itself out downstairs.

Waves of weariness weighted her limbs, but no sooner did she start to give way to the luxury of drowsiness than an intolerable restlessness would force her to change her position, to turn over, so that the rustle of the sheets on her legs brought her full awake again to stare at the ceiling showing faintly white in the light from the street. As part of the pretence that nights such as these were rare and were not happening more often, she set her face against all the dreary devices for seeking sleep, counting neither sheep nor her blessings. She thought first of the next day's tasks, of the shopping and what to have for supper, then of the children and their births. Carole was the first. When she was in her teens and full of her grammar-school stuff, Latin and all that, Harold used to call her 'big-head'. It didn't do to think about what that really meant. Young people think they know it all. You can't tell them anything, especially today. Oh well, their turn'll come. When you want to help them they won't let you. Let them get on with it.

She thought of the man sleeping at her side. At least he didn't snore.

When Carole was born there was all that carry-on until the doctor had said she had to go to hospital, and there had been a day and a night of it and still no-bloomin'-where. They put you in the delivery room to fight it out by yourself. All just routine to them. They had it all the time, one after the other. Never had she felt so alone. Before her time she'd got fed up with the old cows, having their hundredth by the sound of it, coming up and giving their advice all the time. But then, alone in the delivery room, with that nurse and the sister who kept looking in, she would have given anything to have one of 'em there. The nurse was the same age as herself and a working girl, you could tell, but all the same she seemed too young. As for that sister, well! Miss Green or Miss Cream or something, she had been called. "If you'd bear down properly, Mrs. Brockett, we'd perhaps find it easier to bear with you." And the nurse had giggled just as a pain came on, so that she could've scratched her eyes out.

You could never think of that time now without seeming to smell lino polish off the miles of pale brown flooring and the dry dust roasting on top of the steam-hot radiators. When it was over Alfred came with a great bunch of chrysanths and his moustache properly trimmed by the barber. That sister, the nasty one, had walked down the ward when he was there, along with all the other husbands, and it wasn't until then that she'd seen what was wrong with her, for all her posh talk and jokes. Then you didn't hate her or feel afraid of her any more. In the few days after your first you seemed to grow, maybe, twenty years older.

When Carole was little he used to do a lot for her. Not just walking her to the pub all in her Sunday best, and then leaving her outside on the corner to wait, as some did, but all kinds of things, mending her shoes on a last out in the shed and making her a doll's cot out of an old box. Then, as the others came along, it all seemed to change and he did nothing but moan about everything and fight with Harold. He used to fight with Carole too, but she was getting to be old enough now to know how to ignore him. Sometimes she wouldn't answer back at all, just look at him in a way that made you want to take his side for a change, but you couldn't do that. For one thing, Alfred was always in the wrong. You couldn't tell how they were going to turn out. By the time it was certain you were past caring.

It must be getting on for two or three. From time to time the stairs or some other woodwork in the house cracked and creaked. In the distance she could hear a lorry on the by-pass. At this time of night you could tell just where it was by the way in which the noise of the engine faded and then whined out loud again as space and the houses and taller factories in between varied the sound. She thought of the man, high up in a glass and metal box with the noise of the engine around him; the other person wide awake in this quarter of a mile of the earth's surface. In the cold back room the springs of Harold's bed gave out a muffled jangle as he turned over. Holding her own breath for a moment—after all, she had nothing better to do—she fancied she heard the sound of his deep breaths and the light, quicker sighs of the children.

There was a rustle from the grate downstairs as the fire settled to ash and quite went out.

CHAPTER 6

Keep a Second String
to your Bow

FRYING bacon over the gas-ring next morning, Carole found herself calculating just how soon this Tom Stanton could be expected to phone. In order to hide her surprise and annoyance at this, she thought, 'Anyway, he's got a rival.' Since there had been nothing said to suggest that Tom might seriously resent a rival the thought was meant to be funny. To put Tom in his place, she giggled. Like many people who live alone she often laughed aloud or spoke a few words to empty air. Mrs. Lenton had once overheard her as she was pottering about outside Carole's door, open at the time. Carole had come out and smiled a bright business-girl's-to-her-landlady smile which became shamefaced like the under-rehearsed stage gesture of an amateur actress. "Don't worry, dear," Mrs. Lenton had said. "That's why I keep a cat. Then if people hear you they just think, 'There's the old girl talking to her cat again.' If I didn't have one they'd be gossiping around the pubs and the neighbours and before you know where you are I'd be busy trying to talk my way out of Colney Hatch while me dear little nieces and their husbands was selling me up as next-of-kin or heirs presumptuous or something."

Time to leave, and once again the bed would have to be left unmade, pulled back to air in the airless room so that the first thing she would see on coming in again would be the crinkled sheets splashed like whitewash across the corner and making all the rest of the room look untidy.

Carole was entitled to arrive about ten with other senior members of the staff, but it really suited her better to get in much earlier and have a look at the mail and clippings from the financial pages of all the papers. Thus she now hurried towards the Tube station, together with other bed-sitter girls in much inferior jobs and representatives of that type of middle-aged men who still occupy a room in the house in which they were born and have indeterminate jobs as handymen in the basements of the big stores or as clerks in the goods yards of the main-line stations. Our age has abolished the treadmill and brought in the escalator with power-driven steps on which you have only to stand and watch the corset advertisements float past. No need to grasp the hand-rail and tread the boards. The legs can rest and the mind be free to rattle itself around the bars of its own do-it-yourself Newgate without painful distractions.

She stood on her own step of the treadmill and absently pulled her coat straight. For some reason she had been taking more interest in her appearance in the last week, since the night of the dance. As each advertisement glided upwards past her she caught a vague image of herself: a slim girl with a rather pale, oval face set with wide-apart brown eyes whose habitual expression was an odd mixture of shrewdness and a vague, deeply-hidden puzzlement. Her hair generally looked as if it did not belong to her but had been glued upon her head for display by a hairdresser wishing to demonstrate the latest fashion. She had it set regularly at the same little shop in Bayswater.

Although it was late the Tube was crowded, and she had to edge back to an uncomfortable area without a handhold to avoid a large, middle-aged man in a bowler who kept pushing his knee into her whenever the movement of the train gave him the slightest excuse. What was the matter with men? If things got as bad as that with them why didn't they either do something about it or else shoot themselves?

She started to think of men she had known, boys at college and the one or two from her childhood whom she still met from time to time. The pattern of her life had given her a much broader experience than many women of her age, but of this fact about herself she was unaware. Very often it seemed to her that the confident little pony-tailed office juniors who climbed into jeans every evening and hung around the coffee-bars and rushed off to Clacton on the pillion-seats of motor-bikes knew more than she did. As regards her friends who had married, sometimes she felt older and tougher than they were and sometimes much younger.

The train emptied a bit and she got a seat and opened one of her papers. On some mornings it still gave her pleasure to see the glances of men trying to place a young woman who bought *The Times* and four other morning papers and who turned first to the City pages. For some reason she sat and dreamed this morning. Every now and then a memory of an incident involving Tom Stanton and herself would come into her mind and she would find herself comparing him on some self-devised scale of character constructed of the personalities of boys she had known. She told herself that this was absurd, that she didn't know enough about him yet to make a fair judgment, but it didn't seem to stop her doing it. With her trained orderliness of mind she started at the first affair, with dear Laurence. His mother had called him that after Olivier and she had confessed to him that her mother had named her after Carole Lombard. It was just the sort of thing you kept to yourself in the Sixth. Ages before, she'd told her great friend Marie, and when they weren't friends any longer blasted Marie had gone and spread it all over the school. That had been one of the first great lessons life had taught her. As with nearly every other human being, she thought now, the preceding great ones had been taught her in relation to her mother and, to a lesser extent, her father. Then there had been Marie, and after Marie everything that mattered she had learnt from her experiences with boys. The great novelists had only slightly deepened her knowledge of life, though they had broadened it beyond measure. Anna Karenina and Madame Bovary never seemed to have to worry about money or jobs or passing exams, Soames Forsyte always seemed to have time to day-dream about Irene. Nobody ever plonked twenty-three awkward letters down in front of him and told him to answer them himself and not to bother his boss about any policy decisions but be good and ready to carry the can if any of his answers misfired. Count Vronsky and the man who fell in love with Tchekov's Lady with the Toy Dog didn't know what overtime meant. Once she had read Irwin Shaw's story, *The Girls in their Summer Dresses*, and with the tears still wet on her cheeks had come the thought, 'If he'd had to work that Saturday it might all never have happened.' That had helped to dry them. Anyway—she jerked her by now not-so-disciplined mind back—Laurence had been tall and pimply and she had never noticed him seriously until the day of the debate on World Government. After all the smart-alicks had stood up and said their piece and old Fishface had pretended to make notes of what they said and nodded and looked out of the window with his fish eyes filmed over by classful after classful of chalk dust, dear old Laurence had suddenly stood up, blushing, gangling and with his pimples fiery, and made a bloody fool of himself and knew it and had sat down. Old Fishface had done what he could, in a tired way, to save the situation and two extraordinary things had happened such as she would never for a moment have believed possible a few minutes before: first, she had felt so sorry for Laurence that she had wanted to reach out a hand to him right there and then, in front of everyone, and, second, she had had a glimpse into the essence of the working life of old Fishface. 'He's tired,' she had thought, 'but doing his best.' She knew already in her young life what it is to feel tired. But not, of course, what it is to feel tired all the time. At the end of the lesson Fishface had brought out his summing

G

up of the pros and cons and gone out of his way to let Laurence down lightly, but all from some ready prepared corner of his mind, so that you might be able to feel sorry for him but simply couldn't respect him. Then the lesson had ended and the cynics, sensing the atmosphere, had held their fire until later, until they could catch Laurence in the locker-rooms and shout his mumbled phrases one to another around his head. Two other serious-minded pupils had pressed around him to dispute his point of view and Carole had dawdled up closer, impelled by a vague curiosity and a desire to put her opinion forward. There had been one or two taller boys than Laurence in the school but not many. His flushed and pimpled face on its thin neck had stood nine inches above the noisy group around him. He had been trying to maintain the case for absolute pacifism, which had been his standpoint all the time she knew him. He had just made some point, and old Fishface had hovered in the background murmuring about not being too long in getting out of the classroom and then funked it all, of course, and gone off to find his coffee in the staff-room. They were all on the borderlands of childhood and youth and no sooner was he out of the classroom than some heated and excited boy had said, "Let's prove it's against nature!" and slapped Laurence in the face. Even the boys were a bit shocked and, to cover it up, started shoving and pushing about and trying to trip Laurence up. It had been as if some witch had spoken the fatal word and all the young ladies and gentlemen, so intent upon debating their responsibilities as citizens, had been transformed into snarling lunatics. Laurence had gone very white but stood his ground. He had made Carole think for a moment of some awkward animal, a giraffe or camel, set upon by hounds after it had blundered from a travelling menagerie into the market-place. Carole came from a working-class family of four and knew rows in close quarters. Normally she had been neither forward nor over-quiet in her school. Now, without thinking or really seeming to be fully aware of what she was doing, she had pushed to the front, turned to face the circle of them all and shouted, "Stop! Stop it. That's enough!" Everyone had been so surprised that they did. One of the teachers had walked past the door and the group broke up and drifted away, leaving Laurence and herself. When she looked at him a fairy waved a wand, just as effectively as a witch had cast the spell earlier. He had been quite transformed and from being a gosling-necked and ungainly youth became for her, all at once, the tallest boy in the school both morally and physically. That had been the start of it. Then there had been the long, ever-so-earnest walks and talks together and the absurdly shy and innocently chaste fumblings and fondlings. Poor little boobs! They had not even known enough about it all to get out of the district first, which is easy enough in London—threepence on the bus will do it, but they had stood, an awkward and self-conscious fourteen inches apart, with Laurence holding both their books, on some neutral street corner halfway between their two homes, and talked about homework and the necessity for non-violence and the place of the individual in society, until one day a gang had ambushed them from behind the hedges and whistled and catcalled and made filthy noises with their tongues so that both had had a desperate desire to run away out of it all. Then their eyes had met and they had walked hand-in-hand down the street without looking behind them, and the wolf-whistles and so on had become childish and self-conscious and they had won because they'd stuck together.

Then there had been the 'serious' occasion one evening in the rec. They had stood and clasped and gasped and then stood apart and talked about incredibly pompous abstractions, "the necessity for mutual respect," "the glass-of-water theory" and so on, very busy respecting each other's point of view and testing their minds and memories one on the other. Whilst, all the time, Old Mother Nature, caring nothing for theories or thoughts, had stirred her earthy fingers about, unthinkingly strumming discords from their tight but as yet unhandled nerves.

Dear Laurence! It had not ended so much as died away when their paths no longer crossed. He had turned out quite brilliant and won the Open Scholarship. Even his parents and old Fishface were surprised. But not Carole. A girl is pretty certain, just as a woman knows.

She had reached her station and started to walk down the curved corridor, still in a daze of memory.

There had been one or two near-serious boy friends, and many not at all serious. But really after Laurence it had been the end of intellectuals for her.

It was almost a relief to leave such memories outside in the street and to commence work. At odd times throughout the day, however, she continued to think about men she knew or had known. 'What a parade!' she thought guiltily to herself and giggled inwardly. 'A general review of experience, a grand march-past of the troops so that the general can see for himself and make a speech and order the next advance.' She lunched alone, and late, and then strolled down King William Street, and back again, deep in thought. This Tom Stanton, now. Suppose . . . Not his fault he hadn't gone to a grammar school. Laurence had only taken up certain ideas from the environment in which he found himself. Tom had done that too. Ideas, perhaps, were not all that important. Other things were as well, and she blushed faintly and laughed aside, to herself, at the thought, 'Such as his hands and the way his hair grows above his close ears.' Laurence had gone on developing, but only in one way, unless you counted the pimples going and his height and stoop increasing and made it two. They'd met twice—or was it three times?—since, and he had become terrifyingly erudite and produced a book in his own field at twenty-four. Somewhere in the background there was a plain little blue-stocking who had married him and still thought he was wonderful. Laurence had blossomed and mushroomed out only in one direction. She had only had to be with him two minutes to realise that his enormous cerebral development remained tethered to the messy playing-fields of seventeen like a captive balloon in a fairground and that he would never cut loose if he lived to be ninety. Only swell bigger and bigger.

A boy like Tom, hard-working and not spoiled, had only enough vanity needed for his survival. She could live with him and help to form him without the handicap of a brain ten times bigger than her own swaying about over them both and shutting out a view of the blue sky. Besides, he had nice hands and she liked the way he kissed her.

At this point in her cogitations something most odd and unexpected occurred. A young schoolmistress was bringing a party of juniors back from looking at the Monument. She had time to think her customary 'There but for the Grace of God go I', and then they had passed her, all over the pavement of course, in spite of the girl's pathetic naggings. Snatches of their conversation reached her—"Why carn't we go up it, Miss? Could we another day, Miss? Can I get an ice-lolly on Tower Green, Miss?" and so on. At the end of the pack there was a little cockney boy, almost running to keep up. "Leave Miss alone," he gasped. "She's busy, thinking." Since 'Miss' could not possibly hear him this had plainly been said from a desperate loyalty and not from toadyism. He worshipped her and would rather have thrown himself under the chariot wheels than have the dust annoy her. Carole started to grin to herself and then from absolutely nowhere an idea had rushed upon her so strongly that she had almost to catch her breath and pause for a moment and look around for somewhere to sit or to lean: "I'd like to make Tom one like that!"

She put on an idiotic expression of benevolence, for the sake of any passers-by, and turned to watch the retreating school party. The little boy had become involved in some argument, perhaps as a Galahad in defence of his Guinevere, but most likely over something quite different, such as swopping Dinky toys. As he trotted his down-at-heel little feet and dirty knees around the corner he seemed to stretch out a part of her guts after him and, when the party turned the corner, it turned to a rotten rubber-band and didn't snap back at all, just parted and then lay along the dusty, cold pavement to be either gathered up by hand and coiled back in place or else cut off sharp with whatever knives or scissors came to hand.

The very sharpness of this experience in itself impelled her towards the only possible immediate alternative. To marry Isaac Kantordemhague, otherwise called Donald Warwick, and give him sons while they both kept working and made thus enough money to employ nannies from John Barker's and to take a mews flat within distance of the Park and bring into the world a Christopher Robin all set for his own Pooh Bear, Kensington Gardens future.

Not letting herself become fully aware of her own motives, she phoned Isaac on a business pretext and found him free that evening and quite pleased to suggest seeing her for supper and a visit to an Italian film about an *abattoir* worker who didn't like killing animals.

In the afternoon Sir Henry, back from his lunch at the Royal Consort, gave her a lot of work to do, so that there was, happily, not much time to think.

Isaac did not have to have his City page copy in until much later. The City reporters had a conference as soon as the market closed and then the City editor drafted the first copy while the junior subs double-checked on the list of closing prices and so on. Isaac had started by doing this himself, and whilst the others had contented themselves with becoming slicker and slicker copy-readers Isaac had learnt how to write in all kinds of different styles, including that needed for the City page. Now, at thirty, "so soon already," as his mother might have said, he was a good all-rounder, able to spin out a para under half a dozen different names in any one of half a dozen different styles. He even kept his own name for small items from time to time in the Jewish press. By deed-poll his name was Donald Warwick. He had been very struck with Carole at one time and had asked to marry her. For a year or so after that it had been rather too awkward to meet, though their paths crossed from time to time and once he had even come to the office to pick up a press hand-out of Sir Henry's annual report to shareholders. They had exchanged a few words and the office girls had looked enviously at their Miss Brockett standing chatting with that tall, very handsome young man who was dressed in a perfect City man's outfit, grey-striped trousers, black coat and even a pearl tie-pin, but who was so good-looking with a Spanish type of olive complexion and dark curls that he seemed more like a successful actor dressed up for the Royal Garden Party than a journalist looking for copy.

This meeting having been 'on business' and their getting paid for it in fact had made it possible for some reason for them to arrange to meet again and things had drifted back, outwardly, to their former state. But the real, hidden change showed itself in certain new conventions which they now observed.

Donald had begun to establish a witty act of being the broken-hearted, hopeless suitor, but doing it with such skill and theatrical perfection that it was implied that it was not to be taken seriously. Then he talked from time to time of outings and adventures with his 'popsies' and his 'sweety-pies', pretending to consult her about the best approach in some case of an unexpectedly difficult surrender, as if they were a pair of experienced male roués. And among all this was an unspoken convention. They had once, for a brief time, been lovers. It had not been very exciting. Sometimes even now, when she looked at the backs of his thin, brown hands, she found herself remembering the car-rug spread on the grass and ants dashing up to steal the drops from an overturned thermos flask. The

new convention was that they never spoke of this time and it
was assumed that it would never be repeated. The proposal
followed this event by a few days. Carole had known it was
coming, had found herself no better prepared for a decision
than many a less experienced girl. He had started off with
some fumbling references to the events of the week-end and
managed to find courage to make some airy reference to it
"proving that they were suited" but that it "would be better
next time". Feeling a bit tense and hence putting on her best
and brightest university manner, Carole had said, "It certainly didn't go too well, Don. But don't worry; it was really
very far from being 'worse than death'." Only a long time
afterwards had she realised how much she had hurt him. At
the time he only swallowed and went a bit pale and then
plunged on to his proposal. And she'd promptly done him
down again.

Things had become quite comfortable and pleasant between
them now, as they can sometimes do between man and woman
of similar taste and interests. 'But I suppose your curiosity has
to be satisfied first,' thought Carole. Thus they met sometimes
for a dinner and a show and when Don needed a safe escort to
some function or party. If he had been rather over-generous
one year she would send him an expensive Christmas present.
In the meantime he prospered, put on a tiny bit of weight and
remained unmarried as a further defiance of his orthodox
family background.

After Mr. Dentham had put his smoking materials away and
Sir Henry had walked off to get a taxi to his club and then to
some dinner engagement up West, she tidied up ready for the
morning and went to meet Donald. What she really felt like
was a cup of tea, but Donald, of course, took her to some rather
exclusive wine-bar where even a sandwich cost three shillings.
They exchanged City gossip. It was satisfying to Carole that
even at this level each had something to offer the other. Sometimes she had even to conceal from Donald how much she

enjoyed her part of the career girl holding her own in a man's world. 'Of course,' she thought, 'it helps to be the girl who jilted him once, so perhaps it isn't quite like that after all.' It was all very well being objective and not fooling yourself but it did make it more difficult to enjoy yourself.

Donald was talking about himself and his paras for tomorrow for the daily to which he also contributed. "The whole thing there I've now stood on its head, very neatly, though I do say it as shouldn't. I used to be one of the lads who garnered the stuff and put it into some sort of order so that an old ruin called McKenzie could put it into his sausage machine of a brain and turn it all out in a mellifluous, though slightly mouldering, style, both dignified as befitting serious matters like money and yet readily understandable to the moronic investors who read it all. Towards the end he got so that he could do it half-drunk with a volume of Keats open on his desk. He was supposed to be writing a monograph on Keats. Once he had a short article in *John O'London's Weekly* about some aspect of Keats's work, under his own name. Out of all the mountains of crap he must have churned out in his life in Fleet Street he only clipped this and kept it in his wallet. Anyway," Don grinned and made a mime of drawing an enormous breath, "anyway, to get to the point, when the old chap was out of action on what turned out to be his last illness, I got some bits and pieces together and turned them in in his style, honey-soaked facts and figures with a bit of the old 'this-is-inside-stuff-but-I-know-I-can-trust-you' touch. Just bread upon the waters, really, but it turned out the most paying thing I'd ever done, because they offered me the desk job and like a clever little boy I wouldn't take it on their terms but kept my hands free for any other fingers in pies. Nowadays it's a bit of a bind but I could even do it and read Keats at the same time myself. Here, look." He brought out some smudged typescript and put it into her hands. Carole read: "I learn with mixed feelings of the forthcoming retirement from active interest in the affairs of

Angular Fixtures Ltd. of Sir George Barton-Tumbrill. Sir George feels that, at eighty-four, he should make way for a younger man. All those who know him will, whilst welcoming Sir George's courage, feel a keen sense of loss as yet another of the old admirals steps from the quarter-deck and gives the command of a sturdy vessel into more youthful hands. On the whole, though, Sir George has made a wise decision. Enterprise and youthful energy are needed at the helm in the stormy waters in which British industry must today survive. Sir George has shown courage. I wish him well."

"I like the bit about 'old admirals'," said Carole.

"I got tied up with a military metaphor first but there's so many actual generals in the City that I couldn't use it."

It was very cosy in the wine-bar with its shaded lights and comfortable armchairs. The sherry Donald had bought her was very good, but she had not eaten anything yet and she had been tired to start with. For some reason she asked, "What happened to the old man?"

"What old man? Oh, they ganged up on him and squeezed him out. It got too much, apparently, altogether when he got mixed up and thought he was in a night-club instead of the office and started offering the typists a tenner apiece to come and pull him about the grounds of his place in a bath-chair—'Now the weather's warmer you won't mind not wearing anything, will you?' "

"Don, you're making it up."

"You can't make things like that up."

"*You* could."

"Fact, I assure you. Some sort of reversion to pony-carts and governesses, I suppose."

"I didn't mean that old man anyway. I meant the one whose job you took over, the one with his Keats."

"He died," said Donald, changing the set of his large but well-formed mouth and suddenly brushing his black curls tight back from his forehead with a brown and bony hand. "I thought I'd made that plain." The whole tough and light-hearted atmosphere between them vanished as if the cleaners had arrived and switched on some powerful, white and glaring overhead lamp which faded out the parchment-yellow glow from the dummy oak candle sconces and showed everything up plainly, down to the last lipstick-greased cigarette-butt and the worn patch on the spilt-drink-sticky carpet. Donald got up and went to the bar and returned with two more drinks. She didn't really want one but the ghost of the old Keats-fixated journalist hung in the air, so that she was obliged to admit that Donald was right. As sometimes happened when they were together, all the acts flopped and the stage was left empty for the scene shifters and for the actors, tired and in overcoats, to tread their echoing ways home. So, instead of saying, "Are you hungry? Because, I must admit, I am," or "Heavens! Another drink. You'd better get me something to soak it up," or "We've not all got your capacity on an empty stomach," she just said, "Go and get some sandwiches." Not even a 'please'. They might as well have been married.

During the film she cried and, once, squeezed Donald's hand. When they came out into the lighted and crowded air of the street it was with a slight shock, as if this trivial and familiar world could not be the truth of their lives, somewhere there was some deeper reality which was just evading them. It had been a great film, one of the finest flowers of post-war Italian realism. Carole felt filled with a vague dissatisfaction. People might suffer more among the Italian poor but at least the sun shone sometimes over there. And there was a clear line between shadow and light. Here everything was just a neutral grey, cold and damp. "I feel like a cup of tea," she said to Donald, who nodded. His large, sensitive and luminous eyes for one moment seemed to hold an age-old sadness. "This way, my dear. This way," he said, taking her arm. He had about six different manners and voices to go with them, but now he brought out the one he usually only put on for a joke and became so Jewish in manner that he looked as if he had lost his hat somewhere and missed it.

They looked into two coffee bars but they were too crowded and noisy to suit the mood of the moment. They walked, still in somewhat of a dream, full of the feeling of the film, up to a lane near Cambridge Circus. Three metal posts barred the way to all but pedestrians and leaned towards each other for company. For many years people's feet had not been able to wear down the stones around their base and hence they still stood on small humps above the level of the path. Round each the tarred surface put down by the City Road Department had not been moulded up the sides of the humps to the foot of the posts so that they showed rounded stones, large pebbles, grimy and anciently lumpy against the smooth asphalt. A single gas-lamp of the old-fashioned kind leaned out from a blank brick wall on an ornate iron bracket. You felt that the path would at any minute give on to the openness, shadows and mysterious lights and splashings of a small harbour at night. Instead it all turned to an ordinary street with cars parked at either side. "Look, the original cobbles," said Carole as they passed the posts. "It must all have been like that once."

"Not all. A lot of these streets can only have been built much later. Half of them weren't here even in Dickens's day." They found the café Donald was looking for and sat at the back with a sticky table-top of orange glass between them. They started to try and talk the film into shape to lessen its impact on their emotions and make it manageable, snipping off a bit of the plot there and examining it, patting a lump left loose by the director here, and so making it all into a ball which could be tossed across the table and back without fear of damage.

Donald had put his elbows on the table near a mess of dried, slopped tea, cake crumbs and sugar grains. His suit was really too good for such a place. "Mind your elbows," said Carole. He took them from the table and brushed them with a quick and far from elegant gesture and gave a quick cockney's nod and shrug as if to say, 'Lovely, ain't it?' Now she understood why he brought her here instead of taking her to some select supper place or to the ladies' dining-room of his club. After a film like that he couldn't keep up the effort to be bright and charming and hard-boiled that went with such places. He ordered them cups of tea and omelettes in cockney and put his elbows back on the table again. He *wanted* his suit to be dirtied. 'Just as long as things don't get so intense and sincere that he thinks of proposing again it doesn't matter,' thought Carole and couldn't help adding to herself, 'It's a fine place to end an evening that began in that chi-chi wine lodge.'

Donald said, "If the omelettes turn out to taste like the table-top looks, then just tell yourself what a compliment it is to you to bring you to a place like this. If you were one of my popsies I'd have to go somewhere ever so posh."

"You wouldn't have gone to the film with one of your popsies," said Carole.

He was often just a fraction of a jump ahead of her. It was one of the things about him. If only she was able to respect him it might be possible even now. 'But that's just being silly,' she told herself. 'People don't change.'

The omelettes tasted as if they had been fried in old candle-ends and the 'two large slices' of bread with each were soggy and smeared with the sort of margarine whose makers should offer a prize to anyone *not* able to tell it from butter.

Both found the atmosphere as pleasant and lazily familiar as an old pair of boots. While Carole was taking this in and swallowing her foul food with the resigned indifference of the English, Donald said, "See how easily one reverts. The *déclassé* still finds his starting point the most comfortable of all."

The film, their old friendship and that which had once happened between them, the odd and deserted alleyway by which they had approached the cafe, all impelled them towards some serious talk about themselves and their lives.

But Donald knew that this was best approached via some generalised abstraction. Carole under these circumstances could not take the first step. Once raise the curtain on a night like this and The Proposal of Marriage might rush from the wings again and have to be brutally hooked off before the audience laughed. Just this once the masculine approach was the right one. She switched her own mind back from its feminine abstractions and put on an air of listening to her escort. However, she had not been paying sufficient attention. It was her turn to say something. Donald was waiting and looking at her.

"When you say *déclassé*, do you just mean those who've climbed up far enough to see that they don't want to pay the price of climbing any further or do you mean all of us, those on the way down as well? Everyone, from tramps to that public schoolboy we met—you know, the one with the perfectly genuine title, who was pimping for Argentine and American tourists."

"Remember your logic. Because all criminals can be said to be de-classed it does not follow that every de-classed person is a criminal."

"You know quite well I didn't mean that. I meant that it's all very well for those of us who are on the way up the ladder to suddenly say, 'Oh what the hell! I don't care if I go higher or lower after this. I know what it's all about now,' but if we meet someone who is on his way down and has decided to stop off, then are we really his equals?"

"Dear child," Donald began and Carole thought, 'Men can't argue with a woman without being patronising in some way or other, not even Donald.' "Dear child, listen," Donald went on. "Once you start thinking in terms of 'equals', then you've slung in your towel and might as well admit that you were fighting by the Marquess of Queensberry rules all along."

"Please don't go into metaphors, especially sporting ones.

It's difficult enough to follow already. Let's talk about something else, Donald. I'm not feeling clever."

As quickly as if the sour omelette had been some swift-acting poison Donald slumped and shrank into himself. He took his elbows off the table and sat back hunching his straight shoulders. Two faint brackets enclosing the area between his mouth and nose (as if it constituted some comment upon the rest of his face) deepened and darkened as the light found them and shadowed across them. This made his nose seem more prominent and his mouth smaller. If you had seen his face for the first time at that moment you might have thought, 'Petty and spiteful if you're stronger than he is. Cruel if you're weaker.' Carole knew him and could not make this mistake. She knew that if you looked above the brackets (which enclosed nothing but a meaningless area of well-shaved flesh) you found enormous and sad brown eyes and realised that the only person Donald-Isaac Warwick-Kantordemhague was ever cruel to was himself.

"Let's go," said Donald. They got up and he paid the bill and they walked in silence up the street in the direction in which they had been going, leaving the alleyway with its metal posts behind them. The evening together was over. Donald took her in a taxi to her corner and kissed her briefly.

Back in her room Carole opened the rumbling sash window and let the night air waft and trickle in. She washed herself and put cold cream on her face and prepared for sleep. From old habit she lay for a few minutes in bed feeling the quality of the day that had gone, dipping litmus papers composed of previous experience into the feel of the immediate past, seeing if they turned coldly blue or warmly pink and recalling each seemingly important incident and trying to estimate if it were truly so.

Out of it all she boiled it down to this: Laurence was married already and even if he hadn't been she couldn't have taken on the job of helping him grow up, not with that brain in the way of both of them. Donald was her sort but weak and still trying to fight his way out of his family background, which for some reason he seemed to imagine was more difficult for him to do than for all the Catholics and Buddhists and Muslims and Methodists who had had to do the same. Then she tried to hold some of the lovely moments of the film so that she could go to sleep in the security of the total beauty of them, but this didn't work. 'What on earth's the matter with me?' she thought. The only film being shown on her consciousness was not set in Italy but in King William Street and down the centre of the screen trotted a brave little cockney boy with dirty knees, patched shorts and worn shoes. He looked just like a miniature of that cockney boy Tom Stanton she'd met at the dance except that his small heart beat with her own, in time or tune, there was no word.

So *that* was it! Oh well, it was nice to know for certain. All the same it was a long time before she could sleep.

CHAPTER 7

In Springtime! In Springtime!

TOM phoned Carole and they met in a tea-shop. The plan had been to go to some foreign film she wanted to see, but they got talking and gave up the idea in favour of a walk. He didn't have the car, but it was a fine evening, one of those rare patches of nice weather in England, stuck like sudden jewels in the damp clay. They walked down to the Embankment and watched the lights in the water and the people in the glass-walled foyers of the Festival Hall far across the river, moving about like bees in a laboratory display hive.

"Do you remember the old trams along here?" said Carole.

"Yes, and what about the all-day rides you could get? I used to go all over London some Saturdays when I was a kid and had the lolly." They spoke some more of childhood. First as it was in general associated with trams, travel or London and then on to more personal and family aspects. They talked and talked. In some way both dreaded the time, soon to come, which they were also looking forward to. Yet both knew it could not be avoided. They found the little dark gardens where stands the only statue of a camel in London and clutched and kissed on an uncomfortable bench near a gentle, old gas-lamp. When they had to stop, it was by complete and unspoken agreement. Although matters were now plain between them it was still early enough on in the affair for each to have a last scruple about being the first to admit the truth. It was such good luck, how could you dare to trust in it? Each thought, 'What a fool I should look if I was wrong and then said it.' They skated around it with endearments of a traditional kind, yet, even from among these clichés, managed to select those which suggested uniqueness, "I've never known anyone like you," and so on.

He had to watch the time of the last Tube because of not having the car that night. They walked towards Charing Cross and stopped at a coffee stall with its crowded interior white-washed and sheeted by the blank glare of a pressure lamp. Two old tramps sipped cups of tea in the shadows. On a piece of cardboard was pencilled, 'Hot Pease Pud and 2 Saveloys 8d.' It was like something from the 'thirties that older people were always telling them about. They had a cup of lukewarm coffee essence and then Tom went down the Tube and she walked back to her room. Both felt that an important event had happened and that more was to come. Their excitement had something of dread in it. They had fixed up to meet again soon.

Carole sat and brushed her hair at the dressing-table in the glow from the scorched pink lampshade, 'There's plenty of time. Nothing's settled,' she thought. Tom stared at an ad. curved on the wall of the Tube and thought, 'There's plenty of time, really . . .' Though just what it was that there was time for he could not have said.

Some days later they met in a tea-shop just as the rush hour was finishing. It was very quiet at the far end after the bustle of the street. A few other couples whispered over their beans on toast. Steam formed and ran down the marble-covered walls. In the distance there was a rattle of cutlery.

Tom started to think of an opening. Each one seemed too stupid and banal or too intimate, assuming too much. "I've been thinking of you such a lot" was O.K. but it gave him away in a manner he wasn't ready for yet. "Have you been thinking of me?" had the same objection to it if it were to be said in one fashion, and would put them back to their tough, matter-of-fact sparring around if it were said in another. A silence fell. They looked at the crumb-strewn table and stirred their tea.

Things felt awful. They might have been seventeen again. Somebody had to do something. Carole looked up: "I've been thinking of you such a lot," she said, "all the time," speaking in that wonderful woman's way of stating the really important things just as they were with no pretence. In a real crisis, or at a moment when life needs clarification, a woman goes to the point without fear or hypocrisy, as if she did not care at all for the trimmings and niceties so important to her at other times, but only with the immediate physical facts of life or death and their emotional corollaries. Tom was meeting this for the first time just as Carole was finding it within herself for the first time.

It seemed to Tom tremendously important that she had told him this thing. He had been with her, in her thoughts all the time he had been trying to imagine the mysterious life she was leading on her own, a life in which he had no part. His gratitude to her for having given him this happy balm to his vanity arrived at the same time as his joy in it, so that the two emotions piled up as the wash from a ship rides the back of a natural swell, confusing the normal rhythm. His state was such that the pressure arising from the need to cope with the situation, to make some reply, not to give way entirely to his happiness, dammed the wave, and the only emotion to emerge fully was a moment's panic. Carole's matter-of-fact, almost sad tone had put her at his mercy. He wanted to show her that it was all right, that he felt the same and wouldn't let her down.

"Did you get back all right the other night ?" said Tom.

"Yes, did you ?"

Silence again. It had turned out not to be the decisive moment after all, but nevertheless Carole was not afraid. Already, as far as matters such as this were concerned, she knew him better than he knew himself.

The situation became wholly plain when Tom at last looked up and their eyes met.

Then they had discussed going to the flicks. Carole still

wanted to see some new French film and of course he didn't like that sort, except the spicy ones, and they didn't interest him now. In his first experimental approach to telling her the truth he said as much. "You're growing up now," she said in quite a maternal fashion.

In the next few weeks it became more and more like that. Thorpley had once said to him, "Know when to pack up a woman, boy? If you haven't got a moustache it's as soon as she starts saying that you'd look older or more handsome with one; and if you have one, then it's as soon as she starts telling you it tickles and to shave it off. You may think it is just a matter of the moustache but it means she's made up her mind. Twenty jumps ahead of you, and planning what colour curtains you're going to have in the front room." Carole never suggested anything about a moustache, of course, but she did stop him swearing, and every time in a café or a pub or anywhere when he absently put a finger-tip to his teeth to pull away some little flake of flesh she reached out and laid her hand on his wrist. For some reason he didn't mind, not even if it made him look a bit of a clot in front of other people. Apart from anything else, there was her hand on his wrist.

Walking home, or driving out to Ivinghoe Beacon on a Saturday, or elbows on the counter for hours in a coffee bar, they talked and talked. It didn't matter at all that Carole knew so much more than he did, because there was a lot he could tell her about business. There were fiddles lower down in the rat-race that they never knew were in the book in their offices up in the City.

Their bosses knew each other. That was another thing that balanced out nicely: Carole had a posh job with a real big company, but he was a bigger frog in his own smaller puddle.

A funny thing was that when he told her about some of the tricks the boys got up to she laughed, but sometimes if he was telling her about some mug he'd worked a fast one on she'd go quiet.

Spring arrived. Lovers' time, the only pretty ring time and all that. One night he just couldn't fit it in to pick her up in town and had to phone her where to meet him. He took some clients out to see a house and dropped them at the Tube station and then hung on, waiting for her. He'd handled one or two sales around here but didn't know the district well. It had become axiomatic that, whatever the difficulties and inconveniences, they spent every leisure hour together.

A whole batch of people came out of the Tube. A train must just have got in. He was busy playing games with himself to pass the time. 'No use looking at this lot because another seven minutes aren't up yet!' and so on, when he saw her, unexpectedly, among the crowd. Three emotions came together: joy at seeing her, relief that the strain and boredom of the wait was over, and something else very surprising. She had her head down, as she often did, looking at her feet, not expecting him anywhere near just yet, and she did not look a bit like the girl he'd met on the dance floor. In the old days he'd hardly have given her a second glance, one of those crazy, arty sort of girls, not his type at all. Remorse and shame and a mean feeling of having spied on her like some Peeping Tom came on him so quickly that the thought never wholly emerged, but it was there in the back of his mind, 'What am I getting myself into?'

He stepped out and took her arm and led her to where the car was parked and they started on the usual routine of telling one another everything that had happened since they last met. Each knew the agonising sense of exclusion and from this deduced what the other must feel, so it became a duty, as well as being, of course, a delight, to tell every detail and say, " . . . and that made me think of you and wonder what you were doing then. What *were* you . . .?"

He was so anxious to make amends for his thoughts, of which she had remained quite unaware, and she to ask him about his day, that they decided to stop for a moment in a side street before going on to eat somewhere and to spend the evening

together. Tom turned the car into a narrow cul-de-sac of
dreary terrace houses. Some children shouted and played and
old people sat out on the steps in the warm spring sunshine.
It was a lovely evening and a sky dove-grey and mauve rose
up behind the blackened tracery of three gasometers. Spaced
down the pavement pollarded trees stood with their lumpy
tops looking like giants' bludgeons or sections of the large
intestine. But, from each, new young shoots pushed and
sprouted, spotted with the palest of greens. Tom lowered the
windows and the sparrow voices of the kids cut through the
noise of the traffic on the main road behind them. There was a
windy smell of coke from the gas-works and of petrol and coal-
smoke, but also the faintest flavour of a balmy spring breeze.
Somewhere in the world, very far away, ice was melting on
mountain-sides and the frozen moss turning soft and moist in
the sunlight. Gas-works in an evening sky and children playing in the street, the two London lovers held hands and were
quiet for a moment.

Without relevance to anything or doubt that her lover
would understand her, Carole said, "And I never get that
feeling any more since I met you."

"Sounds interesting. What feeling?"

"Don't you ever get it? About us here, I mean."

"No."

"Don't you know the feeling I mean?"

"No." And it was true. He did not. He went on, "If
you're going to talk about feelings, just stick to how you feel
about me."

She was about to explain but stopped herself. For one thing,
it was a sensation about which it is best not to be flippant and,
for another, she knew he would never understand. Also
talking about it might bring it on and she didn't want that to
happen when she was with him. Besides it would contradict
what she had just said.

They started to talk about the events of the day and to say

again how strange it was that the paths of their two employers had crossed. This accident of commercial complexity held a secret meaning, too childish to be put into words and confessed to. It added to the feeling that some fate or gods had a hand in their meeting. Destiny and all that. But of course that was being silly.

"I think your Mr. Thorpley has offered some land to Sir Henry but they couldn't agree the terms. Does he own much land ?"

There was a long digression, of intense interest to them both, about how she had heard of this offer and what she had been doing at the time and whether it had reminded her of Tom— "Yes, of course,"—and so on, and then the conversation wound round again to land.

"He don't own much land, but he . . ."

"Doesn't own . . ." murmured Carole.

"*Doesn't* own much, but he buys it without using his own money and flogs it again at a profit."

"How does he manage to do that ?"

"Blimey ! Don't let's waste time talking about the boss."

"No, I want to know."

"Well, Miss Brockett, financial adviser and chief lah-di-dah to Sir Henry Chumly de Posh, I'll tell you." It was his revenge for the 'doesn't'. Carole felt embarrassed for his sake and hence ashamed for her own. She had had no other motive than to give him a chance of revenge and then sit and listen to the sound of his voice, but as he went on she became interested. It was a level and branch of finance new to her.

"He's a real sharp one, old Thorpley. He watches and gets all the gen where there's going to be some new development take place, or where there's a bit of land near some shops. Then he goes to his bank and gets an overdraft to buy the land. He can offer his houses and the business as security. If he can't get enough to actually build a shop on the site, he finds one of his golfing and boozing pals that's a director of a building company to help out and they begin putting it up on tick. Then they agree how they're going to share the cake after it's cooked. Once the shop's up there's plenty of the big multiples after it and the boss gets some agreement for a twenty-year lease, with a clause about reviewing the rent every five years and so on. Even if the estate is not very fully developed you'd be surprised how the big chain stores like to snap up the shops so that their name is up on it for maybe six months before it opens. Once it happened that the boss didn't get enough to pay his overdraft, so he flogged the lease and the rents due to come on it to an insurance company where he had some pull, and with the money they gave him he was able to pay back the bank and have a few hundreds to split with the builder. The real beauty of it all is that the whole thing has been done without his touching his own money. Except to buy the drinks, of course."

"He's quite a character, your Mr. Thorpley."

"Oh, he is. You'll have to meet him."

"I'm not so sure I want to."

"P'raps I've given you the wrong idea. He's a real nice fellow. He never lets a pal down and you couldn't wish for a better bloke to work for. Long as you do your job, of course. He's real hard on two things: anyone try to fiddle anything from *him* and on anyone not pulling their weight when we get a rush. But he's a real good sort. The drinks he's bought me! And he's taught me a lot about business. He trusts me enough to tell me things he don't tell the others. I always think he might make me a manager of one of his firms later on. But I keep on the book just in case."

"Just in case what?"

"Well, you know. It all might fold at any minute or the boss might get in too deep and have the Fraud Squad on to him. Then I'd build up the book and try and get a real full-time round to take on while I looked around. I wouldn't want to do insurance all the time."

"Why not?"

"Too much work for too little lolly. Cycling round all the back doubles and dunning 'em for arrears and all that. It can be quite a steady number if you don't aim to make any real money at it, though."

"What do you mean by 'real money'?"

"Well, enough, you know." And feeling himself pushed, he said, "Enough to give you anything you want."

They had left it at that but his last answer had been, in the modern fashion, a proposal.

It suited him very nicely to be explaining something to her for a change.

"It's very interesting," she said. "Sir Henry has been selling some land and I had to look up some things about it. He's taken out another mortgage on his house, too." She had a strict code of not gossiping about office matters outside and felt the faintest discomfort as soon as she had spoken. She had had no other motive than to meet him on the level of talk about their employers and not to spoil his boyish pleasure in being, for once, able to lecture her. Later she was to remember this slip.

They drove right out and ate sandwiches and sipped warm beer in a deserted pub which smelt of cabbages and beeswax. 'It has to happen tonight,' thought Carole, 'and it's no good letting him get all solemn about it. He wants to but he's become so virtuous since he really fell in love that he's sure to go guilty and pompous.'

Without speaking they left the pub and drove to a quiet turning giving on to some privately-owned wood with a rotting fence and well-repaired signs about trespassing.

Both felt nervous. Carole thought, 'It's as if it was the first time.' For some reason she wished that it was.

"Is it all right?" asked Tom and she nodded and pressed reassuringly against him. In any case she didn't care. She just wanted to give and give and let the consequences go hang. Even in this there was some element of self-deception. In a way she hoped that it would not be 'all right'. Although he was excited to a point of extreme nervous tension and yet tender to the point of reverence, yet it was still more important to her than to him. But she did want it to go well for him, more than anything. "Now," she whispered.

"Not here. Not in the car," said Tom.

"Why not? The ground's damp. Let's go in the back." She took his hand.

"No, not in the car." They spoke in whispers with a sense of strain and urgency as if engaged upon crime or some dangerous project.

"I don't want to in the car, because—well, because of the other times."

"Don't be silly, dearest, what does it matter where? I love you."

"Not in the car," said Tom firmly, making her think for a moment of a stubborn little boy refusing his food.

Had they been less experienced or very much more, matters might have stopped there for that night. But each was trapped by a code of modern, I've-been-around toughness which clamped laxity upon them as harshly as an inculcated puritan prudery might have enforced virtue. And besides . . .

"All right, silly. Not in the car, then." Between the endearments the practicalities were also whispered. The pink clouds and asterisks of romantic fiction take no account of suspender-belts and buttons, bent hooks and eyes or damp ground. Yet the lovers found, as all true lovers have always found, that the absurd, human details became in themselves a form of honesty between them. "Bring your coat," whispered Carole.

"Wait, there's an old mac in the back." They slid out of the car and picked their way across the darkened grass and fallen twigs, holding hands at almost arm's length so that the business took on a quality of childish innocence, a secret game in the warm dark. "Here will do." He spread the coats on a flat piece of ground.

"Ouch," said Carole, sitting down on a stone. They both giggled and for a time did no more than sit side by side. He had still his business shirt on. "This collar's killing me," he said undoing it and slipping his tie knot down. She lay back and slipped her hand inside his shirt, cool palm flat against his warm chest. Soon he had half undressed her and was stooping to stroke and cup her treasures with the intensity of a miser dazed by the handling of a newly-discovered hoard. 'I knew he'd be gentle,' thought Carole. All the same they were still too ill-adjusted and over-anxious to please each other for there to be anything but an anticlimax.

"Never mind, never mind," said Carole as he set his teeth for a minute and commenced to mumble something. "Never mind, don't be silly."

After a short time they felt chilly and stumbled back to the car. It had all taken only twenty minutes. Carole thought, 'It has been one of those times in life when the act is not very important but has to be done before it can be seen to be so.' "Next time'll be better," said Tom. Carole became even happier. It was usually left to her to make some general comment summing things up or putting them right.

He drove her all the way into town. They slowed down when they passed the pub they had visited earlier and looked up at the darkened windows. "You can't help thinking of all the nice bedrooms inside," said Carole. They made plans to come out and visit the place again. It had become 'theirs'.

Parting outside her place was agony. Simultaneously both had the idea of asking for some small keepsake. Then there was surprise at the uncanny coincidence. So it came about that Carole fell asleep with her fist bunched around a rolled tie and Tom with a pair of girl's gloves in his pyjama pocket. Neither slept until the earliest of the London sparrows started chirping at the pinking, dark-grey sky and the first trolley-buses glided out from the yawning depots.

CHAPTER 8

Business with Pleasure

MR. THORPLEY arranged to lunch with a young man who some friends had told him might be the man for this job, or for some job like it in the future.

He got hold of him on the phone and fixed up a lunch. He suggested the Dorchester but the young chap said that a taxi might have trouble in getting him so far West in time and named a chop-house. Thorpley did not quite catch the name of the chop-house and did not want to show that he had never heard of it. He kept chatting for a few moments and then said, "Some time since I was there. Cooking as good as ever?"

"Oh, rather," said the young man in a voice which sounded to Thorpley languidly top-drawer. "The old Cargo of Spice is still what she used to be."

So he said, "The old Cargo of Spice," to the taxi-man and hoped for the best, and that gamble came off too. The man ran down his metal banner and said, "Fletcher's, is it? Right you are, sir." The place was west of Aldgate pump but east of St. Paul's. He paid off the taxi and saw a narrow doorway with a plaque announcing that one Sam'l Fletcher had founded this coffee house with the proceeds from his share of an investment in a ship to the Indies which had returned with a cargo of spice.

It was so dark inside that for a second he imagined there must be a hanging curtain still to pass, but then he turned a corner and came into a long, low-ceilinged room set with high pews and looking like a meeting house of some nonconformist

sect. An elderly waiter came up to him and set his grey face in
a look of respectful enquiry.

"Mr. Warwick here?" asked Thorpley, hoping that this was
how it was done.

"Mr. Warwick, sir? Yes, sir, at his usual table, I believe."
He shuffled off to show the way. He wore a waiter's black coat
and bow tie but from the waist down a stiff, white apron fell
nearly to his ankles, so that facing you he looked rather like a
bust set upon a marble column. The back view gave quite a
different effect, an old man's white hair cut short but growing
untidily around a worn collar, the shoulder stooped and bent
under the black coat and a pair of legs hidden by the kind of
trousers which give the impression of starting hitched up under
the armpits so that they descend in loose folds and creases like
the back view of an elephant.

'It's all on the front here,' thought Thorpley, 'same as
everything else.' Thus he prepared himself to meet this
journalist, a kind of man he'd never met before. From all he
could make out, this chap wrote stuff for the papers, and
speculated a bit with what he saved out of his payments. He
knew all the public-relations boys and girls of the big companies and could sometimes get you a little para in that'd start
a bit of interest in your own company, but he expected something in return. If one of the papers got themselves a reputa-
tion for just giving puffs all the time for sharepushers, then
their readers would drop off and no one would believe their
'investment advice service' and so on. On the other hand they
wanted real news of what was going on and that meant keeping a look-out for the new men and the companies and mergers
coming up to the top. Try and pull a fast one on the papers
and you might land yourself in real trouble. There were ways
they could do you down in print without even mentioning the
name of your firm. It seemed to be a set-up where you had to
know exactly what you were doing and you had to know the
right men. "You should meet Warwick," his friends had kept

saying. "Warwick's your man. He knows everybody."

The waiter had stopped at one of the pews and a young man stood up and smiled. "Mr. Thorpley?" He held out his hand. "How do you do? I'm Donald Warwick."

Thorpley looked with one quick, sharp glance partly concealed behind the creases of a jovial smile, and took in a tall, very handsome and perfectly-dressed young man. "How do you do, Mr. Warwick? I'm pleased to meet you. Heard a lot about you. No, nothing bad, on the contrary, on the contrary." And he thought, 'Blimey! a Kanger. I might've known it.'

The meal was served by the patriarchal waiter from heavy silver dishes which clanked and clicked sedately. The cutlery was of the same pattern and the knives really sharp. Bull's-eye glass windows and oak panelling muffled the noises from the street and the high pews stopped the discreet murmurs of the City gents from carrying at all. The kitchens were behind double doors of traditional green-baize tacked on with brass dome-headed nails.

From time to time the younger man would nod and smile a greeting to other diners and once or twice even waved gaily, raising his arm high so that it lifted above the level of the high-topped pew-back and showing just the right length of white cuff falling from a thin, sallow-skinned wrist.

Drinks arrived after a whisper from the waiter, "Mr. Crantleroyd wants to know what you're drinking, sir, with his compliments." Then when it came to liqueurs Warwick said to the waiter, "Ask Mr. Crantleroyd if he and his guest will join us in a Benedictine." The patriarch shuffled back and forth and brought an answer and in the distance a black-sleeved arm was raised above pew height and dipped, which signal Warwick answered with an airy wave of his own hand straight above his head, as might a choirmaster and his colleague co-ordinate their antiphonal effects in concealment from the congregation.

Twice during the meal, after a whisper in his ear from the waiter, Warwick excused himself for a moment and went and bent over some other invisible pewful of diners and then returned and excused himself again.

Thorpley kept the conversation in generalities and looked about him and watched. 'I'm learning,' he thought. 'Learning fast.'

The younger man now sipped his liqueur and put both his elbows on the table and without preliminary said, "Now, Mr. Thorpley, what's it all about?"

Thorpley acknowledged the use of his own favourite opening tactics with a nod and a grin. "That's what I like, just what I like. Cards on the table and no messing. Well, now I'll tell you what it's about." He went on to give details of his newly-formed property company, of its holdings in smaller estate and land agent's concerns, and explained his own favourable position in regard to local land purchase—"I'll not make myself out to be bigger than what I am to such a sharp young gentleman as yourself. A big frog in a small puddle, that's old Thorpley for you." He went on to hint at his plans for buying his way into Sir Henry's company and the offer of land for development. He told the truth of his luncheon with Sir Henry and Illstone. Then if, or when, this smart boy checked up he would find it was all just so. They spoke some more of the property market and of Thorpley's plans to have Sir Henry's plant turn to the making of metal building components and necessities. "Tell you what," said Thorpley. "I was wondering if you could fix up for me to meet Mr. Illstone again. I still think we could do business. Trouble is I don't know where he can be found and . . ."

Warwick took the point. "I don't mind speaking to him for you if I can get hold of him. I think I know where he'd be at this hour. We'll try in a moment."

Thus Thorpley had to learn how to suffer, with a great show of amiability, a long delay, whilst his companion sipped his liqueur and languidly questioned him about events in the world of property deals. He felt a nervous physical desire to jump up and bustle them both to a telephone, to get on with it all, sharpish.

At last Warwick got up and led him to a darkened alcove smelling like a small museum, down some steps near a cloakroom. It was one of those arrangements Thorpley disliked, because he always imagined you could be overheard, where you told someone the number you wanted and then sat down until they motioned you to a vacant booth and you had to tip them a shilling. There were only three telephones visible here and each had been cunningly fitted into a sedan chair whose handles and seats had been removed. The bright bulb lighting the padded interiors like showcases in the dim room added to the sense of being in some cellar museum. Warwick spoke to some old ruin, who shuffled out from among rows of hooks, bowler hats and umbrellas and crossed to a tiny switchboard. Leaving Thorpley standing staring at an empty sedan chair, the younger man stooped his way into one and closed the door behind him. After a time he opened the door and shouted to the attendant, "No go, try the Dorchester," and after a few minutes, "That's no use either, try the United Services." This was evidently successful, for he closed the door and could be seen talking and smiling as he hunched into a corner of the cubicle. He waved apologetically at Thorpley and made a thumbs-up sign to indicate that all was going well. Thorpley moved nearer but keeping a careful distance from the thin glass of the tiny door. All the same he could hear what Warwick was saying every now and then. "Yes, rather. . . . No, not seen him for ages. . . . 51/3, I believe, but expected to drop if tin rises, which it will next week when the truce ends in Malaya. . . . What? . . . Oh yes, quite. Yes, he's with me here now. All right, I'll tell him. Yes, rather a rough diamond, you know. . . ."

He came out with the very air of a dandy who might have

been the original owner of the chair and said, "It's all fixed. Illstone suggests you meet him in the Grosvenor Buttery at six if it suits you."

"Do fine, do me fine," said Thorpley. They went upstairs again and back to their table to pick up newspapers, gloves, brief-cases and an opened packet of cigarettes Thorpley had tossed hospitably on the cloth. Thorpley transacted some discreet business with the elderly waiter, of which Warwick apparently remained quite unaware, and the two new business acquaintances parted. Even on such a dull day it seemed brighter outside.

Charlie Illstone found Mr. Thorpley good company. They had dinner together in Soho and then drove to The Knuckleduster. Fellow didn't pretend to be at all a gentleman, which counted for a lot, and he laid his cards on the table in business matters, took no offence if he didn't get what he wanted first go and went straight on to tell one of his good stories. Illstone continued to insist on these good qualities of his host. Almost as if he were, in reality, whispering to some acquaintance of his own set who had found him by chance in such odd company.

The Knuckleduster lodged in the dubious area between northern Mayfair and southern Paddington and fell, sociologically, halfway between a night-club of the more exclusive kind and a plain drinking-club. You could join at the door but it cost you two guineas, not five bob. Ladies unaccompanied by a gentleman were not served unless of the category which wore black semi-evening dress, good-quality furs and an air of remote indifference. Unless she were foreign a woman too was expected to have mastered enough higher-standard English to call champagne 'bubbly' and learnt not to say, "I must spend a penny before we go, dearie," but just to float away mysteriously and do it.

That which made The Knuckleduster unique was that it was housed on the second storey of a large house instead of in a

I

cellar. The *décor* made attempts to overcome this handicap with dark red draperies, which absorbed all the light from the chandeliers and shadowed corners behind what looked like plush-covered cow-stalls lit only by reflected beams from indirect lighting sconces. A band was trying to imitate the glissading, tobogganing glide of Glen Miller's 'Starlight Serenade'. This was a bit difficult with only two saxophones but the imitation passed. Most of the customers were in early or late middle-age and the old corn kept getting requested— roasted, stewed or on the cob, who cared? "And, waiter . . ." "Sir?" "Ask the orchestra leader if he and his men would care for a drink." 'These Foolish Things', 'Stardust', 'Melancholy Baby' and so on. Sometimes even 'Ramona' or 'Charmaine' for some old dowager.

Thorpley was known here and grinned and waved to people. Two of the serene, black-sheathed women glanced over and away again. The two men were given a table near the dance floor, away from the shadowy recesses reserved for couples.

"Not a bad spot," said Thorpley with the manner of ownership peculiar to those bringing a guest to some public place hitherto unknown to him.

"No, not bad at all. You can breathe here. Not like some places."

"True enough, Mr. Illstone, true enough. Got to keep breathing, haven't we?" For some reason both men laughed although they were not yet drunk. They looked at one another and nodded as if they were two tough divers, asthma victims or soldiers who had known a gas attack, for whom the remark had some hidden significance.

Thorpley ordered champagne and sandwiches. A girl dressed in a brief skirt with a tarnished golden fringe like the edge of a stage curtain and a pair of skin-tight black satin pants terminating her long, nyloned legs came to their table with a tray of cigars and cigarettes. "Cigarettes, sir?" she asked in American after the school of Stratford-atte-Bow. She'd got the idea of the costume from the pictures too. She'd made it herself and come with it on, stepped out of her coat and got the job.

Thorpley tossed a quid on to the tray and scrabbled up a packet of cigarettes. "Keep the change, dear, keep the change."

"Thank you, sir."

"How do you keep those stockings up, dear? Can't see a suspender-belt."

Thorpley winked at Illstone, who chuckled. He was a card, this chap.

She might have been just telling him his hat-check number. "With Sellotape, sir. And get the sticky off with lighter fluid and cottonwool," she added, pouting, in a little-girl innocent fashion.

Thorpley got out his lighter and waved it at her and roared until a gust of smoke caught his throat and he coughed without turning away, so that the side of the champagne-cooler was spattered.

"I can manage, thank you, sir," said the girl and swayed her wares away to the next table.

"Oh dear, oh dear, 'with Sellotape'!" spluttered Thorpley. "We do see life." He stopped quite suddenly, poured them both out another drink and said, "Listen, Mr. Illstone. Listen close. I'll give you sixpence over tomorrow's opening price for three-quarters of your slice and share for share for the rest in my new Thorpley Hearths and Homes Company." Illstone commenced to smile.

"Wait, wait for it," Thorpley went on. He continued to bargain and cajole until Illstone agreed to a cash price only slightly above that which Thorpley had had in mind all along.

They touched glasses and smiled, Illstone rather self-consciously.

The Knuckleduster became full of an ear-hammering rhythm and the air seemed hot and close. Six girls in sequined

G-strings with an ostrich plume nodding over their rumps high-kicked and screeched out the words of some song. Then came the 'novelty numbers'.

A comedian told blue jokes in a red spotlight and a girl contortionist smiled at the drinkers from between her own legs. The band played 'Jingle Bells' and the chorus trotted round like ponies in and out of the tables. It had become even closer and the powder on the girls' buttocks, as they rotated past the chins of the customers, caked and flaked.

"I told you you'd like this place, Mr. Illstone," said Thorpley.

For some reason, perhaps the heat, or the effect of drink wearing off or some buried feeling of snobbery reviving, Illstone became annoyed. "A bit too noisy for my taste," he said.

Thorpley excused himself and pushed his way to the tiny bar. When he returned to the table he led one of the ladies in black by the hand. "Mr. Illstone, this is a friend, Miss Grangedene."

"How do you do?" said Illstone, half getting up.

"Don't get up, please," said the girl.

The conversation became very stiff and formal, because the niceties of the situation were beyond the social powers of any of the group. It was clear that Thorpley intended to round off his evening by spending the remainder of the night with 'Miss Grangedene' at her grange or her deanery and that he would be very much a paying guest. At the same time etiquette demanded that none of this should yet be admitted. Of the three each despised the other two. They talked about the floor-show and the girl turned brightly towards each man in turn as he spoke, smiling as if she hung on words of wisdom, and leaning forward over the table so that Thorpley kept lowering his gaze. Things still didn't seem to be getting anywhere. It was up to the woman to come to the real point of the problem.

She laid one hand on Thorpley's sleeve. (Though her features were fairly well formed and her face vulgar but not unintelligent, her hands were puffy and predatory.) She managed to whisper, "What about your friend, dear?" Thorpley wasn't sure but didn't like to admit as much.

"Far to go, Mr. Illstone?" he asked. Illstone named a distant suburb.

"Excuse us a minute, girlie," said Thorpley. The 'Miss Grangedene' had got lost after her whisper in his ear. The two men stood and crossed to the Gents. "You goin' straight home or shall I ask her to get hold of a friend?" asked Thorpley, cards on the table as ever.

"Oh, I'll cut away now, thanks. I've rather a long drive," said Illstone. He looked slightly surprised and could even have been so. These real posh types took some weighing up.

They returned to the table and Illstone shook hands with the girl. Thorpley saw him to the outer door, downstairs, and they discussed a few details of the next day's business. Miss Grangedene remained alone again at the table, staring at the tablecloth and sipping her drink from time to time, her actions and attitude demure and the lowered eyes as hard and brightly empty as the plated steel ice-bucket at her side.

Thorpley came back and sat down. He took her pudgy, little hand between both of his sweating palms and said, "Now there's just the two of us, girlie."

"Pity about your friend." This meant that work for two had rather unexpectedly become work for one. A contract had been broken.

"Don't worry, girlie, don't worry. All on the expense account. You know me." She did not know him well. They had only done business together once before, but her profession had made her perceptive within its somewhat limited field of action. She had him placed, not one of the mean sort as those who were real millionaires or near it often were, but a good, boastful kind of spender, generous, flamboyant and cruel. As far as her rather dim memory took her, he was a straight-forward piece of lumber, not demanding any fancy stuff. For a moment she'd had him mixed up with another fat man who always brought a riding-crop and costume of his own in a pig-skin brief-case. He'd been a good spender too. She snapped her attention back to Thorpley, who had com-menced speaking again.

"Don't you worry about your friend or mine, dearie. If you've really told her to stand by, I'll give a little present for her as well. There, how's that?" She shook her head and smiled at him in a pretence of reproof as if to say, 'You naughty, extravagant boy. But there, you've such a generous nature you can't help it!' Thorpley let go of her hand and drank. He leaned across the table and slopped some wine into her glass.

"Don't worry about him. I don't. Just business. He's no pal of mine. I don't make pals of any of those posh ones. They all think they're so smart. It's only that they hold together. Sort of club they've got. Old school tie. They think they're smart but I know, I know . . ." He swayed on his chair and raised one red, fleshy forefinger in the manner of a lecturer and adopted an air of great cunning and shrewdness. "I know a boy as is cleverer than what all that posh crowd are. Thorpley's cleverer. Old Thorpley is. They don't know it yet but I'll buy and sell the lot of 'em before I'm through, buy and sell 'em twice over." He waved his arm and brought it down dramatic-ally and rather too hard for comfort, palm flat on the table. "They're sharp enough, I grant you, but then they've not had to come up the hard way. Dads to buy 'em seats on the Stock Exchange. Went to the right schools. Not like me, not like poor Thorpley . . ." He shook his great head from side to side and the lower lip of his scoop of a mouth actually trembled in the flow of self-pity and sentimentalised self-dramatisation.

Miss Grangedene shook her own head and sighed, deeply touched by the pity of it all. Her work for her client had begun in earnest.

"Another thing. They marry ladies of their own sort and then all that side of the family, the in-laws, is more contacts for 'em. *Their* wives know how to entertain and back them up and all that. No wonder they stay in the saddle."

"It's a shame," said Miss Grangedene. "It's not right." She thought, 'I knew we'd get to bloody wives sooner or later. Tell me the old, old story.'

"You don't know what it's like, girlie, to have to make your own way up and know when to crawl round those bastards and when to throw a scare into them, and learn all the fiddles in the meantime so that you can get yourself enough lolly to operate on in comfort. You don't know what it's like . . ." 'Don't I just?' she thought, but aloud she said, "I like your sort best. You're a real man."

"You said a true word there, girlie. I'll show you later." She giggled in a ladylike manner which carried its own slight reproof. Things were not at the stage for such plain speaking yet. Protocol had to be maintained or where would the fun come in later? Besides it wasn't the kind of talk you expected at The Knuckleduster.

Thorpley had left his car at a Lex garage, so they took a taxi. His companion was only a stage below the top category of her profession and had both a room to which she brought her lumber and a flat where she could entertain house guests of a more distinguished kind for a week-end or longer.

Her short-time room had faded wallpaper with a design of pink roses, a dirty wash-stand and a large dressing-table with a flecked mirror set at an angle which reflected the bed. The air was sour with dust, damp blankets and powdered armpits.

From time to time a door slammed elsewhere in the rambling house and there were careful footsteps and the sound of lowered voices.

Thorpley became sentimental, almost maudlin. "It's a cruel world, girlie. A cruel world and we're in the mucker. You know something? You know what? I'm not such a bad chap, really. It's a lonely job, battling away on your own, day in and day out. I like you, girlie. Tell you what? You know what? Well, I'll double the usual! There you are! What d'y' think of that? Poor old Thorpley's not a tight-fisted old swine, eh? Whatever else they may say about him." He carried on in the same way for some minutes, sitting on the edge of the bed and swaying slightly from time to time. She thought, 'One of the sort that likes to crawl a bit first.' She was gazing at the ceiling and the wobbly light fixture which really ought to be mended.

As the age-old ritual jerked on its way from stage to stage he lowered his voice more and more, as if there were some danger of eavesdropping or he were once more a boy courting in the front parlour of his father's house. Then he suddenly stopped speaking altogether.

'What fools some of them look in their shirt-tails,' she thought. Around the light-fitting in the centre of the stained ceiling the plaster had crumbled away, leaving a mysterious black circle with chewed edges. She hoped it wasn't dangerous. If there was a fire there might be trouble with the coppers or something. "Yes, that's it," she said, with eyes fixed on the bare wires vanishing into the plaster, "that's it. Ah! I like a real man."

CHAPTER 9

Mistakes Cannot Afterwards be Rectified

MR. DENTHAM, as chief accountant, was the first to know about it when the certificates plopped into his morning post In-tray for registration. It was the largest transfer of shares that had ever taken place in the history of the company. Sir Henry was not in yet, of course, but in his excitement he went towards his room. He had to tell somebody and it would be a breach of faith and a betrayal of his lofty position to say anything to one of the clerks. In the quiet inner office the morning light filtered faintly down the white-tiled shaft. Miss Brockett was standing sorting Sir Henry's own post. He trusted her for everything now.

"Sir Henry not in yet, then?" She looked at him. He never was in at this time, and it would in any case be impossible for him to enter without passing Dentham's desk. Dentham wanted to delay the news, to make a great mystery of it. Once it was told, his moment would be over and the excitement gone.

"What is it, Mr. Dentham? Has something gone wrong?"

"I don't really know, Miss Brockett. I suppose it's all right. I suppose you and Sir Henry knew it was coming." It was really too early in the morning for Carole to try to be pleasant and so Dentham allowed a touch of his jealousy to show, drawing a cloak aside for a second to show the hilt of his dagger. The only trouble was that everyone knew it was a rubber dagger.

"Sir Henry looks like having a busy day," said Carole, thus including him as a senior member of staff into the current secrets of the highest levels. A small enough gesture but it sufficed for Dentham. He put the documents on the desk between them. "Twenty per cent of the company's shares've just changed hands, Miss Brockett, and I've only the broker's note. I can guess where they've come from as I suppose you can, but I don't know where they're going to."

Carole herself was startled and too young to be able to attempt even to conceal her surprise. Dentham spotted that, of course. He was silent for a moment. It was beyond his powers to think of a simple sentence which could convey the slight lessening of his jealousy, at the fact that Carole knew no more of the event than he did himself, together with an apology for his rudeness. Nor could he conceal from himself as well as from her that the news caused him not only surprise and excitement, but fear.

When Sir Henry came in they told him the news and showed him the certificates. He went a bit pale but didn't say anything, "not in front of the staff", after all. He asked Carole to try and get hold of Mr. Illstone and fix a lunch as soon as possible and then went on with some routine business matters in a rather subdued fashion. Carole was unable to locate Illstone at his office, his club or at home and asked Sir Henry for any suggestions as to where he might be found. "Never mind, my dear, never mind," he said. He seemed a bit grey and shrunken. She felt sorry for him. Returning to her only referment or measure for experience these days, she thought, 'I wonder what Tom's wonderful Mr. Thorpley is like when *he's* worried.'

By one of those unnerving coincidences Sir Henry then said, "See if there's a Mr. Thorpley in the *Directory of Directors* or *Who's Who*, and ask Dentham if he's ever heard of him." She searched, but the name did not appear anywhere. "Rather thought you wouldn't find anything," grunted Sir Henry.

"Is it the same Mr. Thorpley with whom you lunched last week, Sir Henry?"

"It is indeed. Why, do you know anything about him?"

"Not really. It's just that I know someone who works for him."

"I see. Has he many people working for him? Is it a big show he runs?"

"He seems to have a finger in a number of different pies but I don't know much about him really, just that . . ."

"Just that what, Miss Brockett?"

"I think he operates a good deal on credit, at any rate as far as real estate and land are concerned."

"So do most of us," said Sir Henry rather brusquely. She knew he was rather worried these days and had made plans to sell his own piece of land to some local speculative builder as well as taking out a fresh mortgage on his house. The money was all put into his company. He wanted to raise enough to buy the land for the new wing to the factory, and the credit squeeze and the new Bank Rate was making it difficult.

The intercom from the switchboard buzzed and he threw the key. "There's a Mr. Thorpley asking to speak to you."

"Talk of the devil," said Sir Henry to Carole and nodded, so that she discreetly left the room.

"That you, Sir Henry?" came Thorpley's voice. Funny thing, on the phone he sounded like a much younger man. "Can you lunch with me today?"

"I, well . . ."

"I'm inviting you, Sir Henry, as a substantial shareholder, a substantial shareholder, which I now am." 'So that *is* it,' thought Sir Henry. 'Have to meet the bounder now.'

"Righto." He made it sound quite airy and light. "How's the Royal Consort at half-past one suit you? Fine. Good-bye, Mr. Thorpley."

"Good-bye to you, Sir Henry."

It was a shame to be in the City on such a morning. The

pigeons waddled about like ducks in a farmyard and sunned themselves in every quiet court. The bus drivers wore their grey summer jackets or shirt-sleeves and the typists out in the lunch-hour sunshine were in summer dresses.

After the glare it was almost a pleasure to be in the window-less, cool washroom. "Good morning, sir. Lovely morning. What I've seen of it."

" 'Tis indeed, Harris. A most pleasant change." Harris popped into his cubby-hole and fetched a clean towel. Sir Henry combed his already well-groomed hair at one of the enormous mirrors. Harris continued to hover about respect-fully. Their eyes met for a moment in the mirror.

" 'Scuse me, sir. I was going to ask if you'd heard anything for the Gold Cup?"

"Killarney Boy," said Sir Henry. "But I'm not doing him myself. Can't afford a flutter these days. Hard times, Harris." Harris chuckled with his old-retainer's manner. "They are that, sir. They are that."

Sir Henry walked slowly to the door, thoughtfully letting Harris lurch and punt himself ahead on his good leg in time to swing it open and earn his tip. " 'Kew, sir. 'Kew very much," and he returned to his cubby-hole to study the list of probable runners and betting, raising his eyebrows and pursing up his lips in thought, to indicate to some self-projected audience that he was in his own office and following his real vocation.

Without Charlie present, this lunch went rather differently from the first. For a start, it was Sir Henry's round. Although the invitation had come from Thorpley he had paid for the lunch last time. Then, they went straight in without any time in the cocktail lounge first, because they had met in the hallway as soon as Sir Henry had emerged from Harris's kingdom below ground.

Both men ordered tankards of bitter, then Sir Henry a plate of cold beef and salad and Thorpley a rare steak, in spite of the heat. For some reason Thorpley, the master and advocate of 'cards on the table', started this time with a long rigmarole about himself and his point of view. "I've always got my best results, Sir Henry, by throwing everything in but the kitchen stove and then standing back to catch the splash. I've had to fight my own way up. I'll not hide it from you. My old dad was a coalman. He never got good money like they do now. What he did get he boozed away. I've seen him come in, in the winter, and stand his coat up in the corner and laugh. It stood up on its own with the ice and black dust froze solid on it. 'Not for me, not for me,' I said then and, by God, I've stuck to it." And so on. Sir Henry was a bit taken aback. His only solution, dismissed as soon as it came to his mind as impracticable at the moment, was to turn the conversation once more to golf, since this had provided the lowest common denominator during their first lunch. Then, whilst Thorpley burbled on with some tale of his own early struggles, he thought, 'The fellow's trying to get my sympathy, since he failed to frighten me last time.'

It seemed as if Thorpley must have sensed his thoughts, for he dropped it all with a final sad shake of his head, as if over the grave of his father and his own past, and suddenly raised his voice. "Listen, Sir Henry, you hold forty per cent of the shares and now I hold twenty. I want you to sell me yours and get out. There you are, that's my kitchen stove thrown in. I'll tell you, quite frankly, that I think it's time you retired anyway. What's more, if you sell now you can get out honoured and *ree*spected—honoured, *ree*spected, and with a good price. They stand at 41/3 now, since Mr. Illstone has kept to his agreement and not breathed a word about his shares coming my way. I'll give you a tanner over that, conditional on my getting the lot, of course."

"I've no intention of retiring just yet, thank you. And, to speak frankly in my turn, I'm not at all sure it would be in the best interests of the company to sell out to you if I were."

"You can't offend me, Sir Henry. One of the things, the

lots of things, you've got to learn about old Thorpley is that you can't offend him."

He put down his knife and fork with a dramatic clatter and pushed his face over the table. "A man as is mortgaging his house all over again when he's getting on like you are so as to plug the holes in his own company is good and ready to retire."

There was a silence whilst Sir Henry thought, 'Has he got some pal in the blasted building society or bribed a clerk somewhere in their office? Can't 've come from anyone local down my end nor from the office.'

"Now all your worries could be over, Sir Henry, if you'd take my offer and let me have your holdings at 41/9. Then the new building plans can go ahead on my land and that'll boost 'em a bit. Tell you what. So long as I get the controlling interest you can hang on to the rest and sell at the top of the rise later. Go bull on your own stocks. They'll rise all right when I see to it that there's plenty of rumours of extensions to plant and so on. You'd be on the inside still."

"I'm sorry, Mr. Thorpley, but I won't sell and that's the end of the matter, I hope. If I can't get your land I'll put off the new wing for a time. No hard feelings."

"No, no hard feelings. If I can't persuade you, I can't. Only I'm sure you'll regret it."

They finished the meal in a gentlemanly fashion with talk of golf and general business trends. They avoided the dangerous fields of property and land, but somehow the question of sudden rises in share values cropped up. Sir Henry was anxious to be pleasant. It never did to make an enemy unnecessarily. "There's never been anything in my knowledge to equal old Bernard Baruch's Northern Pacific squeeze." Bringing in an almost historical or classic event in commercial history was meant both to flatter his guest and to move the conversation into pleasantly safe channels for a time until they could decently part. Thorpley, however, did not play the game like that. "Barook? I've just about heard of the name. Some Yank, that's all I know. Poor old Thorpley's an ignorant bastard really. Never had much time to read, only contracts and the prices and all that." He patted the back of his own hand in ironic self-pity. Sir Henry had no alternative but to continue as planned after the faintest of smiles to acknowledge his companion's self-depreciation.

"Thought everyone knew that story. One of the classics, as it were. Baruch kept bidding and the price of Northern Pacific went up from 300 dollars to 1,000 dollars in a week. The bears were in a complete panic. He won and the bears were allowed to settle for something short of complete ruin. Forget just what."

"I'll have to read about that fellow when I get time," said Thorpley, who had no intention of doing so. The knowledge he needed was not found in books.

"Yes, he's a fount of wisdom, he really is. He said once—" Sir Henry raised his voice to indicate a quotation—" 'There is something about inside information which seems to paralyse a man's reasoning powers. A man with no special pipelines of information will study the economic facts of a situation and will act coldly on that basis. Give the same man inside information and he will disregard the most evident facts.' "

"That's the truth, that is. Wrap some duff gen up in enough mystery and any wide-boy will believe it. Yes, it's true right enough." The lunch party seemed set fair to end on a note of grown-up and friendly rivalry, one might almost say of mutual respect. After some more unimportant talk the two men rose from the table. Sir Henry excused himself and went down to Harris's echoing tiled cavern below whilst Thorpley said he was going to treat himself to a drink. Sir Henry arranged to look in at the bar on his way out but planned to refuse any more to drink.

No matter how well regulated a man's life he cannot escape some of its accidents and collisions. Had one of the cisterns in

Harris's charge burst upon his head Sir Henry could have done nothing to prevent it. Coming up from below, Sir Henry met just such an unexpected and unpredictable mischance.

Instead of waiting quietly in the bar, where a polite good-bye could have been exchanged and the two men could have shaken hands, Thorpley was in the lobby. Sir Henry noticed something strange in his manner and then his luncheon companion came up to him. His red face had gone white and his thick lips were stretched over his teeth, thinning themselves into a viciously down-drawn line. He appeared to have some difficulty in controlling the movement of his great jaw, as if a connecting cable had broken in the working of the excavator bucket. Sir Henry looked at him and was reminded of a shell-shock case he'd seen once—or was the memory of even longer ago, of a face in some fight with a schoolfellow at Charter-house?

"You listen to me, Sir Henry. You listen close. If you don't sell to me now at 41/9, one fine day you'll sell to me for a pound." He appeared to feel the need for a stage director, for he paused and waved one stocky arm and looked round as if trying to think of some way, short of physical violence, of adding dramatic weight to his words. "For a pound! for one quid. Less maybe." Sir Henry glanced round to make sure none of his friends or acquaintants were, by unlucky chance, in the lobby. He started to murmur some vague words intended to have a calming effect on this madman, but Thorpley went on with a rush, "Giving me the old madam about 'classic deals'. I'll show *you* something classic before I'm done with you. You bloody gents think you're so smart. I'll buy and sell the lot of you one day. The lot of you." He turned and walked away to the bar. It was one of the most unpleasant things to have happened to Sir Henry for a long time. The fellow had never shown any signs of being mentally unstable before. 'Hope he's not going to make a habit of coming here. Have to dodge him from now on. What on earth was Charlie thinking of to have anything to do with him!'

Sir Henry was old, tough and experienced but all the same shaken by the unexpected event. He would *not* sell. He was stubborn with an old man's stubbornness.

Both Dentham and Carole noticed something odd in his manner when he came in. Later he sent for her. He had a little list of names scribbled lightly in pencil on the pad in front of him. Something in the atmosphere made her think for a moment of some dreary film when the distinguished amateur detective asks the Earl to draw up a list of everyone in the stately home on the night of the murder. "Sit down, Miss Brockett, please."

He doodled a bit on the blotter and said, "A rather unpleasant matter has cropped up. The ship's sprung a leak."

The gap in the generations proved too wide. Their minds did not chime over this unusual matter of business and Carole felt that momentary panic common with the self-made when faced with a situation outside their understanding, however secure the present job and the immediate relationship. Sir Henry was a gentleman and found a way at once of explaining without having to admit that there was any need for it. "Somehow the details of my personal transfer to the development fund have leaked out. I can hardly believe that this has happened via the mortgage agreement and in any case such information would not prove how the money was to be used. No, the more I think of it the more it seems to me that something's gone wrong here. It means we've got to get rid of all the temporaries in the typing pool. You'd better get together with Miss Felton on that, and I want to ask you if you can throw any light on the matter at all." Carole was a bit surprised but far from being upset. She gave her mind to the problem in hand as befitted a loyal employee to one who had given her her first real job and trust. Where Sir Henry had scribbled she called a mental roll: the filing girls, Joan, Claire

K

or Estelle? No. That left the clerks and Dentham. Impossible. With an irritated feeling of being forced to betray some deeply felt principle she reached the conclusion, 'It's a man's job to think this out.' Aloud she said, "I can't think who; I don't know, I'm sure."

Sir Henry seemed to become conscious of his doodling and completed one geometric pattern by crossing a square boldly through and then filling it in solidly in crumbly black pencil. "I may be wrong, of course. All the same, tell Miss Felton as tactfully as you can that we're to use that other agency for temporary typists from now on and let me know if you hear anything which would give us the slightest pointer."

"Of course, Sir Henry."

Some hours later, when the end of the day's work permitted her mind to snap back as a released spring to its only natural position, she sat sipping tea, reading the evening paper and absently marking items for clipping the next day from the financial page, but really thinking of Tom. She went over everything they had done and said and caught for a moment the whole sensation of the time near the gas-works and driving home. But there was some uneasiness associated with the memory which she could not place. Not about *that*. That would all come right. Something to do with work. The shock made her rattle the tea-cup against its saucer and feel very cold. She thought, 'Oh, how awful!' and aloud whispered, "No." Tom must have told this Mr. Thorpley what she'd said about Sir Henry selling his personal land and raising more money on the house. Then during the lunch Mr. Thorpley must have used his knowledge in some way. She was caught out in the most stupid betrayal of confidence, and the only other person to blame besides herself was the man she loved.

To think 'I must see him' was hardly necessary, for it was the accepted thought for this time of day in any case. But it took on now an intrinsic meaning as well.

The arrangement for today had been that she should phone

him at Speedy Homefinders, and if he was out on a job a message would be left for her. A young girl's voice answered her, "Good afternoon! Speedy Homefinders."

"Is Mr. Stanton there, please?"

"Is that Miss Brockett?"

"Yes."

"Just a minute, please."

"Hello." There was a man's voice much older and gruffer than Tom's but with something of the same intonation, and later, she realised, the same mannerisms.

"This is Mr. Thorpley. I heard that young Tom wanted to leave a message for you so I said I'd do it myself. I always like to help out my boys, they'll tell you, he'll tell you, young Tom will. Anyway he's out with a client and asked me to tell you he'd be outside the Tube station like last time. I told him not to keep you waiting. He's only got to see to a rough valuation for me. 'Cut it short,' I told him. 'Don't keep your fee-anzee waiting. You seem to have a real winner there,' I told him. 'See she don't give you the slip.' You don't mind, Miss? I'm not interfering, mind. Just that I think highly of him. One of my best boys. Perhaps he's told you? Thought he might. Not too modest, our Tom. It don't do to be. I'd like to meet you some time myself. I like that boy and you've done a lot for him. In such a short time, too. Like his hands and finger-nails. Surprised? Oh yes, I've noticed. Old Thorpley's not such a fool as he may sound at this moment. I've noticed all right. I see a lot, I do. More'n folks think I do. Now *you* say something," and he chuckled in charming self-depreciation of his own verbosity.

Carole was slightly off-balance. There was the shock and worry of the realisation of her own indiscretion and Tom's, she hoped, unthinking betrayal, and now this extraordinary personality had poured a totally unexpected monologue into her ear. She called up her defensive university voice and bright young manner as she always did when insecure and unsure. "Thanks awfully, Mr. Thorpley. I'll go and meet him. It's awfully good of you."

"Not at all, not at all," said Thorpley, rudely imitating her accent. "Must go now, awfully sorry. 'Bye for now." He hung up. Carole was more astounded than upset for the moment. For his part Thorpley was thinking, 'One of those, is she? Tom'd be well out of that. But he mustn't pack her up just yet.'

All the plan of driving to the same street by the gas-works and then out to the same pub went for a Burton. He knew something was wrong the moment he saw her walk. Nevertheless they talked about other things for a few minutes while he turned and waited for the lights. Then she said, "Tom, why did you tell your Mr. Thorpley what I told you about Sir Henry having to sell his land and mortgage his house?"

"I didn't. I mean . . . Oh, I remember now. I just said something about it when we were talking about the price of posh places in Surrey and Sussex having gone down a bit lately. Why? Is it important?"

Carole's heart had given such a twinge when he had braced himself to tell the truth that she had to harden up quickly now. "You know jolly well how important it is."

"We were just talking about land and it slipped out. Why don't you tell me what's happened?"

"I don't know what's happened, just that . . ."

"Then what are you on about?"

"Let me finish, can't you?"

"Well?"

"I think your precious Mr. Thorpley has been trying to buy his way into our company and on to the board and he told Sir Henry that he knew how short of ready assets he is at the moment. I just can't tell Sir Henry it leaked out because of something I said to you. I just can't. He's always been so decent to me."

"You're making too much with it. It'll blow over. I didn't

know it was going to be used like that. I didn't think it mattered. I . . ."

She thought, 'He made the effort to tell the truth at first and now he's rewarding himself with a lot of little lies for trimmings.' The need to protect herself from her own disappointment compelled her to cruelty.

"You needn't've said anything about it at all. You wanted to impress your boss with all you knew, that's all."

"I suppose you never try and impress that *Sir* Henry of yours?"

Both had become a little frightened at the speed with which the slide to disaster was taking place. The lights changed and he jerked the car forward, flogging it up into third at a rush and then having to brake down so that it pitched. "Oh," said Carole and immediately wished that she had not. She'd fight fair and not come the helpless, terrified female in the face of masculine ill-temper. It was too late. He pulled into the kerb, looked around and ahead irritably and crawled up to a side turning and nosed down it for a car-length and stopped.

"I'm sorry, I'm ever so sorry," he said. If he had added, 'Sorry, lady,' he would have sounded exactly like a little cockney boy caught after breaking a window.

Carole had to raise her shield firmly over her heart. "I was not in the least frightened, if that's what you mean. I was just thinking of the poor car and how horses must have suffered in the days when we all travelled pulled along by them."

"Horses! You are a silly." This had lately become an endearment between them, stemming from Carole's frequent use of the adjective. For a golden moment the path to escape from the awfulness of their row flashed temptingly before them. Just to pretend that it all hadn't happened and slip back into "You silly" and "Oh no, I'm not" and "dearest" and so on. Or at least to leave matters for a time and take the argument up again at some comfortably unspecified future time. Their hands touched where they lay on the hot cord of

the car seat. Someone had to make a move. Both looked
straight ahead out of the windscreen and down the drearily
respectable street. For some reason both noticed with a com-
pulsive but intensely boring interest that one side of the street
had houses with a flight of steps leading up to them and the
other side didn't. Yet there didn't seem to be a hill. What a
thing to be thinking at such a time! 'I reckon they'd go for
about nineteen hundred or two thou,' thought Tom and
Carole, 'I wonder if the "up six steps" people give themselves
airs.' They were both breathing with slight difficulty. Tom
reached up and pulled open the sunshine roof of the car. It
would be nice if you could do the same with your chest sometimes.

"Why did you do it?" asked Carole with something of the
pathetic and irritating courage of a poor actress repeating a
line of some bad play which has just drawn groans from the
audience.

"I told you. Why don't you drop it? Can't you leave me
alone?" He set his jaw for a moment and then turned to face
her. "I told you. He was on about land and about some big
deal on the Stock Exchange that he's been on lately. I, well,
I . . . *He's* always been the one to tell *me* things. Even
though I've kept on the bloody book he knows more about
insurance than I do and he had a bigger book than mine once,
himself, years ago. It's a change for me to be telling him
something and, besides, I didn't know you'd get dragged into
it. I didn't want that. That's the last thing I wanted."

"Last thing you meant to happen, you mean."

"Drop it, can't you? I told you I wanted to give him some
gen for a change. Show him he's not the only one who knows
all the answers. I didn't think what it'd lead to or I wouldn't've
done it. I told you once. Why bloody well go on about it?"

It was, of course, just this which he had not told her but
which she had told him. By having refused earlier to follow the
tempting path of escape there was now a real way out before

them. "Don't worry, dearest," said Carole. "I'll think of something to tell Sir Henry. Perhaps I'll have to tell him the truth. I couldn't get another job nearly as good, but that doesn't matter. Don't worry. Now let's go and eat somewhere."

"Kiss me first."

"All right."

"I've got an idea. Let's drive round some of the boozers that old Thorpley uses and see if we can run into him. We can have something to eat there if it's the Ploughing Team or that other one. Then we can have it out with him, if you like. Besides you've often said you'd like to meet him. Now's as good a time as any."

It was not exactly Carole's plan for the evening, but she agreed. "Now's certainly as good a time as any."

"He might be in the Ploughing Team and he might be in the Warrenchester Arms or the Hand and Racket. We'll try the old Ploughing Team first. Know it?"

"No," said Carole. She wanted to say, "Don't let's meet him now. Not tonight. I was wrong to agree. Let's be sure we are all right absolutely first." Instead she said, "I spoke to him today, when I phoned up your office."

Tom was surprised and, in a strange way, a bit intrigued and uneasy. "Oh, what did he have to say?"

"Nothing much. Just where you'd meet me and so on." It was quite impossible to tell the whole truth without becoming involved in unimaginable difficulties and complete systems of subtleties.

To have told the whole truth would have led into complexities involving Tom, herself, their relationship, Thorpley and the general social background of which all three were a part, and spreading into areas in which she herself was not sure where truth lay. Hence she lied to him, only by omission, but all the same it was for the first time.

"For *goodness' sake*, how far is it?" said Carole. "If he's not

in the first of these pubs you're talking about for *goodness' sake*
let's give it a miss. It's too silly driving about after your Mr.
Thorpley without any definite arrangement."

Having chucked away all weapons and laid aside his
buckler once their first frightening row was over, he was now
quite defenceless and hence took all this as some bitter hurt, a
reflection on his driving ability, knowledge of how to find the
boss quickly enough or personal adequacy in general. "I often
go after him in the evenings. I mean, I used to before I was tied
up with you every evening."

It seemed that they had made up only to argue again.
"You don't have to spend every evening with me if that's how
you feel!" They continued with jabbing words, searching, and
often finding, the tenderest spots but avoiding certain exposed
areas where to take advantage of the special knowledge each
had of the other would be a self-degrading betrayal. In the
course of this tense, childish, at times almost hysterical,
bickering they got out cigarettes, which Carole lit for both.
When he stopped in the parking area outside one pub she
leaned out of her window, saying, "Left-hand down a bit,
plenty of room yet," and so on in an ordinary, if somewhat
strained, voice, and then turned back to face him and hissed,
"I don't know why you're so anxious to find him tonight
unless you think he can think up some excuse for you that you
can't for yourself." Then for the third time in the last twenty
minutes she said, "You know you only did it to look big in his
eyes. You never thought of me at all."

All this time he was finishing parking, switching off the
ignition and leaning back to lock the back doors. She made to
get out but she changed her mind, not wishing to enter the pub
with everything still unsettled, and turned round again so that
their heads bumped slightly and he had to slide back rather
suddenly into his place again, unable to hold the twisted, half-
risen position. He knocked his elbow on the steering-wheel and
rubbed it. He had begun on his angry reply to her last thrust

and this incident came in the middle of a tirade. "Sorry," he said as their heads bumped and Carole murmured something about "my fault" as he caught his elbow. Thus in the very flood of their anger their eyes met and the absurd and trivial necessities of life had to be acknowledged. Then they went on with hurting one another, for this too was a necessity of the moment.

They gave up looking for Thorpley and he started to drive her back into the centre of town. "You needn't bother," she said as soon as the direction was apparent. He didn't answer but sat looking very straight ahead and driving with great concentration as if he were a learner again. "Tom, I . . . I'm sorry."

Generous in his relief, he said, "You were right. All the same I never knew you'd get brought into it." She nearly said, "I'll bet you didn't" in a joking way but could not run the risk of that tone while the dreadful feel of their first argument still hung about the car.

They went up West and strolled among the crowds round Leicester Square and walked up Greek Street and through Soho to see if a little café she had told him about was still there. "When I was a student. It was my very first meal I ever bought out for myself. Not counting fish and chips and so on. It sounds impossible but I always had school dinners or later took sandwiches when I was at commercial college. Then when my grant came through, there I was, a London girl and a student of eighteen, and never so much as ordered a poached egg at Joey's. Some of the provincial girls were more blasé than I was."

"Go on!"

"It's true. You should've known me then!"

"I can imagine." But he could not and was, at that moment, being gnawed at by the lover's hopeless jealousy of the beloved's past.

For Carole the familiar check tablecloths and dim lights

were a form of security. Both the waiters had changed since
her day but the owner still helped the waiters out when there
was a rush and went out himself to fetch drinks from a pub on
the corner. Tonight it was too late for the before-theatre
crowd and not late enough for late-supper people. The pro-
prietor nodded respectfully to Carole from his corner behind a
marble-topped counter on which were set baskets of bread,
half-filled water carafes and a cash-register. The strain of the
evening told on her and she felt better able to cope with life in
a place whose atmosphere she had conquered years ago.
Another new waiter who had noticed the *patron's* greeting to
her came towards their table. She decided to tell Tom that
they'd go Dutch treat and have something really nice. 'This
bit's all right,' Carole found herself thinking for the first time
for weeks. Tom was not the first young man to whom she had
introduced this place, which had nothing special to commend
it in the way of cooking or convenience. She ordered cold
consommé followed by *filet mignon* and Tom an omelette and
mushrooms. The food was good and for some reason they both
felt ravenous. They had a bottle of wine brought in. Their
tiredness changed to a rather strange feeling, light-headed but
solemn and intense. Both knew that now there must be other
things said, but this time not in anger.

Carole was still partly withdrawn into her protective inner
world, pretending that she was having dinner, one of many
dinners, with a boy friend, one of many, at *her* restaurant. She
didn't feel like coming out to talk seriously yet. This bit was all
right.

"There's some things we got to get straight," said Tom.

"I suppose there are," she said.

The waiter came and laid the saucer with the bill on it
discreetly on the corner of the table. Tom turned up a corner
and said, "Blimey, I hope they know you well enough here to
give us credit!" She knew he had enough money on him and
they had already agreed that she'd stand the wine as her share,

but something about the remark upset her. A vague un-easiness hovered around the word 'credit'. Events were now forcing her out of her private world. Something was trying to force its way into the front of her mind. She felt really cold for a moment and then hot with shame. Tom was saying some-thing more about the bill being either quite reasonable or un-reasonable but all she could hear was her own voice that morning saying, "I think Mr. Thorpley operates mainly on credit." Tom had not asked her to keep quiet anything he had told about *his* boss. He'd just assumed she would. Nothing had come of her remark to Sir Henry but did that make her any better than Tom? And here she had been pompous and superior, and, yes, cruel to him over a slip, when she herself had made the same sort! The only thing to be done now was to tell him.

She made the effort to face what she truly felt was one of the bravest actions of her life. "I think, I mean I said something to Sir Henry too about your Mr. Thorpley operating mainly on credit." She shut her mouth tight and looked straight ahead.

"Oh, that would just flatter him," said Tom. "Does too. Shows how smart he is."

Carole was now unwilling to forgo the rewards of courage and virtue. "I meant I'm as bad as you are." It sounded a bit childish.

"Oh, we know that," said Tom. She looked at him and they both laughed as if to say, 'What a pair of fools!' They laughed again, so that the tired, middle-aged man behind the counter glanced over to their table and stayed watching for a moment the pretty sight of two young lovers happy. Tom stood up and paid the bill and they left. They were in a hurry to leave that place and go somewhere and make it up properly. In due course it was properly put right; but something had happened that day all the same.

CHAPTER 10

There's Always a Catch in it

Mr. Thorpley chose that day to breeze around and inspect his local interests. He left word that Tom was to meet him for lunch in the Jolly Farmer.

To get there Tom Stanton had to go near the part of the old town, now assimilated as a suburb, where Carole's family lived. This started him off thinking about her good and proper. Sometimes he wondered what he had done to deserve a girl like that. Every day, all the time he was with her, he could almost feel himself learning and understanding more. Yet she didn't put on any airs with him and not even before they'd fallen for each other had she tried to cover up anything about her family. Not like some.

This imagined presence of his mistress pervaded the whole area with a peculiar nostalgia, an unreasonable longing not just to recapture his own past but hers as well. He took a detour and entered the area of 'The Poets'. Here was where she had lived as a child. She'd told him all about it. One Sunday soon they were coming down here together to meet her family. All the streets were named after different poets. The Brockett family lived in Byron Road, where there were bigger houses with passages. Most of the rest of 'The Poets' was little terraced houses where you opened the front door straight into the parlour. Wordsworth had the off-licence on the corner and Shelley a bit of waste ground in the middle of which stood the British Legion Club, painted a dull and peeling green with coarse grass growing high around the rotting sand-bags left to lie there for fifteen years since the blitz. He felt tempted to get

out of the car for a moment and walk around one of these
dreary corners and try to imagine Carole as a schoolgirl skipping and playing hop-scotch or, in order to make sure that the
searching tongue had jabbed to the limit of the aching tooth,
picture her later, tall and gangling, in an unbecoming gym-
slip, little budding breasts hidden in a white blouse, joking
with some boy friend on the way home. And he hadn't been
even anywhere near at the time! His heart ached. He slowed
the car but some element of shame-faced common sense kept
him from stopping and getting out. He could not place the
pain in his heart, which seemed even about to take his breath
away. For all that, he was more fortunate than some men in
that he lacked sufficient imagination to feed his pangs. He
lowered both front windows, as if the better to smell the air she
had once breathed. It was a close, muggy morning with hardly
any wind. The whole area was dead flat and the sluggish
breeze swept across it, picking up a smell of cabbages and coal-
smoke on the way. On the right of Tennyson there was a row
of new council houses with doors painted in different bright
primary colours, trying to look like something out of the
Festival of Britain, and along the main road, into which he
must turn in a moment, there was quite a different sort of
property, rushed up in the 'thirties by an estate company. He
had had a hand in selling one or two of them for the boss in the
last seven years. The people who lived there never crossed the
road. They did their shopping at the Jubilee Parade, a three-
penny ride down the by-pass. The old-fashioned shops of 'The
Poets', which were much nearer, might as well have been in
another town.

Tom pulled into the wide parking area of the Jolly Farmer.
He recognised the boss's car. Before going in he stood for a
moment, pushing Carole and all that business right down so
that he didn't go into the boss in a dreamy state. The tyres of
the cars had squeezed the dull clay soil up between the coke
cinders. On one side of the pub was waste ground littered with

broken bricks, rusty bicycle frames and water tanks and old
tyres showing their white cord skeletons. On the far side came
a row of cottages, over a hundred years old and most likely
built when all this was farm-land, to house the married
labourers. They didn't come on the market often, not much in
it when they did. He had taken clients into one or two. The
street doors opened straight into parlours as tiny as ships'
cabins, full of furniture and with a damp smell like turnips;
enormous family photos in sepia always hung on the walls.

He started to walk across to the entrance with the wide road
at his back. The endless procession of traffic made the ground
shake slightly. The air, too damp to sponge up the dark diesel
fumes, softened the roar and rattle of the engines and settled
heavily again around the dusty number plates and hissing
exhausts. There was a curious smell of hot tin and chemicals
from some near-by factory, and in the distance, someone
dropped an iron bar on to concrete, so that the clang lifted
above the dull clatter of production to strum high up among
the heavy cables looping across the sodden countryside on their
grey pylons.

When Carole and he got married they wouldn't live in a
part like this, even if it meant changing his job.

Thorpley was perched on one of the stools as usual and
waved to him.

"Here, over here, boy. What are you having?" They
talked about some small local deals and Thorpley brought out
his big news.

His habit, especially after a few drinks, was to emphasise any
instruction or announcement with dramatic gestures and by
raising and lowering his voice from a shout to a conspiratorial
whisper, but now he spoke casually and conversationally.
"Tom, how would you like to be manager in charge of all the
four offices this side? How would you like it, boy, eh? It'll
mean ditching in your insurance book, but I'll more than make
that up to you. What do you say?"

Since Tom had been more or less functioning as a manager for some time the proposal was not so startling. All the same he felt pleased and, even before he could reply to Thorpley, was thinking of how he would tell Carole the news, as if this were the only important matter to be considered. The boss was watching him. "I . . . thanks very much, Mr. Thorpley, I don't know what to say for the moment."

"Oh yes, you do, boy, yes, you do. 'Yes'. That's what you've got to say."

He bought Tom a drink and went on to give details, right down to little things like taking over the boss's own room in the main office on High Street and getting rid of one or two sales-men who were not pulling their weight.

"After all, Tom, you're the senior now in any case and it's a thing you've got to learn to do sooner or later." Tom nodded in a very serious fashion. He'd felt a bit bad about it, almost shocked, when the boss had first brought it up about having to sack blokes, but now he knew it would be O.K. He even felt a little thrill of a peculiar kind he had not felt very much before.

"You'll do it all right, boy. I know you will." Thorpley took a good drink of his gin and tonic and lowered his voice, turning his body round on the high stool like a great engine on a turn-table. "You know why I picked you? You know why? Well, I'll tell you why. I've had my eye on you for years, boy, for years, that's it. It's not that you're so much smarter than any of the others, in many ways you're not. Remember that Peartree Road job?" He reminded Tom of the details, which he had never forgotten and never would, of his first major error. "You cost us a nice packet and got us landed with a crook as knew his way around and sat in the blasted house for three years just paying the interest on the mortgage and 'showing willing' to the beak every time he was dragged to court. Could've gone on for years."

"I'll not be caught that way again, Mr. Thorpley."

"I know you won't, boy. Never the same way twice, eh? Not you anyway. That's one of the reasons I chose you." He went on in the same way for quite some time. Tom thought, 'It's not so much that he's trying to flatter and butter me up. More like he's trying to cover up the real reason for giving me the job.'

Thorpley suggested that they move up to the sandwich and snack end of the bar. He made a business of trying to persuade Tom to go on to gin and tonic but both knew he would stick to beer. "I can't afford to let go lunch-times now," said the new manager, risking his first comic prance of unconcern on the springy high-board. "It's all right for you, Mr. Thorpley, now you've just unloaded it all on to me!"

"You know me, boy. I'd never hold a little slip-up through being fuddled against you. 'Long as it didn't cost us all too much, of course." Both men laughed and Tom felt the high-board of his promotion giving and pushing under his toes just as he wanted it to, his own weight making it move. Thorpley seemed to be waiting until he had finished a bit of his sandwich and had another drink before he went on talking. When he started again Tom once more felt that he was trying to cover up in some way his real reasons for having given him the job. He went on and on about how long Tom had been with the firm and of little incidents, which even Tom had forgotten, of his earlier good sales and failures, of how prices and values had shifted over the years they had been associated. Then he started a lot of stuff about the City and his new plans for taking over some small company and turning it into a plant for making steel window-frames and other building necessities of metal which could be bought by Thorpley Enterprising Builders, the shares in which were held by the builder he had worked with for years off and on, and the controlling bulk by Speedy Homefinders. The boss was on the board of all three and, of course, Managing Director of Speedy Homefinders. Tom couldn't follow it all and, indeed, it seemed at times as if

the boss didn't really want him to. Anyway the general effect
of this spray-gun play of words was that things were going to
get bigger and better and Tom's life with them. "So you see,
boy, there's a good time coming, a good time coming for us all.
Hang on to old Thorpley's coat-tails and you'll go places."

Tom started again to think of how he would break the news
to Carole. They had long ago laughed over his first attempts to
impress her with talking about being a partner and so on. It
would be good to go over that time together now that it was all
more or less true. Starting to think about Carole in working
hours had been a mistake. He was so taken up with the
imaginary dialogue with her that he stopped listening to the
boss and Thorpley had to squeeze his elbow and say, "Excited,
are you? Don't let it run away with you. You listen to this
bit, you listen close. Here's where you come in. I'm going to
need plenty of ready, a good backing of the old needful, there
where I can get it out quick to flash at them, to bring it off. I
can't go into a long rigmarole about the property we got on
our books and the assets of the old Homefinders and all that,
not with these gentry I can't. I've got to have the lolly right
there by each settlement day, once a fortnight, just in case.
Once through this bit of rough and we'll be sitting pretty, but
in the meantime I've got to have the cash. Now, boy, cards on
the table is best, nearly always best. Listen, I want you to
realise as many assets as you can, just as if we were getting
ready to wind up the business and do a moonlight flit, which
we're not. Sort right through the lists and flog everything you
can as quick as you can without letting it get out too much.
We're finished buying any stuff on spec at the moment even if
you get on to a snip, unless you're sure you can flog it again
real quick. Then get together with old Soapy, our legal
gentleman, and work out what you can get the rents of all that
lot of stuff back of 'The Poets' raised to. I've spoken to him, so
he knows what he's got to go over with you. I'm sure there's a
few hundred a year more can be got out of them even though

our legal gentleman says we pushed it up to the max. as soon as the Rent Act was passed." On the word 'gentleman' he paused and gave the term a half-bored, ironic tone as if even the title were some absurd legal formality which must be complied with in conversation, like saying, 'This is my act and deed,' when there were only the two of you in the room.

Tom's mind had already started to work on some of the details involved in carrying out the boss's instructions. He wouldn't have much time to see Carole. She'd have to understand and try and fit in somehow. The boss was talking again, "The thing is that I don't want to have to worry about what's happening this end. Not all the details, just a check-up with you once every week. 'Course I'm always there whenever you want me for a word of advice but I've chose you because I know I can trust you to get on with it."

Tom thought he had spotted why the boss had rushed it all at him and kept on with different reasons for having given him the job. "Mr. Thorpley, I . . . I don't see, well . . ."

"Come along, boy, cough it up. You know old Thorpley's way by this time. Cards on the table."

"All right, then. Cards on the table, Mr. Thorpley." In his own voice it sounded embarrassingly self-conscious. "It seems to me I'll be rather sawing off the branch I'm standing on. I mean, especially if I have to give up the book as well. If we're going to sell up all that stuff and not expand the business I'll be losing commission all the time, just when . . ." He was about to add, "just when I'm thinking of starting saving to get married," but he didn't want it to come out in this way. Besides he wasn't sure yet.

It had taken a bit of courage to say it all and he started, half-defiantly, to say it all over again the same way but the boss stopped him and started to laugh, slapping his own fat thighs and gasping and spluttering over his gin and tonic. "Like I always say, you can't have your cake and eat it in this world, boy. Maybe in the next, but not in this one. If you wasn't so smart I wouldn't have anyone to pick for the job, but then if you wasn't so smart you'd never think of asking questions like that one. Oh, it'll be all right. Explain in a minute," he started to gasp and catch his breath in earnest. "Don't worry, you'll be all right. Explain in a minute, just let poor old Thorpley get his little laugh over with!"

He recovered himself but held a rumbling chuckle in reserve ready to let it billow out and swamp the conversation again if needed. "You won't lose by it, boy. Keep your wits about you and when the dust has settled a bit you'll find yourself manager of a real company, twice, ten times, as big as what Homefinders is or'll ever be. You haven't done so bad sticking to old Thorpley all these years, have you?" He pushed his face out towards Tom, his eyes so screwed up among creases of shrewdly harrowed fat that they seemed to be closed completely. To lessen the effect of grimness the background chuckle was pushed to the fore and brought into use like a machine-gun to cover the advance.

"Well, have you, eh?"

"No, of course not, Mr. Thorpley," said Tom. "It's just that . . . well, just that I don't want to drop too much in the meantime. And, besides, you're asking me to give up the book. I paid out for that round, and, what with the time I've given to Homefinders—not that I grudge it mind, Mr. Thorpley—I've not had a chance to work it up much. I just about keep pace with my lapses and pay-outs."

"There's three things you can do, boy, if you think it out. You can sling in having anything to do with the old firm and walk out on old Thorpley for good and build up your insurance round and so on. You'll be pushed to make real money at it. Then, you could sling in the book and become manager here, like I told you. The other thing you could do would be to keep on as you are and that'd mean working all day and all night and not getting in any pleasures such as a young man is entitled to expect from life."

Tom was thinking of Carole. He wanted to ask her advice
but also he wanted to announce to her that he was now the
manager. He started to repeat to himself the opening phrases
he would use to tell her. This brought her presence near and
he suddenly found the boss looking at him and saying, "First I
thought you were thinking it over, but you've gone into a daze
and it must be over that girl of yours. Well, ask her what she
thinks, then, go on, ask her. She'll say the same as me. Take
on this job and stick by old Thorpley and you can't go wrong.
See if I'm not right."

Tom never kept much back from the boss; he'd tried it once
or twice and, for one thing, you couldn't do it. He was smarter
than you were. This was different, though. Nothing to do with
him. Only now did he realise that he was to pay a price for all
the times he'd boasted to the boss about girls he'd had and
made him envious talking about pick-ups at dances and so on.
He now had no natural right to stand on his dignity about anything to do with his sex life.

"It's . . . that's a personal matter, Mr. Thorpley," he
brought out, and felt himself blushing at the daft sound
of it.

The boss went into another of his laughing and coughing
fits, slapping his thighs and saying, "Oh dear! Oh dear!" over
and over. Since he was feeling a bit foolish and wanted to
know just how big a fool he looked he started watching the red-
faced splutterings taking place a few inches from his own nose.
Although chuckles and the effort needed to stop them from
choking him seemed to be occupying all the boss's powers, his
eyes had a curious inward-looking quality, as if he wore a
movable rubber mask which he was twisting about all ways
whilst really thinking of something else. It struck him at last
that in fact that was just what was happening. Mr. Thorpley
used these attacks of cackling to find time to think. His eyes,
pondering and shrewd, filled the spaces where the mask of
Comedy should have shown black blanks.

Tom's realisation gave him little advantage. He was as unprepared for the boss's next move as if he had never noticed it being planned. Mr. Thorpley stopped laughing as suddenly as one switching off the sound of a telly set to answer the phone.

"Don't marry that one, boy. Don't marry at all if you know what's good for you but especially don't marry that one. You wait a few years and then take a step up. Marry some girl from a posh family that has what they call 'good connections' but not much lolly to keep up with 'em. Daughter of some retired army officer or wog-basher with only his pension, that sort of thing. She'd know how to get you on a bit and help you meet people as would be a real help to you in business. That one you got now, she's got on in her own way but she don't know where to go next. She's got it but she don't know what to do with it, you might say." Tom had put down his glass on the bar and stood staring at the dark, stained wood. He felt numbly resentful and also unhappily exposed and uneasy, almost frightened—the feeling of being at a medical and stripped to see if you were fit for call-up, but this time there weren't any other blokes around in the same boat. Thorpley went on about it and it began to get under his skin a bit so that he had either to lose his temper or find a way out. Thinking of how to shut up the boss without either upsetting him or letting on how upsetting he was being made him stand outside himself for a moment. That was how it happened that he imagined Carole further down the bar on a high stool or, as in a dream, floating somewhere around just above and behind his head, watching and listening. He had to stick up for her! He began to feel angry with himself, with Thorpley and with Carole. What business had she to come interfering with his work and his relations with the boss? He had to get on, didn't he?

In a strained voice, which an observer or newcomer to the conversation would have imagined to be calm to the point of

disinterest, he said, "You've never even met her." He left off
'Mr. Thorpley', just to show.

"I've spoke to her, boy, on the phone and you've told me a
bit and I know her job and her boss. On the face of it you
might think she'd be right for you. Got it in the noddle and so
on, no doubt, but, like I said, that sort don't know where
they're going and she'd soon make you the same. You mark
my words. Soon make you the same. Then it'd end somehow,
not as you wanted it to, or else drag on and not end, more
likely, which'd be worse. And besides, it . . . it . . ." He
paused and sipped his drink. It seemed to be his turn to stare
at the mahogany bar as if it were a crystal. "Besides, going
steady and getting hooked is a mug's game, at your age anyway. Maybe at any age. Oh, I know what it's like when
you're young. Think you can trust each other and all that.
Promise never to keep anything back about how you feel. I
know, I know. Now, look. You've sold enough places and
been in enough homes to know it all already if you'd use your
bloody eyes, boy. How many couples, with or without kids,
have you known that wouldn't give their eyes—well, say,
one eye for safety's sake—to be out of it? You know the old
song, 'I wish I was single . . .'" He paused and seemed to
cheer up, raised his eyes from the bar and started to sing under
his breath and glance round the company of boozers as if
inviting them to join in, knowing that this, the saloon bar full of
a week-day, lunch-time crowd of business-men, was not really
the time and place for a sing-song but at the same time showing
that he had no worries, was successful and his own master,
could please himself, not bother to hide his origins and his
familiarity with the world of coach trips to Southend, cockles
and 'Knees up, Mother Brown'. His glance around the primly
suited salesmen and shoe-shop managers was rather like that
of the barrack-room bully who reels in and switches on the
lights and invites the blinking recruits to join him in the chorus
of a song known only to regular soldiers such as himself. One

or two men who knew him smiled and raised their glasses and winked and nodded in a knowing and doggy fashion, others shrugged slightly and turned their backs. Tom felt as embarrassed as he'd ever felt since that unforgotten day, years ago, with that barmaid, Mary. The boss raised his voice, as if to make him feel worse, and went on with the next line, "How my pockets would jingle, I wish I was single again, again. I wish I was single again!"

He suddenly shut up, just as it was really getting too much, and swung round to face Tom. "I'll give you a picture," he said, "and then you tell me what's wrong with it. These muggins get to the age when they feel the urge, then before they know where they are some girl has got 'em hooked. Always remember, boy, that a woman is cleverer than what you are and she is here to increase and multiply, as the good book puts it. That's her aim, her only aim. And you're just here to help her—a begetter and a provider, that's what you are to her. A woman don't think much about anything else although she may pretend to. How she's cleverer is that she can not only fool you but fool herself so that she gets what she wants and can still make herself out to be a martyr over it. Then there's kids. You keep paying out and paying out and all the stuff you've made your little love-nest with is slowly ruined by them rolling on it and jumping on and off it and you can't afford any new, what with shoes and school uniforms and so on. Then as soon as they're in their teens they'll start looking down on you because the place is shabby and all that. Couple of years of that and then they're away and you're ready to retire without a thing saved for a bottle of booze even. That's the picture, boy, and you know it is if you've eyes. Listen to 'em in here jokin' about it all. Got to, or do 'emselves in, and they haven't the guts for that. I know what you're thinking. I'm not slow. I can see it in your face. You're wondering about me, about old Thorpley. Don't you worry about old Thorpley. I go my own way and enjoy life and my old woman lets me get

on with it. That's all there is to it. All there is. No need to ask
questions. That's all there is to tell." Tom started to say
something and before he could get a word out of his mouth
Thorpley repeated, "All there is to tell you or anybody. All
there is to it." It seemed he didn't want time wasted in dis-
cussing that part, as if it would all be more to Tom's benefit if
some other aspect of his advice were discussed or argued
about.

"I was going to say, somebody's got to have kids or it'd all
stop."

"Quite right, boy, but you and I are not the sort. Anyway,
like I said, you wait until you're a bit older, then if you want to
you can have your pick." Quite suddenly he stopped talking
about marriage and said, "You're going to take on that job,
aren't you?"

Although he was used to Thorpley's tactics, and even at
times tried to imitate them, the younger man was surprised.
"Yes, Mr. Thorpley, I am," he said with the faintly solemn
note of young people who wish to show that they feel the importance of a decision or an occasion. Mr. Thorpley was
pleased and they clinked glasses together with a fresh drink.
They discussed a few more details and Tom had to leave to
meet a client and to start on his new duties. "Bye-bye, boy,
best of luck," called Mr. Thorpley after him. He watched
Tom go out through the swing doors and turned back to face
the bar, shaking his head benevolently and admiringly as if to
say, 'A grand boy that, but I can't do anything with him.
He won't listen to me.' This theatrical movement had been
performed for the benefit of the company in general, or for
some imagined audience, but he glanced up to find himself
facing the middle-aged Irish barman, bald, with pale blue eyes
in which the lamps were only lit when the packet-boat had
cleared Holyhead once a year, dressed, in the modern pub
fashion, in a soiled white coat like a male nurse in a mental
ward. "A fine boy," said Thorpley, aloud in order to excuse

himself before the hint of undimmed shrewdness in the defeated blue eyes. "A fine boy," and he nodded heavily in a pantomime of paternal pride.

"Yes, indeed, sorr. Takes after ye'. Takes after ye', plain to see."

CHAPTER II

It Must Often Happen
Like That

IT became more and more difficult to see enough of Carole, what with being manager and the boss sending him chasing off on strange messages and odd jobs and still expecting him to keep selling up stuff and chivvying the collectors to get the rents in where there was trouble getting an eviction. Some of the jobs (' "messages" is more like it,' thought Tom a trifle bitterly) were nothing to do with property deals at all. It was worrying not knowing exactly what you were doing or what was going on. You might make a boob of yourself and never know it.

For two days after he was made manager they had to be content with long phone calls. Then he managed to get away about seven and drive into town and pick her up. It was all against the traffic. A new, delayed stream of car-owning senior clerks, managers and salesmen who had stopped late and then had a drink up West were now driving home to scorched suppers and sulky wives. Tom wanted his own supper. A lot of little things had gone wrong that day and he had plenty of worries waiting for the morning. He'd had a bit of a moan to old Thorpley about the difficulty in getting a decent price for two old bits of property without garage space, what with the high deposits needed for old stuff from the blasted building societies and the state of the decorations . . . "That's what I made you bloomin' manager for, boy," was all the boss had said. "If I've got to worry about things like that I might as

well do it myself." Now, he'd known the boss long enough
now to know that he never blasted you unless he thought it was
the best way of getting some action or unless he felt really
worried himself. Suppose this marvellous scheme of his should
all go wrong. He might put himself into Carey Street as a
limited company, so that his own personal household stuff'd be
safe, and wind up Speedy Homefinders to pay off at whatever
rate in the pound the Court might fix. Then where would Tom
be for all his hard work? He jabbed down the brake pedal as
some flaming idiot swung out from a side turning on a scooter.

His gloomy thoughts gave way to irritation as life pressed
itself upon him too closely for him to savour them at leisure.
What the hell was he doing, anyway, chasing up to town after
. . . he was about to say 'this girl' to himself but changed to
'her'. Love, even in a shallow nature, will not be mocked.
He thus avoided total betrayal and also the saying of her name,
which could not be muttered in anger, any more than a
prayer might be by one devout.

When he met her, and for a short time after, it was all right.
Her eyes were so bright and he supposed his must be the same,
each of them signalling that it had seemed like years and then
both laughing at themselves for being such fools.

Soon after that it started to go wrong. They got caught up
in a lot of theatre-bound traffic and he had to make two nasty
right turns to get to her blasted special café. What was so
special about it anyway? Then there was nowhere to park and
a copper stopped him, leaned in at the window and told him
off because he'd slowed down to see if there was room to
squeeze in at the kerb and pulled out again suddenly, without
signalling, so that a bloke behind had to brake hard. He had to
sit there and take it, because if you argued back to them they'd
smack you on a charge. He was humiliated in front of his girl.
It was all her fault anyway. "Do we have to eat there?" he
asked in a very irritable voice.

"Anywhere you like," she said, pressing against his arm and

side and so not giving him any excuse to turn his annoyance on her.

When they finally found a spot and walked back, he found himself going all over the boss's advice about marrying too young and so on. Then they had to wait a long time for the food to come, sitting side by side and crumbling bread pellets. He knew she sensed his anger and that it was making her miserable and this made him feel worse, guilty as well.

They started to try and talk of unimportant matters and then fell silent again. Tom almost stopped listening to her talking about things that had happened in the office and about some friends of hers that they had made a foursome with one Saturday. From time to time he said "Yes", or "No", or nodded. She must've known he wasn't with her completely, but didn't want to admit it to herself, or else to risk annoying him further by nudging him into full attention. This lent a brightly strained note to her voice and so added to his vague feeling of guilt.

Without really wanting to, he began going over what the boss had been saying about marriage. What the hell was he doing sitting here with this girl? Dashing up to town like a bloody maniac to see her and waiting to eat in some stinking café in Bloomsbury just because the place meant something to her for some silly girl's reason. As the word 'silly' came into his mind he started hearing her voice again, trying desperately to sound cheerful and interesting over something to do with the window getting stuck in her bed-sitter and what the landlady had said. The boss knew a lot and he'd said, "Always remember, boy, a woman is cleverer than what you are. . . . She's only here for one thing: to increase and multiply. That's her aim. And you're here to help her and be a provider, that's all you're here for . . ." He found himself getting so annoyed with the sound of her voice in his ears that his chest felt funny. He even began breathing more quickly than usual. He suddenly wanted to shout at her, to do something awful like standing up and upsetting the table and running out, leaving her there startled and crying, to hurt her somehow. He turned to face her and, nervously, she faced him. Her eyes looked a bit frightened, but wide and trusting. She tried to go on with her chatter for a moment. He felt such a desire to shout, "Shut up!" that he fell almost into a panic trying to control himself. "Shut up a minute, please," he said, in a voice so hoarse and funny that he hardly recognised it as his own. "Let's . . . I mean, please marry me, Carole."

CHAPTER 12

Things Get a Bit Much
at Times

SIR HENRY'S ability to throw off the cares of business and to lose himself in the affairs of his home and estate rarely broke down, and then only in the stilly watches of the night. When things were going smoothly he was often able to look in on the City only for an hour or even to stop at home for two or three days, keeping in touch by telephone and leaving Carole Brockett and his trusty Dentham to run the office and seek his decision in any unexpected crisis.

Such days and their domestic comings and goings were organised by him with the zest and detail of a large troop movement or of a complex commercial venture. At a late breakfast one such morning in an alcove of the sunny garden room, he said, "What's today's arrangements, dearest?" His wife announced plans for a visit to the market town, for interviewing a possible part-time gardener at his cottage and for looking in on some friends for tea. Then she planned to hurry back. A friend of her own youth was coming to stay for a few days. In explaining all this she became very confused, repeated herself several times and placed her possible movements in an obviously inconvenient, even unworkable, order. "Well, now, let's see," said Sir Henry. "What about transport? Better take the 'tilly. Say we leave at about ten. We can have a spot of elevenses in Downsford at Anne's Pantry. Get the shopping and be back. . . . Where were you thinking of lunching?"

"I hadn't really thought," said his gentle wife. She said to

herself, 'How ever does he think I manage when I'm alone?
But then I only get vague and muddled when he is here to plan
it all. He likes doing it so much. After all these years I'm not
even sure if I'm still putting it on or if his being here really
makes me like that.' Her husband was saying, ". . . or there
if you like, what do you say?" and she was able to look at him
with a perfectly genuine expression of flustered indecision, for
she had not been listening to a single word.

Sir Henry started to make notes in the broad, grey margins
of *The Times*. "When will you have your bath?" he asked. "I
wondered if you could have it early whilst I was driving to the
station to meet Isobel. Then she's sure to want one as soon as
she arrives, before dinner. It wouldn't really leave me much
time for my own. I *could* be a bit late down, of course, if you
wouldn't mind holding the fort with Isobel for a bit." The
time-table and movement order for the bath became more and
more involved and tied up with shopping matters and the
speed at which the 'tilly could safely be driven back. Then
there followed a discussion of the part Sir Henry was to play in
the interview with the possible part-time gardener. This
needed a great elaboration, because normally one would have
left Mary to have broached the subject and broken the ice
with introductory remarks about how they had happened to
hear of the fellow. Then it would have been left to Sir Henry
to mention money, man to man, and hint at how to dodge the
tax-man and the pension people so that the old boy's pittance
was not cut and to give some indication of the work involved
and the state of the garden. The snag was that Sir Henry
could do all these things but the last, since he knew nothing of
gardening except that the flowers looked pretty and that a
gentleman always had a garden. His father had had one. But
then his father had never had to go driving around cottages
looking for a part-time gardener. There had been no 'servant
problem' then.

The planning session continued thus for some time and then

Sir Henry said, "I'll go and bring the 'tilly round to the front and put the shopping baskets in while you go and get ready."

He walked out across the yellow gravel to the doors of the double garage. Though he was unaware of it his stride was longer and slightly slower than in the City. Fresh country smells and the dew-wet grass of the garden were all around him and the morning sun lit the tufted trees far into the distance, as in an old engraving of Sir Gawain riding out in armour across the meads towards some forest of old England.

Side by side in the front seat, with the baskets and an old crate in the back, they drove along the leafy lanes. This continual driving and counter-driving down the narrow tracks of black tar dusted with yellow gravel formed a large part of living in the country. Sir Henry had long ago logged all the times taken to complete journeys to his neighbours' houses, to the near-by villages and towns. When movement orders from his wife became especially complex he could go into great lengths to explain and break down the journeys from point to point and estimate the total time needed and the most economical routing.

Very little of the countryside was visible. The banks and high hedges turned the roads into green-lined chutes which blinkered the eyes' scope even on high ground. In the woods the narrow runways widened and became vaulted tunnels and the noise of the engine pressed back more closely from the trunks and the black arms supporting a pale green luminous roof.

All parts of the scheme went through nicely to time. They had elevenses as planned at Anne's Pantry. "Coffee's not bad," said Sir Henry, and, lowering his voice and smiling, "Feel one's doing one's bit at the same time for the impoverished gentlefolk." His wife smiled with just the right mixture of amusement but gentle reproach and nodded a warning as the enormous hips of Anne herself squeezed past at eye level, their wide slopes turfed with several square feet of some heathery tweed seemingly woven with actual spikes of gorse and bracken stems.

"Don't be unkind, dear. She's done awfully well, and, of course . . ."

Then there had been the shopping to do, with a nice division of labour as Mary saw to food and curtain material and some odds and ends and he went to order winter oil to be delivered for the central heating and arranged for a builder to come out and look at a leaking roof to one of the out-houses. Then they had a quiet lunch together in the back room of the George and Dragon. The move was to arrive early and linger over a sherry in the bar and tell the barman to let the manager know they were staying to lunch. Then he'd organise things a bit and they could be sure of a damn fine lunch. Dining-room was a bit dreary, of course. "You're quite right, quite right," said Sir Henry. "The whole place seems to have been varnished in dark brown Windsor soup."

All the arrangements for the evening went off well. He had a few minutes to spare before setting out to fetch Isobel from the station and phoned the office. There'd been nothing much in the post and the closing prices were firm. He'd had a feeling he could get away with it for a couple of days that week and relax a bit. You must develop a bit of an instinct over the years, kind of sixth sense. Something of that sort. Luck in it as well, of course.

All the tight schedule for the bathroom worked out according to plan.

It was a quiet dinner party. The women talked of holidays abroad and of the lives of their grown-up children and from time to time made an effort to include him in the conversation.

Mary had to keep excusing herself and going out to the kitchen. They were without servants at the moment except for Olga, a D.P. girl from the agency with small bad teeth and a greasy Lithuanian dictionary in her apron pocket.

Over liqueurs they talked of servants they had known and of mutual friends and the old days.

In the middle of this cosy, companionable and secure conversation the phone rang in the hall.

Carole welcomed the break in the quiet routine of a slack afternoon at the office. Nothing had happened much up to then. Sir Henry phoned, just after old Dentham had lit his four o'clock pipe. She gave him a report on the post and confirmed his own estimate of the market and the day's trading. She was amusing herself with her files of clippings and studying an analysis of how Hatch System operators might have fared over the past twelve months, when one of the juniors came in, dithered in the doorway and said, "Excuse me, Miss Brockett, but Mr. Dentham told me to tell you that there's a Mr. Warwick outside to see you."

The office was ill-designed to receive callers. Anyone of importance was shown through to the only place possible, Sir Henry's room, and Carole could hardly use that to receive her visitor without so infuriating Dentham that he would find some way of being unco-operative and rude the next day. Besides, it might be some personal matter, though it was unlike Donald to call except on business. She crossed through the typing room and felt the envious eyes of the girls on her, the smart one who didn't have to sit typing all day and getting a back-ache. Some of them had glimpsed Donald, too, through the heavy, glass doors and that made the minxes worse than ever. He really was good-looking and in his too perfect City clothes looked rather like something out of an advertisement for an expensive town car.

She had to smile at Dentham as she passed through Accounts. She tried to indicate in her expression that it was all very awkward, wasn't it, with Sir Henry out and someone from the City page of a paper calling, and that if she couldn't manage she'd be sure to ask Dentham's advice. All this was work for nothing, for he chose to ignore her and put on an air of intense concentration and preoccupation and ran his finger down the page of an open ledger, looking unseeingly into the middle distance and moving his lips slightly. Carole sighed and went to meet Donald, who was standing in an uncomfortable no-man's-land between the heavy, glass doors and the dark, marble-floored hallway. Behind him stood a central, open lift-shaft encased in an ornate latticed grill like some rare exhibit of the Great Exhibition of 1851. Donald's rather languid manner and the formal clothes in which he always armoured his personality in working hours added to this effect. Carole was wondering what he wanted, so important that he couldn't phone, but it was as if her mind resented the sudden discipline in the middle of an easy afternoon and deliberately misunderstood its orders. Instead of thinking about the reasons for Donald's presence there at that time she found herself thinking just about Donald. He looked so much the City man, and yet a bit too slim and intense and his hair just a trifle long for the part. He'd certainly found his niche, a job where he could buy and sell and invest just like his father but much more successfully and yet really call himself a journalist. He had it coming and going, both ways, seemed to have his cake and eat it too just as every fool aspires to do. To the thick-necked City types he was a faintly romantic figure who knew both their world and one of his own too, and to the hag-ridden hacks in the King Lud he was that traditional figure of envy— the moneyed young bachelor, never short of gin money. And yet he wasn't happy. He wanted one thing he couldn't have. 'Me,' thought Carole rather smugly, and floated through the doors.

"Come in, Don. What is it? If it's going to take long you can come and sit on the corner of the table in my little glass hutch if you like. There's barely room to swing a cat, but . . ."

"Oh, I'm not thinking of swinging you," said Donald.

She knew exactly what this was meant to convey. He

resented her jolly and chatty office manner, he could not be bothered to drop his own working *persona* just for her, especially since she did not seem at all anxious to drop hers for him. As well as this, of course, in a way, he hated her because, in his way, he was in love with her.

Carole had the ample generosity of the happy and secure. On Friday she was meeting Tom to choose an engagement ring. She knew why Donald had to be jaunty and rude and, perhaps, even try to hurt her. She felt a bit ashamed of her smug little thought coming through the door a moment before.

First things first, however. "What is it, Don? Business or pleasure?" she asked.

"Business," said Donald, and at once she found herself dreaming again, released from having to give her full attention to anything but 'real' life. She compared him with Tom, both men so different, both twisted by the struggle to survive and advance beyond their starting point. She knew Tom was almost as twisted as Donald. (It is hate which is blind; love is only partially sighted.) The difference was that Donald was slippery as well as twisted. In any case, when you love, you love, there is no question of choice. These and similar philosophical abstractions from her recent emotional experience occupied her mind to such an extent that she hardly heard the opening of Donald's remarks, and, quick as he always was, he said, "Look, I haven't really time to have to say it all over again, so please stop thinking about your latest boy friend and listen. There's a strong rumour that a Mr. Thorpley is going to make a public bid for all the floating shares in your outfit. I lunched with him a few weeks ago and he hinted as much, and sold a few of his own holdings that he'd got from old Illstone and started a mild scare. That's when you dropped a bit just before last account day, you see?"

Carole was listening now. "Yes," she said, "I see."

"Now, I'm seeing him later," Donald went on. "Some time ago we made a gentleman's—save the ruddy mark!—agreement that I should have the scoop on his public offer. Never thought much about it at the time. Didn't imagine he'd make the grade so soon. Today there's this strong rumour going round about a public take-over bid coming and on top of it I've had this message to meet him. Ties up, you see?"

"What kind of man is this Mr. Thorpley?" asked Carole, and she thought, 'Now I know what it means when you read, "She had her own reasons for asking." '

"Oh, rough diamond, you know. On the way up and doesn't mind being a doormat for anyone who can help him; thinks he can always kick them in the teeth later, I suppose."

Carole nodded and their eyes met. She suddenly wanted to say, 'Who the hell are you and I to be talking about "rough diamonds" and so on?' but all she said aloud was, "When are you seeing him, what time?"

"About eight. I've had to see about holding a bit of space. It's a rotten time for me. We usually get together in the office and pool our bits and pieces and make up the page then." He went on, in a somewhat self-centred fashion, to explain details which were irrelevant.

"I ought to phone Sir Henry at once," said Carole.

"One of the things I came for was to ask you for the number of his rustic hide-away or stately home or what-have-you. When the whole thing's certain I'm going to phone him, officially, as it were, on behalf of the fourth estate, and ask him his views. Then he will say 'No comment' and I'll try and get some sort of arrangement to see him again by dangling something about further information I'd rather not discuss on the phone. Then I might be in at the birth—or should it be the death?—when he does say something."

Carole was worried and faintly resentful of Donald's flippancy. "How will I know what's happened? I'm meeting someone, I'm going out later."

"Well then, you'll have to phone me at the paper after nine or so. If I'm not there I'll leave a message."

"All right, Don."

"Don't look so worried, Carole. If your firm folds you can always get another job or even marry me." He tried to so mix his tone and manner that it struck the right chord of lightness and bitterness, but failed to do so.

"Drop it, Don. If you're going to start being all airy and light with me as well as everyone else, then there's not much point in it, is there? Don't treat me like that."

Donald flushed and made a self-deprecating gesture. "Oh well, cheerio, Carole," he said. "Must fly now." Somehow whenever they were together now it never seemed to go very long without becoming awkward. It was something to do with that afternoon long ago. She shook herself into attention as Donald mumbled some phrases about not waiting for the lift and started towards the head of the stairs.

She suddenly realised that she had been rude to him again. And he had come partly out of concern for her interests as well as his own job. Also his whole manner implied a complete trust in her discretion which is not always so common from man to woman. All she had done was to sneer at the super-ficial armour which he probably needed to put on in her presence to protect the bruised vanity of the rejected suitor. Love's strange yeast was working within her, making her more perceptive towards all men and impelling her towards a long-ing for truth in all relations, not just those with the loved one. She found herself running a few steps down the dusty marble stairway after Donald. He heard her approach and turned.

"I'm sorry, Donald. It was no way to speak to an old friend. You can treat me how you like and use what manner you like. I've no right to object."

"Being a gentleman I can be relied upon not to take ad-vantage of the more ambiguous aspects of what you've just said, Carole." It was plain that he had been hurt sufficiently to refuse to admit having been hurt at all. There was nothing to be done then but laugh and run upstairs again.

She was duty-bound to tell Mr. Dentham something of what might be happening. He pursed his lips and said, "Sir Henry'll never give in, never. He knows a lot of tricks and he's a strong man." He had the air of the batman of some famous general holding forth to a war correspondent.

Carole managed to get through to Sir Henry's place, but the only person in was some foreign girl with an extraordinary accent, who just said "Yes" to everything, whether it made sense or not. She'd have to try later and that might mean a public call-box and fuss over the right change for such a distant call. Might as well wait until she could hear further details from Donald. She too was convinced Sir Henry would not give in. But was he really strong or just stubborn? She began to wonder what exactly was the difference between the two, since it was she herself who had drawn the distinction. 'There's only one sure way of telling,' she thought. 'If a person isn't pig-headed over small, unimportant things, then he isn't stubborn by nature, and if he digs his heels in over something bigger, then he is showing strength.' "But he can still be wrong, of course," she said, falling into her trick of speaking aloud.

When half-past five came she felt oddly little difference in the atmosphere of the day. The vague uneasiness brought on by Donald's news and her own failure to reach Sir Henry never lifted. She said good night to Mr. Dentham and a few others of the staff and they seemed to avoid lingering to talk about the news and hurried away with lowered eyes. It reminded her of the last year of her school-days, when she had begun to feel the war and sense its presence no longer as a child.

All this went when she met Tom and saw his smile and walked with him to the car, aware of every casual movement of his body with every nerve of her own. Then, no sooner did they start talking about things that had happened and what to do that evening than it crept back again. Tom noticed at once, although he was a man. "What's wrong?" he asked. She started to tell him all about the crisis in the firm and the possibility that Sir Henry had overreached himself and about the public take-over bid coming soon. "From your Mr. Thorpley, by the way," she added. Halfway through explaining it all she had suddenly thought that she had never really told Tom about Donald. Neither of them had ever questioned the other about the past and other girl or boy friends. It was one of the things about Tom that made him different from other young men of his type and background. He took her as she was as a person, without involved and pompous theories about what a girl should or should not have done or do. 'Some artists and a few intellectuals are like that,' she thought. 'But Tom's certainly neither of those.' She gave his arm an affectionate squeeze. There is room for every kind of lesser affection within the limitless tower of love.

Having no clue but the gesture itself, Tom misunderstood and said, "Blimey, I'm having a rough time myself these days, but I'm O.K. You're the one seems to be feeling the strain."

She felt it was impossible to go into a long explanation about Donald at that time when they were both tired and hungry. All the same she'd have to tell him soon. She said, "Let's drive out somewhere, to that pub, if you like. Or else somewhere we've never been before." No sooner had she spoken than she remembered that she'd have to phone both Donald and perhaps Sir Henry later. It was going to be awkward from far out, perhaps miles from a call-box, and she'd have to explain. They sat in the car for a moment and Tom lit a cigarette and then just sat lazily looking ahead at nothing down the street. "Oh, let's get going," said Carole irritably. She felt very tense and worried and the atmosphere of the afternoon started to creep back. Things were happening, in the distance, far away out of her control. People she did not really know were making decisions to affect her whole life. As well as having a faint flavour of the war in it, the feeling reminded her of waiting for examination results and imagining the examiners seeing through her answers into her mind, or the time Sir Henry gave her her first promotion and got out her folder and she found he had been making notes about her for three years.

"Blimey! Let's have a smoke in peace," snapped Tom. "It's all right for you. I've been driving about all day."

"Oh, it's all right for me, now, is it? I thought I was the one who was feeling the strain." They went on to snap at each other a bit more. They might have been already married.

Carole was the first to stop, and found to her annoyance that she was having to blink very rapidly. Tom started the car and seemed to change his own emotional gear the minute they were properly moving, for he said, "You know what I think?. I think you've been in that job too long. It's starting to get you down . . ." He made a gesture to her to keep back for a while the angry words he had just provoked. "No, I don't mean it's too much for you or anything like that. You know I think you've got it in the top storey all right. What I mean is that you're too concerned about the blasted firm. There's other jobs. You could get another one easy."

"Easily," said Carole. She felt a second's panic, for it seemed a risky thing to do and she had spoken more from habit than from any wicked desire to provoke him or to fly in the face of danger, balancing the weight of his irritation against that of his love.

However, Tom just said, "Easily. Getting better, though, ain't I?" She felt a bit ashamed. Tom went on to talk about some of his worries as manager and the state of the property market. Just as there were more houses coming on the market and more and more people wanting to buy them the building societies were getting tighter and tighter on advances. Often with other people she stopped listening and just said "Yes" and "No" when they seemed to be called for. This had never happened when Tom spoke to her. Now, however, she found herself drifting away from him, just as if he were Donald or some other friend who did not matter all that much. She began by wondering how it was that the fear of something

awful happening had lifted when she first met Tom and now
had come back in full force. Other emotions, such as delight at
being with him, annoyance with him for sitting calmly
smoking instead of responding enthusiastically to her suggestions to drive out somewhere, a feeling of meanness at having
pulled him up over his grammar when he was tired and
worried, were all simply built on the platform of this basic fear.
'One might have thought,' she said to herself, putting on a
pompous tone inwardly for her own amusement as she often
did, 'that these other feelings would be strong enough to push
out the first one and not just overlay it.' Why was it so strong?
She seemed to hear the voice of one of her old lecturers saying,
"A problem correctly formulated is a problem half solved."
She jabbed and probed around a bit, hurting herself from time
to time but not getting any nearer to the answer. The steady
flow of traffic out of town went on, with long waits at the lights
at each intersection. Tom was still talking in the nervous and
jerky fashion of people who are overtired. He repeated himself frequently and chuckled aloud at his own jokes, nudging
her and telling the climax over and over. A dashboard clock
glowed in the shadows in front of her and she stared at it,
hoping thus to help concentration on the problem of her own
emotional state. 'Assemble the data once more,' she said to
herself. Very well then; something had happened when she
first saw Tom. All the fear of the afternoon had gone and she
had lived in the moment, aware only of his presence. Then
what could have happened? 'Got it,' she thought. 'As soon as
Tom started to talk about his business affairs it brought back
my own. Then mine, at the moment, are worrying and rather
awful, so that brought on the feeling again. Q.E.D.' And no
sooner was this demonstration of logic completed than she
knew it was not the whole truth. The fear was not just of work
but of something else, deeper. Tom's voice went on and she
listened to the odd word or so. The luminous dashboard clock
glowed coldly but cosily in the shadows: It made her think of

the phosphorescent trail of some large fish swimming away through far seas, alone. She was on the edge of a discovery. The slippery fish of self-knowledge wriggled and squirmed in the swaying landing-net of consciousness. She nearly had it, in fact for a momemt she did realise exactly what it was she feared. This moment when she grasped the fish in both hands had come as soon as she told herself, 'What you're up to with all this staring at the clock is trying not to understand rather than the opposite. That's why the subconscious is all set to run you away with fishy symbols.' Caught unaware by a trained trawler crew, her fear was thus landed and held, and flopped and smacked itself on the clear deck, but only for an instant before escaping over the side again so that the memory of its shape faded.

Tom was saying, "So you see, I don't know what to do for the best. The swine don't like us for some reason, and yet it's us who get them all their business." What on earth was he talking about? "No," said Carole, "they don't." She hoped thus to keep things going and pick up some clue in a moment.

"You're not listening," said Tom. She had just time to note that his tone was neither reproachful nor angry. He stated a fact just as he might've said, "The traffic's not usually so thick at this time."

"You're not listening. I was saying how the big building societies don't like us and yet it's us as gets them all their business. I know what it is. They're so bloomin' keen on 'status' as they call it and they think estate agents not only know all the dodges but might go broke any time. Then they know we're wide-o to just how tough it is for them to get possession if we fall behind with the payments. Consequence is that we can get bigger advances for steady mugs in factories earning half our screw than what we can get for ourselves. So I don't want to have to crawl to them. If I can keep my end up as manager for old Thorpley and fiddle a few sales, split commission on the side that he don't know about, I reckon in a

year to have enough to buy us a place outright. 'Course a lot
can happen in a year . . ."

If she pretended that she wasn't really interested in the fish
but had her whole attention upon what her lover was saying
and how plausible it sounded, after all, then the slippery fish
might be lulled into false security, not realising that it had an
experienced trawler captain to deal with, and a wave might cast
it, surprised and gasping, on to the deck, unasked and un-
netted. And so it happened in this case. She was just starting
to collect her thoughts for a proper reply to Tom, to discuss the
possibilities of a maisonnette or even a flat in under a year's
time, since surely with all his contacts he must get to hear of
them, when into her mind came the deep-sea fish, snapping its
jaws and chilling her with a cold and slimy spray: 'What you're
really afraid of is not just that slipping-up-on-the-job-and-
people-knowing-it feeling. What you are afraid of is telling
Tom all about Donald. Not what happened that afternoon.
Tom is Tom, that wouldn't worry him; he'd be rather
flattered at being told and know I'd make it up to him later
when we had a chance. It is about Donald and me hitting it
off—well, intellectually!' This last thought, thus formulated in
words, seemed so unbearably arch and superior that she
blushed hot and was glad of the dark and wished she could lay
her flushed cheeks against the cold, glass disc of the fish-faced
clock. At the same instant all the afternoon and business fear
vanished so completely that she could hardly recall the
sensation. It was stored away and labelled as 'that' feeling,
along with half a dozen other quite dissimilar emotions and
forms of fear all labelled 'that' in the same way. The Carole
who explored the mind of Carole alone knew which 'that' was
meant at any given time. Personal filing systems of this kind
are always inefficient, and for a good reason.

Long before they were nearly out to their pub it started to
rain. Tom pulled over to the kerb outside a metal Pepsi-Cola
sign and a stainless steel cigarette machine chained to a rusty

spike set in the raw cement as if it might graze too far away in the empty small hours. "I can't go on without eating," said Tom, announcing the fact defiantly as if expecting some protest from her. "Besides, it's raining."

Inside the car was familiar and smelt of Tom's cigarettes and of the warm rexine car-seat cover, as it had that first night after the dance, so very long ago. It was dry inside and raining outside and she had reached the stage of tiredness where she just did not want to move. The clock now looked only like a dashboard clock. She felt that if she left the car now she might not only step out into an English evening drizzle but off the world and into outer space where the world itself is less than a dust mote in a fading sunbeam.

"It doesn't seem a very nice place," she said. Sensing a surge of masculine, empty-bellied irritation about to be discharged at her she added quickly, "You deserve a decent meal. Here they'll only have beans on toast or something dreary like that."

"Beans on toast don't sound so dreary to me," said Tom.

She had used a wrong word. Normally she didn't even have to think about being careful with him. Their relationship was so much a part of her consciousness now that she hardly had to think about putting a censorship on arty words. He'd been quick to pick it up, having been foiled of a chance to launch reproaches by her words, "You deserve a decent meal." Why had she come to make the slip? Thinking of how nice it would be to sit in the car a bit longer and not have to get out? *Weltschmerz?* The truth of the matter was far worse. She slid over to the hump between the two worn dips in the seat to the near side, where Tom was standing holding the door open and turning his coat collar up. 'Heavens!' she thought, 'I forgot I wasn't with Donald!' This linguistic betrayal and its significance so chastened her that she clung to his arm across a blank stretch of cement pavement to the steamy door of the café.

The half-glass door bore an 'A' formed by net curtains stretched to stiff fan folds and barred by a green and blue plastic sign saying, 'Open for the sale of the cigarette that SATISFIES'. In the broad window, designed to display shop goods, balanced a large cardboard cut-out of a tall blonde in a red swimming suit standing on the bright yellow deck of a white yacht and holding above her head a bottle of soft drink. Some technician had managed to convey an impression both glamorous yet sexless and, in defiance of the laws of gravity, inertia and physiology, the single raised arm lifted not one breast but two.

The café was surprisingly full, but almost entirely of teenagers. Blue jeans and bright sweaters sprouted and waved in the sour, steamy air like foreign plants in the great glasshouses of Kew. Divided from the other customers by an insufficient number of years, Tom and Carole could neither exchange tolerant and benevolent glances nor ignore the self-conscious chatter about them. For a few moments they could not have felt more ill at ease had they blundered out of the rain into a select private hotel. The owner, however, knew that he had two real meal orders instead of Cokes and cakes, and bustled to their table.

Ordering took the edge off it. The kids started showing off and pretending that the older couple were not in the room. Every now and then a boy or girl would steal a glance to make quite sure that Tom and Carole were watching the gay abandon with which they said some feebly outrageous remark or danced a few steps to the blare of the juke-box.

"All the cats pretend to despise the squares," said Carole. "But if there weren't any squares to try and shock and show off to, then there'd be no fun in being a cat."

Tom smiled and gazed around vaguely. Carole started to think again of how to work things tactfully so that she could phone Donald and perhaps Sir Henry later. She started absently to count the change in her purse, checking the number of pennies, to fool herself that a lack of the right coins might be the only real obstacle. She thought, 'When things get better they get worse as well.' This meant that when Tom and she had first started going out together she had thought nothing of saying, "Excuse me while I go and make a call," and had hinted at what it was about or made up some lie just as it suited her. Now that things were at a different level she had to be more careful.

Emerging from some inner dialogue of his own Tom said, "I'm on the look-out for a maisonnette, too. You get so that you don't like always being in caffs and that. It must be nice to have your own place and . . . and . . ."

"Yes," said Carole, "it must." Plainly he was setting out to salvage what was left of the evening and knew this line of talk to be most near to her heart. The actual business of a possible house for them had been gone over in the car and was simply a worry and annoyance to him. He'd been sitting thinking it all out, how best to cheer things up and from there how to bring her, selfish, introspective pig that she was, nearer to him, to their joint existence, love-state, engagement, or what-have-you. At that moment the juke-box stopped. The young people had been listening and paused for a moment in their chatter so that there was silence. She thought, 'Being in love with Tom, perhaps with any man, is like watching one of those clocks under glass domes so that you can see all their works spinning.' She was in love with Tom and, at that moment, she felt very fond of him as well. 'The two,' she thought, 'need not necessarily go together.'

"Of course," said Tom, "maisonnettes is going up and up too. Area like this one, for example, you'd need three or four hundred and good status to get a mortgage. The blasted societies don't like maisonnettes unless they've got both occupiers on their books. Worst comes, you can't pull half a bloomin' house down and sell the site or build fresh on it, see?"

She checked herself, being about to say "Freshly", and said, "When we've eaten let's work out just what we've got between us and how long before we can buy a place."

"O.K.," said Tom, "when we've eaten. Long enough bringing it." And he looked towards the doorway to the kitchen. Carole faced outwards to the street. The back of the cardboard girl on her yacht had been repaired with gummed paper of a darker brown. She wondered why anyone should bother. Just grumbled and did it as soon as it broke, without thinking about it, she supposed. Not everyone was like her. She had also the side view of a mechanical pin-table on which leaned some of the habitués, watching the bright steel bearings bounce and click downwards, and sticking their bejeaned and angular young hips out into the aisle. The machine sloped up to a glass panel on which were painted orange horses on a green field and numbers and the name, 'Kentucky Derby Stakes'. As the bearings made contact with the obstacle posts a hidden system of relays rattled and ticked and the horses flashed and faded to give the illusion that their relative positions changed. Full of love for Tom, so recently renewed and fortified by fondness, Carole found her feelings of irritation and misanthropy vanish. 'It's not good enough for them, all this,' she thought, looking at the lanky arms linked round the slim waists and the young faces lit in the orange glow from the machine. Just what she meant by 'all this', she could not have defined.

The food when it came was surprisingly tasty and cleanly served. One of the youngsters stuck his head out of the curtained door and swung back, tossing a lank, fair lock out of his eyes, and said, "Stopped raining." As suddenly as a flock of birds they all crowded away, setting the owner to slamming his cash-register till back and forth and letting a bitter draught sweep in from the door as they held it open until the last sweater girl had swayed out. Laughter and the noise of scooters starting came from the street. It became very quiet in the café.

Tom pushed his empty plate away. "Nice to be young, eh?" he said.

"We're not exactly pensioners yet," replied Carole rather sharply.

"No, I just meant, no worries and all that. You know."

"I only know I had bigger worries at that age than I have now. At least I thought they were bigger, so it's the same thing." She was thinking, 'I wonder if he'll remember what we're supposed to do now we've eaten.'

"What'll we do now?" said Tom.

CHAPTER 13

Meeting the Boss

"If only you'd phoned me I could have put you right in the picture," said Donald to Carole. They were lunching together in some dark chop-house he'd taken her to. The high-backed wooden benches reminded her of Daumier's sketch of a third-class railway carriage.

"I just couldn't get to a phone. I was tied up. I was with a friend and we were way out, nearly in the wilds of Bucks, and no phone boxes in sight. I didn't want to have to make a real thing of it and spoil the evening. Besides it was teeming with rain. I just couldn't, I mean . . ." She had not yet told Donald of her engagement. If she had, would that have helped to explain matters at all? She couldn't say to him, "Things were going badly. I panicked a bit. I couldn't risk making him jealous of my work, of you, come to that. I'd funked telling him all about you, so I punished myself by not phoning. And now this mess."

This suppressed monologue forced some of its pathetic and pleading note of vehemence into her actually spoken excuses, so that Donald said, "Heavens! I'm not your worthy employer. If you didn't phone you didn't phone. I just thought you weren't all that interested. Took it as a good sign, if anything. You're rather the career girl, you know. Oh! don't get me wrong." He held up a languid hand in protest, as she started to bridle. "All I meant was that I think you've been in that job too long. You're a bit young to turn into one of those women who've married the firm. You know, glasses and a bun and knows all the secrets. Only person who can speak to the boss and tell him what he ought to know and so on."

"You're the second person to tell me that," said Carole.

"Doesn't necessarily make it true," said Donald. "All the same you don't want to become too attached to that job or you'll feel all the sillier and lost if there's no job to be attached to."

"What do you mean, Don? Things aren't as bad as that, just because our shares have dropped a bit. It's this scare about our new plant and a rumour about Sir Henry losing a big contract."

"That's not the whole picture at all, Carole. The truth of the matter is that Mr. Thorpley, who bought a slice of shares in your respected employer's enterprise from Illstone, sold a few and started a rumour about the loss of contract, hence the drop in your price. Last week he did the same thing and now the shares stand at, what's the latest?—30/- isn't it? A good half year's drop from 41/3. Then, of course, either our friend Thorpley or some other interested party whispered around the market that your Sir Henry had mortgaged his own stately home in Southdownia as heavily as he could and poured the cash into a hole in the dyke, like the brave little Dutch boy. That didn't help much either. What's the matter, ducks? You've gone a bit green about the gills. Now, if you *had* managed to phone I could have told you that Thorpley was going to hold up his public take-over bid and work the same trick again in the meantime. That's how they got the final push down to thirty bob. I phoned your worthy boss and hinted as strongly as I could that I knew something to his advantage to share with me in return for usual exclusives on any public statements of his and the customary vague re-collection of a favour done should the opportunity ever arise of doing me one. Old boy didn't seem to want to play ball at all. When he started to become rude about journalists I hung up, in the general interests of what, for want of a better word, we call our profession. If you'd got in touch I'd have let you know and you could then have told Sir Henry as much or as little as you felt the ethics of your job and your personal feelings for him—oh yes, I know you have some, one always does have for the man who gives one one's first real job. All too late now, of course. The mid-afternoon'll be carrying this." He pushed a smudged typescript covered in printers' instructions across the table and Carole read, "Take-over bid by Thorpley Enterprises for M.M. Components. Mr. Thorpley, Managing Director of Thorpley Enterprises, which is the parent company of Speedy Homefinders Ltd. and of Hearth and Home Ltd., has announced a public bid for all shares in Miscellaneous Metal Components Ltd. These now stand at 30/- and Mr. Thorpley's bid is for 35/- a share conditional upon his securing 60 per cent of all holdings.

"Mr. Thorpley has recently attracted some attention by his dynamic and creative business activities in the property and development fields. His colourful personality and forthright methods have been the subject of favourable comment among business and City circles. It is understood that should Mr. Thorpley's bid be successful he is planning to divert some of the M.M.C. plants to the manufacture of metal building fixtures. Investors would do well to ponder the offer and . . ."

"He'll never give way," said Carole. "He's stubborn."

"In that case we are going to be treated to the spectacle of a battle of rather puny giants. Sorry if I've upset you. I know you're somewhat attached to the old boy. If you are you'd better do all you can to get him to accept and knuckle under gracefully. He's still got a few cards he can play. He could get a reasonable price and retire from the scene. He's getting on anyway. Don't know what'd happen about your job."

"I'd never stay if Sir Henry left and this Mr. Thorpley took over."

"Oh, you've met him?"

"No, just spoken to him once on the phone and I . . . I know someone who knows him."

"Well, it may all never happen. What you're to do now is to breeze back to the office quickly and tell Sir Henry the glad tidings. He'll want to make some public reply no doubt and I suggest you tell him if he gets in touch with me first I can have it printed in the Stop Press of the same edition as Thorpley's bid, thereby, as every child can see etc., etc."

Carole had started to feel slightly annoyed as soon as Donald had touched on her attitude to her employer. The irritation had increased as he had said, "What you're to do now . . ." She did not take orders from Donald Warwick. Now she found his whole manner suddenly intolerable. Both of them knew that his style of speech, rather like a Bertie Wooster with brains, was phoney and normally Donald parodied himself and mimicked half a dozen other types of speech and class mannerisms when they were together. Today, just when it was about something important, he had kept it up all the time.

"I'm not going to do your dirty work for you," she said and, halfway through, tried to give it a serious-joking tone to take the edge off her rudeness.

Donald flushed. He seemed to be hurt again. Carole had a moment to realise that she was quite wrong. He was furious. He looked at her without the slightest hint of the humility of the suitor. His mouth twitched and the petulant brackets curving and enclosing his lower cheeks wriggled like snakes, momentarily out of his control. His eyes lost their deeply-hidden sadness. The only other time she had seen them do so had been on that one afternoon, for a moment only. This time they stared with ugly anger. She met his gaze fully, for she was not a cowardly or timid girl nor was she in love with the man across the table from her. It became plain that some fresh moment of truth was about to come. Perhaps an even deeper level of relationship was about to be exposed. Work and money might mean more than flesh. Carole felt an absurd twinge of fear. 'You're being silly,' she told herself. 'What on earth is there to be afraid of?'

Donald started. "Who's asking you to do my 'dirty work', as you choose to call it? Speak to me about 'dirty work' when you're in the convent or earning your living scrubbing floors. Anyone'd think you were a shareholder in this firm or Sir Henry's mistress. I honestly don't know what you're playing at, Carole. This is all separate from my asking you to marry me. You know damn well we see things the same way. You know . . ." His face had gone a disturbing shade of white. "You know you've always let me think we were on the same side of the fence. What the hell! Anyone'd think there was money in it or something! I've done you plenty of business favours. I'm not even asking you to do one in return, let alone any 'dirty work'." The repetition of this unhappy phrase set off his fury again. "What've you got to be so damned superior about, I'd like to know? Been the house-guest at the ancient pile down in the Southdown Bus country? I thought not! Then what the hell are you? The illegitimate offspring of an old retainer's daughter and Sir Henry? Just because he had some blasted rank in the First World War, which he has had the good grace to drop as a civil title, I must admit, it doesn't make *you* the daughter of the regiment. Why you should think . . ."

He stopped as suddenly as he had begun. His white face turned, at the same time, a most distressing red. He looked down at the tablecloth. "I know you don't like my airy-fairy, blasé act. What you don't realise is that . . ." His redness faded and he started to go white again, but this time not with the pallor of anger. "What you don't realise is that I'm insecure when I'm with you. I don't want you to know how much you disturb me, so I become all the more bland and shallow, and all that nonsense." And he gave the last few words the appropriate illustrative accentation. "So now you

know. If you didn't already." He sensed her flash of pity and
played his advantage quickly, "I'm sorry I lost my temper and
was rude." He sounded like a little boy repeating the formula
ordered by teacher or parent. "I don't often lose my temper.
You really nicked me. I . . ."

She had only herself to blame. If she hadn't wanted matters
to shift to this level of intimacy she should not have asked for it.
If she gave way now, Donald would petulantly refuse her offer
and if she did nothing she would have to go back and sit in the
office knowing that she was thus silently withholding information of concern to Sir Henry, and for the most absurd
reasons.

"I'm sorry, Don. Things are getting a bit much for me
these days and then I'm . . ." She found that it was very
difficult to say simply, "I'm engaged. It's taking my mind off
my work." Things were now such that she would have to
wrap it up somehow and also give more details. *That* would
have to be put off, then, too. The lunch finished awkwardly
and without a decision on the matter of what to say to Sir
Henry.

It turned out to have been an unnecessary worry. When she
passed Dentham's desk on the way in he stopped her.

"Miss Brockett, I suppose you know that there's a special
board meeting been called?"

"No, Mr. Dentham, I didn't."

"There's been a public take-over bid from a property
company. I thought Sir Henry might have told you."

"No," said Carole and, her general dissatisfaction with life
being just sufficient to overcome her scruples of pettiness, she
added, "Thorpley Enterprises, I know," and put on a faintly
worried expression, her mind on higher matters than chatting
with the accountant.

"Sir Henry's stubborn," said Mr. Dentham and this really
meant, 'I've known him years longer than you. You are a
child, an upstart and, worst of all, a woman.'

Carole went through to Sir Henry's outer office and, hearing the door, he buzzed for her to come in. The grey light filtered down the tiled air-shaft and the yellow dome of the ceiling light gave it a quality of unreality and bleakness. Sir Henry's face was the colour of pencil rubbings on a white blotter; with his black coat and white shirt he seemed to belong to the chilly, ghost world outside the window rather than to the warm room with its heavy desk and pale glow from a dusty and inaccessible dome lighting fixture.

He did not ask her to sit down. "I suppose you know what's afoot?" he asked and Carole nodded. "I've decided, that is the board have agreed, to reject this offer and to advise the public not to accept. That's all it amounts to. I want you to draft a public statement for release and let me have it as soon as possible and then see if we can't get it into the City pages of the early evening editions. You'll have to move. Think you can manage a draft fairly soon?"

"Yes, Sir Henry. I know someone, too . . . That is, I know one or two people on the press who might be able to help."

"Fine, good girl! Leave all that to you, then. I've got some rather hectic phoning to do."

When she had finished a draft press release, advising all shareholders not to accept the public offer, mentioning a special company meeting and hinting at development plans, now well advanced, which would make all the difference to dividends next year, she phoned Donald. "Be here in about half an hour," she said and thereby forced her own hand.

"Very nicely done," said Sir Henry, glancing at the typescript. And he suddenly added, "We'll win yet." To protect herself from an absurd emotion she found rising in herself Carole started to think, 'It's too ludicrous. Making it all sound like a grand battle and I the duty WRAC officer to the tough old general.' It was time to take the plunge. "There's a Mr. Warwick, Sir Henry. Perhaps you know him?"

"Heard of him," said Sir Henry.

"Well, I've just spoken to him. The news of the offer is going to be in his paper first. He has some arrangement with Mr. Thorpley about it. I don't know what. I suggested that if he came here we could have our statement in the same edition. . . ." She started to embark on what might well have become a fatal attempt to gild the lily by giving a long and incoherent explanation of how she came to know Donald. Happily Sir Henry cut her short.

"I know the chap you mean, Miss Brockett. I told you I'd heard of him. Send him in as soon as he arrives. Oh, and tell Dentham I want to see him. This'll do nicely, nicely, thanks," he added, tapping the paper she had brought him. Carole smiled and left.

When Donald arrived she took him through the office. Dentham watched them pass with a concentrated indifference, fiddling with his papers and turning to dictate to a girl at his side in a resigned fashion. *Someone* had to keep the wheels turning while the higher-ups and their little pets fooled about.

Sir Henry saw Donald to the door of his own room. They had only been together about five minutes. Donald stopped at her desk, leaned over and said, "Thanks. All goes well. Think your boss is making a mistake, though. He's not on the bridge. Doesn't *have* to go down with the ship, after all. Not that anyone ever does, really."

"There's nothing to thank me for," said Carole. Dentham was watching. She tried to put on a public-relations girl type of smile. Donald sensed it all at once. He held out a formal hand and said, "Thank you, Miss Brockett," in quite a loud and business-like voice. She walked with him to the swing doors and out into the marble-floored landing with its lift cage. There was a muffled rattle of adding machines from other offices.

For some reason the place brought upon her the feeling of their last meeting here the day Sir Henry was not in town and the take-over business had first started in earnest. From out of the blue came the thought, 'If I was really loyal and really doing my job I'd've phoned Sir Henry that evening, Tom or no Tom.'

"Donald," she said, "if I had phoned you, do you think it would've made all that much difference? I mean, what could Sir Henry have done in any case?"

"If," said Donald, "Manasseh Ben Israel had not hit it off so well with the Lord Protector I might not have been here to phone and if Marston Moor had not gone quite as it did the Lord Protector might not have been there to receive Ben Israel's petition and if . . ."

"All right. I get it." If he could not see that she wanted reassurance and not a lecture or a demonstration of his skill at playing historical might-have-beens, then let him go. She pressed the lift button and a mysterious and ancient grumbling and clanking began below in the basement while thick wires slid and trembled like rising snakes in the ornate centre cage surrounding the well, open on all sides. Donald was not to be trapped by the change in her manner. "Looking at this lift reminds one that we stand, in this place, at this time, midway between the New World and the Old. You simply couldn't find a lift as old-fashioned as this in a block of offices in New York. In France or Italy you might find a lot, but with one great difference: when you pressed the button nothing would happen. The thing about the British is that they not only have an ancient tradition but they keep it in repair. Their lifts are still called lifts and not elevators and still work. Somewhere or other there must be an ancient craftsman who knows how the thing was designed to work, just as there are still men who can thatch a cottage roof so that it really keeps out the rain, but take care to cover it with galvanised chicken wire to stop the birds nesting in it and the rats from eating it away. In the Americas they'd just put slates or tiles and in Europe either do the same or put thatch and forget the netting. Here we . . ." At this moment the lift itself creaked into position, only an inch below the floor level it had managed to reach in the year 1908, and Donald boarded it, after testing it with his toe in the manner of an anxious swimmer at the cold sea's edge. Carole laughed in spite of herself. Donald was fun to be with sometimes. He sank from sight down the clattering shaft with a gay wave, which turned to a salute, humming the air of 'Rule Britannia'.

Carole turned to go back to the office, to work and worry. She suddenly thought, 'He gets like that, charming and entertaining, whenever things are going well for him and he feels on top of things. He's excited, like a little boy, and tries to hide it with a lot of extra wit and cynical talk.'

Discreet and unspoken excitement flashed under the lowered lids of junior members of the staff. Foreboding and fear overlay the customary quality of politely concealed dislike in the glance Carole exchanged with Mr. Dentham. Something was going to happen soon but nobody knew quite what. Carole had to work closely with Dentham for the rest of the afternoon. Sir Henry wanted a complete estimate of all liquid assets and even a stock position from the factory and a statement of debtors and creditors down to the last bill from the stationers. It was worse than preparing for the annual Company Meeting because they had nothing ready. Sir Henry kept coming out to see how they were getting on. He complained to Dentham that two of the ledger clerks didn't seem to be doing anything but chat to the filing girls, couldn't he keep them busy? Even Carole had to agree that this was a bit unfair when Dentham could hardly raise his eyes from his own calculations. He went over and spoke to the clerks and the bolder of the two laughed and shrugged before sitting down. It was soon time for the staff to go home. Dentham arranged for tea and sandwiches to be sent up for himself and Carole. It was six before she noticed that he had not filled and smoked his afternoon pipe. She remarked on it. Her workmate seemed surprised and said, "Couldn't enjoy it, in any case, Miss Brockett. Not with all this going on and working at this pace." By seven they had some sort of a figure ready for Sir Henry and took it in to him. He thanked them and left hurriedly, and evidently not for home, for he asked Carole to phone his wife and say he would be very late. The same foreign girl answered and then a rather nice-sounding old lady who thanked her for the message. She phoned Tom. She felt an intense longing to see him, to get away from the atmosphere of the office for a time, to hear his voice. When he came to the phone he said, "Fine. We'll eat and then I've fixed up for you to meet the boss at last. He said he wanted to meet you, so we're to see him in the Jolly Farmer later, about nine, O.K.?"

"I've been working very hard, Tom. I'd rather not tonight, and there won't be time for me to change. . . ."

"What do you want to change for? Stay as you are. You don't want to worry about Thorpley. Just stay as you are." He began to sing, "Stay as sweet as you are," into the phone. She found this intensely irritating. She started to protest again that she was unready to go out and meet people that evening. Tom said, "I'll tell him that we might not make it, then. You'll feel better when you've eaten." He hung up and she knew that he regarded it as settled and that he would not say anything about any possible cancellation to Thorpley.

Mr. Dentham locked up and they travelled down in the clanking lift together and out into a darkened City emptied of its crush of clerks long since. Some odd kind of bond had grown up between them as a result of working together so hard all afternoon. "Good night, Mr. Dentham," she said. "I hope your wife isn't upset. I'm sure I'd be furious if I had a supper all ready and then my husband didn't come in."

"Oh, it won't be like that, Miss Brockett." He gave a polite laugh to show that he understood and was prepared to meet her halfway. "Young Mr. Callard of Sales lives near us and he's promised to look in with a message."

There was nothing more to say and they parted. She

thought, 'How little we know of anybody, really. How little we can ever know.' The vague uneasiness induced by the events threatening her employer mixed with an ill-defined sense of personal dissatisfaction. She seemed stuffed with secrets and false pretences. She thought, 'I haven't told Sir Henry yet that it was I who let slip the news of raising money on his house. I haven't told Tom about Donald nor Donald about my engagement to Tom. I didn't even make it quite plain how it came about that Donald was to have the first news of Sir Henry's answer to the take-over bid.' She continued, whilst walking slowly to the Tube station, to prosecute and judge herself. It was so long after the rush hour that the carriage was nearly empty. It swayed and roared and clattered more than usual and smelt of stale cigarette smoke and thrice-breathed air like a theatre foyer after the audience has left. Behind her was all the worry of the day's events, about her the knowledge of her own moral cowardice and ahead the evening with Tom's Mr. Thorpley.

Facing her an advertisement for woollen garments grinned brightly above an empty, black window, past which writhed and twisted grey-dusted cables. "The pig in a wig did a jig, and the wig was made of wool." A drawing of a pig which fiddled and skipped took up half of the poster but it was the empty jingle which got on her brain. Suppose this Mr. Thorpley started trying to pump her about Sir Henry's plans? Would she get a moment alone with Tom tonight to talk? "The pig in a wig did a jig, and . . ." Quite unexpectedly she realised that she was not looking forward to seeing Tom. It would be nice to think that this was just a customary journey home, rather late but otherwise unexceptional, that she was simply on her way to her bed-sitter, where she could draw the curtains, eat, put on some mules and sit reading and smoking with her feet up. The train swayed and jerked on its way. At least at this time she had a seat and was not squeezed and trampled upon by half the population of London. She drew her coat more closely around her. She felt tired and hungry after the long day. 'Oh well, this bit's all right,' she thought.

When they met she told Tom all about the events of the day. Tom just said, "Oh, the boss's up to a lot of things in the City these days. I reckon he'll be a millionaire before he's done. He's a smart one. Of course I look after most of the property angle of things now." This last was said not without a casual pride. She had a sudden glimpse of his whole attitude. Thorpley was to him the great successful one, to be imitated if possible. The fact that it was her firm which might go under the hammer was just a funny coincidence. Her job didn't matter but his did. Just when she very least wanted it to, the pig doggerel came back . . . "and the wig was made of wool". So triumphant and smug about it! Who makes a living drawing things like that? Do *they* ever worry about telling the truth and not cheating their employers? The lettering of the poster had been in imitation of a child's reading-book. When would she and Tom have a family?

To compensate for still keeping quiet about Donald she gave him every detail of the afternoon, all about staying late and working with Dentham and how the two bosses might have now to fight a real duel. She wanted to bring it round so that Tom and she stood outside it all, watching the machinations of high finance and the struggle between their respective bosses with interest and amusement. But it wasn't like that a bit, not a bit.

Mr. Thorpley didn't look quite as she'd imagined him. Underneath all the bluster he seemed very anxious to please. He slid off a high stool at the bar and came to meet them saying, "Well, the little lady in question, at last, at last! No wonder the boy's kept you to himself. What a smasher, eh, Tom? If I was two hundred years younger you'd have to watch out, I tell you."

Then they all three sat at the bar with Carole between the two men. It might have been an awkward atmosphere with such a difference in ages and the peculiar relationship of Tom and Thorpley, the boss off duty with one of his boys, but the older man took charge and told jokes and kept things going. Carole was faintly ashamed to feel all her university side rebelling against spending the evening in the company of such a man. 'That's just being snobbish,' she told herself. Especially just at that moment, for Thorpley had been holding forth about where they should live and how he might help them. "One of my juniors, lad named Smith, don't think you knew him, Tom, before your time, said to me once, 'How would you go about finding a place, Mr. Thorpley, if it was you that was looking for somewhere to get married?' You know what I said? You know what old Thorpley said? Shouldn't't've done it really, I own, but there it is, I couldn't resist it. I just said, 'Any one of a number of ways, boy. Not one of which is of the slightest interest to you, not having any ready money.' 'Course it was sound enough advice in its way. I was telling him he'd got to get the lolly first. And so he had, so he had."

He turned around on his stool to face Carole and grinned. He pushed his face a bit nearer to her so that she was taken unawares and wanted to turn towards Tom, get him between her and this man. "Hadn't he? Hadn't he, eh?" asked Thorpley and laughed. "You'll have no worries there, on that score at least. Tom'll soon have enough saved up; if you keep him from spending it, of course!" He laughed again very loudly and reached out and touched her wrist and patted it paternally. " 'Ain't that right, boy?" he said to Tom. "You'll have plenty stacked away soon and then you can take your pick of the love-nests, 'ain't that so?" Tom nodded rather vaguely and excused himself. "Hurry back, boy," said Thorpley. "I've a call myself but we mustn't leave your *fee-an-zee* alone at the bar." He turned back towards Carole. "Seriously, now, I've one or two places in mind as might just do you two. I'm glad to see the boy settle down. He's a good boy, that one. I want to see him get what I've missed. Don't say anything to him yet, but I've a place in mind, just coming on the market, as'd do you both fine." He patted her wrist again. He looked round towards the door of the Gents to see if Tom was yet on his way back and lowered his voice. "To get round this business of his status, I'd buy and you could pay me back, say, two per cent or something like that, instead of five or six from the Council or a building society. What do you say, eh? Old Thorpley's not so bad as expected, eh?" He lifted his hand from her wrist and patted her thigh in a fatherly fashion. Fixing her eyes with his own, as if to dissociate their consciousness from the gesture, he repeated, "Not such a bad one as all that, eh?" He patted her thigh again like a jolly old dad. But he left his hand there just a bit too long.

CHAPTER 14

Sunday Tea

Tom finished his Sunday dinner and went upstairs to change and dress with unusual care. Of course his mother noticed. "When are you going to bring her here for tea?"

"Soon," said Tom, "soon. Job to fit these things in. I'm going over to her family's for the first time today."

His mother sighed and fussed round him in the hall, brushing his coat with a seldom-used brush from the wobbly hall-stand. "Should've thought you could've brought her here first." Tom left hurriedly. He'd evidently said the wrong thing again, but then that was always happening.

He picked up Carole at the usual corner. After the last time they'd made an agreement not to talk about jobs and business matters at the week-ends, but since it had to do with somewhere to live he said, "Mr. Thorpley was on to me about a house in Blossom Road. Said he'd mentioned it to you, something about his buying it and us paying him back. I told him that there'd have to be a proper agreement. I mean, you can't just walk into these things. I mean, anything might happen. He might need the cash or something might happen to him and then we'd be evicted by his executors or something. 'There's got to be a proper agreement,' I told him."

"Very sensible," said Carole somewhat coldly. She turned to look at him and then added, "We don't want to start off under any obligations to Mr. Thorpley, thank you very much."

"Now you're saying just what I've said. I told him, I've just told you, I mean I said there'd got to be a proper agreement."

"Can't we do it without him at all?"

"I suppose so. I hadn't thought, not really, I mean. What've you got against the boss anyway? Of course we know he's not as high-class as yours but he's always been straight with me. He told me he liked you. I don't see why you're so down on him, I really don't. If there's a proper agreement and we paid him a reasonable interest, then it wouldn't be such a big favour as all that. He's done me bigger ones than that in the past and he often does. That's the way we work. Take the very car we're riding now. If he liked to turn strict about using it outside business hours, well, I mean . . . And besides he'd no sooner suggested it than I said about a proper agreement."

"For God's sake shut up about the agreement," snapped Carole.

He felt that she had hurt him unfairly and concentrated on his driving in silence. They were getting near her home now and, although he now knew the area, he asked her if there was a short cut down a certain turning. She shook her head and he kept on the same course. In a moment the car was travelling down the street which had been the scene, and partially the cause, of his nostalgic attempt to recapture her childhood and past in his mind some months before. He looked round. Now was the time to ask her all about it; perhaps to stop the car and have her point out spots and places of especial significance in her personal history. Then he could hold her hand and listen to her voice and thus make it all right, get the better of his jealousy. He slowed the car with some vague idea of actually embarking upon this childishness. She glanced at him enquiringly. To strengthen his resolve by inducing within himself the feeling he had known, he looked round and tried to think of her in these same streets years before. Nothing came to him from the view. The streets looked just like streets and the houses no more than low-value property. The name board of a rival estate agents, which had been set up by two young men who had walked out on Speedy Homefinders and set up for themselves, stared out from an unkempt garden. And that was all. The magic had gone. This meant that the pain and indefinable longing had gone as well. He ought to have felt relieved. He felt a strange regret instead.

"Turn right here," said Carole.

"All right, I know, I know," he said irritably.

When they got to the house it was a bit rougher even than he'd imagined. Of course she'd never pretended it was any different. Not her fault. All his own imagination, brought on by feeling about her as he did. Two kids, a boy and a girl, hung and swung on the gate. "Carole! It's Carole," they shouted.

"Careful, you'll have the fence down," said Carole.

They hugged her and the little girl said, "Is this your boy friend? I have a boy friend too. His name's Robert."

They went into a dark hall. They had to edge sideways past a bicycle. Its handlebars had knocked some of the plaster out. Carole's mother came to meet them. She didn't look a bit like dear, precious, silly Carole, only the eyes.

He had to switch off all the valuation side of his mind. The place needed about three hundred, at very least, spent on it.

They went through to a kitchen-living-room of which the overall impression was of steam and dully dirty brown varnish. For a moment he thought they had some builder in for a job of work and were giving him a cup of tea. An old bloke in shirt-sleeves got up from the table and held out a bony working-man's hand. Carole was saying, "This is my father, this is my mother. Mum, this is Tom I was telling you about . . ." He could've sworn that he'd seen the old chap's face somewhere before but he couldn't place it. Most likely he'd been doing decorating or something in a house where he'd brought clients round.

They all sat and talked. Carole's mother kept watching him. The two kids kept running in and out on some game of their own. He was glad when they went to play with some friends in the park. But then things seemed to get worse. The house fell quiet and there was no way either of keeping the conversation going or of interrupting it. Up to then he had been able to make some joking remark to the youngsters, or about them, and Mrs. Brockett to say, "Excuse me," and go and tell them off. Now there was nothing but the four of them round the table.

"I'll make a cup of tea," said Carole's mother.

The person most out of it now became, all at once, the saviour of the situation.

"You're taking on a right handful there, I suppose you know that," said Alfred Brockett to Tom, nodding his thin, putty-coloured face at his eldest daughter. The nettle having thus been seized by one of their number, the gathering were able to converse more freely. No formal announcement of her engagement had yet been made by Carole. What with one thing and another they hadn't even got around to buying the ring yet, as they had intended to do weeks ago.

Before their arrival Mrs. Brockett had said to her husband, "It must be serious or she wouldn't be bringing him here."

Even the most dried out and decayed of marriages remains a marriage, and Alfred had replied, "Kill or cure, I suppose she thinks, bringing him here. When he sees us he either sticks or runs for it." She had met his eyes and there had been a moment's perfect understanding between them, at least over this matter. Then the shutters of habit, spliced and wired with bitterness and old hurts, had closed down again.

Now the conversation was able to jerk on its way and to skate around the dangerous area of the exact nature of the relationship between the two young people.

"Oh, she's a handful, all right. I've found that out," laughed Tom. Mrs. Brockett arrived with the tea from the scullery. The cups clattered, steam rose from the spout of the pot. Emboldened by social success, Alfred ventured on stumbling and heavy irony. "You be firm with her, boy.

That's my advice. Then you'll find remarkable results—she'll do just as she likes!" Everyone laughed and Carole looked modestly down at the worn 'best' tablecloth in the manner of the one being spoken about.

Things warmed up a bit after that and it was soon time for proper tea. The kids came back, tired, quarrelsome and hungry. Tom tried to talk to them but they seemed to have changed their attitude towards him.

Carole sat opposite, along what was clearly by tradition the 'children's side' of the table. He looked at her and thought how here she was in her own home and he was here too watching, part of it all. She leaned across to help spread a slice of bread and butter for her little brother so that her dress stretched taut and creased under the arms into sharp folds which fanned out over her firm breasts. In that way it felt as bad as ever, but something else had gone and he couldn't be sure just what. It all reminded him too much of what he meant to get out of. He was going to get on as the boss had done.

In spite of all she had told him about her family, the romance of her job and her central bed-sitter had hung about her presence for the lad from the suburban estate agent's. Now the romance had gone. He had to face her entirely as a person. The family scene threatened him with a vision of humdrum domesticity. 'Of course I still love her,' he told himself indignantly.

Carole's mother shoved a plate of bread and butter under his chin. "You're not eating much, Tom," she said.

After tea the children went out to play while the light still lasted. The grown-ups stayed talking round the table while Mrs. Brockett cleared away the tea things. After a minute Carole started helping her mother to wash-up. That left the two men at the table, forearms stretched loosely out among the crumbs.

"Care to slip out for a drink at seven?" asked Carole's father.

"Yes. Glad to," said Tom. "We'll wait till the ladies are finished, eh?"

"Blow them," said Carole's father. "We'll get out into the boozer. Get to know each other. What do you say?" Assent was obviously expected. Tom said, "O.K. Glad to. Let's wait for Carole, though. She'll be done in a minute."

"Oh, I meant just for a chat man-to-man," said Alfred Brockett. He had been caught in his shirt-sleeves by this young smart-alick who kept himself to himself so much at the tea-table. "Besides," he went on, "I don't want to take Carole into a public-house round here. If we were all out for the day somewhere it'd be different." He had just this minute made up this scruple and Tom seemed to guess it.

"I quite understand, Mr. Brockett," he said in his best salesman's voice. He seemed to hear Alfred mutter something about, "Glad you do . . ." but could not be certain.

As generally happens when two strange men find themselves thrown together by social circumstances, the two started talking next about their work.

"Carole was saying you were something to do with insurance and houses and that," said Alfred.

"Well, not exactly. At the moment I'm local manager for Speedy Homefinders. We own a lot of property north-west of here. Perhaps you've heard of us?"

"Oh yes. Just doubled some of your rents, haven't you, since this new blasted Act?"

Tom felt that surge of annoyance which is the disguise assumed by a faint and unrecognised feeling of guilt. He was too much the salesman to show it. "Well, Mr. Brockett, rents had become quite uneconomic, you know. I don't think you'll find that we have been unduly harsh with our own tenants."

"Oh, I'm not saying your lot's worse than the others. Just as bad, that's all."

An awkward silence fell. Tom tried to re-take lost ground by a few less pompous remarks, but the rift still yawned.

The subject was just dropped and they tried to reach some
common ground over football and so on. Tom had the easy
salesman's type of small-talk, but all the same the two women
noticed something when they came back into the room. "Now
what?" said Carole to her father, standing straight in front of
him. He shrugged and smiled at Tom, as if to say, 'You see,
that's what we have to put up with from our women-folk.
Trying to stick their noses in and make something out of
nothing.' Tom, too, felt that Carole had made a mistake. You
shouldn't speak to another member of the family like that in
front of a visitor.

There was a moment of silent discomfort. Mrs. Brockett
knew the only thing to be done. She took Tom's arm and said,
"Come into the next room and get the telly warmed up and
tuned for me. The kids'll be back soon and if we can sit them
down straight in front of it till bed-time we might all have a
minute's peace." Tom fell at once into the rôle of being the
civilised person out to help his hostess to smooth over a social
unpleasantness. He rose to the occasion and started talking
about what programmes came on at that time, and what sort
of a set was it, and so on.

The children did not appear. In the end Mrs. Brockett and
Carole had to go out looking for them. Tom offered to come
too so that he would not have to be left alone with her old man
and could be near Carole, but Carole's mother showed less tact
than she had done earlier on and kept insisting that he should
sit and watch the telly. "Why don't you go and fetch a couple
of bottles from the off-licence, Alfred?" she asked brightly.
Tom was about to say, "Good idea, I'll come with you. Then
we'll be back about the same time after you've found the
youngsters," but Mrs. Brockett went on, "Come on, Carole.
Let's find the kids and leave these two to get on with it."

The lines cut now by sex instead of generation.

The telly roared and chattered and flickered and flashed. It
was a strain to try and keep things going in any case in that

racket. Much easier just to smile and nod and follow Mrs. Brockett's suggestion.

Carole tried to fix it. She allowed her mother to take her arm and move them both towards the coats hanging on hooks above the bikes in the cramped hall. She looked at Tom and smiled, with a kind of smile she didn't want her mother to see, switching the division back from age to youth, from one generation to the potential begetters of the next.

When Tom and Carole's father arrived back from the wine-shop the women and the two children were already in. For a time everyone sat and watched the telly. Then it was bed-time. Carole went up and helped her mother say good night to the kids.

The two men sat silent whilst quiz programmes and com-mercials shimmered and glittered across the bedazing screen. The women came downstairs. One thing about all sitting round the telly, nobody had to risk starting off on any dangerous subjects again. It all got a bit boring, though. Carole's mother fetched in coffee and sandwiches. Then they left.

It wasn't until they were in the car that he felt the force of what had happened. All the mystery had gone out of Carole. 'Of course,' he told himself very indignantly, 'I still love her.' It was for the second time that afternoon.

"Now," said Carole. "Just what *was* going on with my father?"

"Nothing. I mean, he seemed to think it was something awful to suggest that we should all go down to the pub. 'No daughter of mine' he said and all that."

"That's silly," said Carole. "He doesn't really mean it. He wanted to assert his authority somehow. You caught him in shirt-sleeves. Then, of course, he only stayed dressed like that to show off. I'll bet Mum was on to him about it before we arrived and that'd make him more stubborn than ever." She seemed to forget about the really important thing, which was how he fitted in with her family and about her old man being rude to him the first time they'd met. "That's something she's never understood," Carole went on, looking straight ahead through the windscreen. "She knows a lot. More than I do, *and* she's my mother, but that's something she's never understood."

"Why do you think it's just being silly of him to object to you going to a pub?" Tom couldn't think of anything else to say in order to bring the talk round to what mattered to him. He knew it wasn't really a question of her old man being 'silly' at all.

"Oh," said Carole. "He took me into my first pub. Wanted to show off his brainy daughter. He made me talk about my exams to a lot of his old British Legion boozing pals. I loved it. I suppose I should have hated it but I didn't. The funny thing is that we were daggers drawn then and having terrible rows all the time. It was a sort of favour we did each other, like two enemy armies exchanging wounded prisoners. Besides he's worked in a pub since then. Washing glasses."

Then he remembered the face. Carole's father was the glass-collector at the Lord Roberts. He hadn't been in there for a long time. He started to recollect the last occasion and to try to remember if it was then that he had seen Carole's father, but the memory was too dim and confused. All he could remember was the deal that he'd been on, that day. Carole started saying something and he hadn't been listening. ". . . if you didn't. And besides we won't live near them and *we'll* never get like that."

Tom had only just the sense to stop himself saying, "Well, I hope not. I'm not so sure, though. Getting married wants a lot of thinking about." In fact he embarked upon this statement, so that he had to check it and change to, "Well, I hope we'll see something more of them."

This seemed to both of them a somewhat odd remark to make about his future father- and mother-in-law. Its main implication, however, Carole saw at once. He wanted the present situation to continue for a time, indefinitely. Having a girl friend and visiting her family suited him better than visiting his wife's family.

"Tom?"

"Yes."

"You haven't told me everything that happened between you and Dad. What else did he say?"

"Nothing. I told you, just about how you mustn't go into pubs and all that."

"You're sure that there was nothing else?"

"Blimey! Carole. How many more times? I've told you that that's what he said. If there was anything else I'd've told you."

"All right, you needn't sound as if I was cross-examining you."

"Well, don't sound as if you are, then."

He did not suggest driving her all the way back into town. He stopped outside a convenient Tube station and it then became necessary for someone to break the silence.

The most customary thing was to start fixing up how and when and where they could next meet. Not starting to do this straight away suddenly gave both of them the feeling that something frightening, irrevocable and important was about to happen, that a terrible mistake was going to be made and that nothing could be done to prevent it. Each thought, 'Well, I don't see why I should have to give way first.'

A car hooted behind them. It was a bad place to stop. Carole said, "Oh well, I'd better go. You know what the trains are like on Sundays." Tom leaned across, managing not to touch her at all, and opened the car door. She got out. Tom slid over the seat, looked up at her for a moment and then hauled himself up and out to stand facing her. Still their eyes did not meet. She turned to go.

Tom said, "I'll phone." She nodded without turning

round. When she reached the Tube entrance he knew that he had only to run after her, not even to speak, just to catch her up and let them look at one another, for it all to come right again. He took a half step. Without looking round, Carole bought a ticket and went to the head of the escalators. It was too late.

Tom drove slowly home. As it was a blasted Sunday, the pubs were already shut. He felt like a drink by himself and a quiet think.

When he arrived home his mother was waiting to hear all about Carole's family. "Did you think to suggest that we should meet Mr. and Mrs. Brockett?" she asked. Tom had to say not and add, "What with watching the telly and so on there wasn't much time for talk."

"What's Mrs. Brockett like?" asked his mother.

"All right. Got on fine with her."

"What's the house like, then?" she said.

Tom didn't answer. To take his mind off things he went over some accounts ready for the morning and planned his week's work as far as possible. He was still winding things up and selling stuff. Every day, about five, the boss'd phone him and ask the position. It must be something big going on, because up to now one of the things the boss was always ready to do was to take a chance and put through deals on credit. He made you think of a juggler with a set of clubs. If he once failed to catch one the whole lot would come spinning and crashing down.

Later his mother came to say good night and put a cup of cocoa at his elbow. She had another try and brought his old man into it as an ally. "Perhaps next Sunday you'll both come over here, Tom," his father said. You could almost feel her nudging him. Tom looked up vaguely, keeping his lips moving, and saying, "Six per cent on three thousand is . . ." and then, "Sorry, what was that?"

"Your father," said Mrs. Stanton firmly, "was just saying

that it would be nice if you could bring Carole here next
Sunday. Now that you've been over there, I mean."

Tom was a business-man and had learnt to listen to what
people said, even at home, about something like this. He
thought, 'She hasn't the sense, or can't be bothered, to hide
that it was all her idea and not his.' Aloud he said, "I don't
know yet. If things go on like this I'll be working next Sunday
sorting out my accounts and not going anywhere with any girl
friend."

"Don't work *too* hard, son. Time you knocked off for
tonight, anyway," said his father, plainly glad enough of an
excuse to drop it all.

His mother had to admit temporary defeat but for some
reason seemed more cheerful. It was as if the men of the family
had consciously combined against her, yet lost a battle. "Good
night, dear," she said.

No sooner were they both safely upstairs than Tom fell to
thinking about Carole. He felt that he had behaved badly,
that he had been mean. Right from the very first she had never
tried to disguise a thing about her family. It just wasn't in her
to do it. Then why did he feel let down? What the hell was he
expecting? That they'd all be kings and queens or something?
He sorted the remaining papers, started to plan his opening
remarks to the first possible buyer he was due to meet on
Monday, and put all his papers ready for the morning in the
top-quality leather brief-case his mother had given him on his
last birthday. Then he went to bed. Just before falling asleep
he thought of Carole almost certainly doing the same at that
time. This brought it on very badly, but he made himself
think, almost say aloud in the darkness, 'Oh well, she should've
said she was sorry for snapping at me like that.'

Across five miles of asphalt, bricks and mortar, slates and
television aerials, with the lights at the intersections winking red
to amber-and-red to green with hardly a person about to see

them, Alfred Brockett and his wife happened to have Tom's name on their lips.

"He's a spoilt only one, that's plain enough," Mrs. Brockett was saying.

"I put him down as a smart-alick," Alfred replied. "She could do better than that," and they both nodded. "But it's no good saying anything to her."

Mrs. Brockett was about to say, "No good *you* saying anything, I agree," but managed to check herself. It was a slightly unreal and theatrical pleasure to them to be sitting and agreeing about something. For many years the only common ground had been bitter remarks about their neighbours and the manner in which their friends brought up their children. About anything positive or to do with their own families they argued, disagreed and fought.

"Still, you can't say she's exactly rushing into anything, our Carole," said Mrs. Brockett. They both smiled at the thought of their daughter's self-constructed nunnery.

Alfred had drunk far more than his share of the beer which he had fetched with Tom earlier on and then had rushed out and bought himself another bottle. Now he ventured, "Perhaps things'll work out all right for her. She's got her head screwed on."

Both knew that this was meant to convey, "Things haven't worked out well for us, perhaps they will for her." Mrs. Brockett might have been expected to bristle and answer back, but she just said, "Let's hope so," and went upstairs to bed as if it was assumed that Alfred had no interest in following her and would potter about and make himself a cup of tea. This, in fact, he did. No word more was spoken. Thus the two raised a temple to the future happiness of their eldest child and laid upon its altar as sacrifice the admission of their own failure.

CHAPTER 15

Lucky in Love

LOOKING back on the period later, Carole supposed it had lasted about a fortnight to three weeks. At the time it seemed to take place in that realm outside customary human reckoning. She went to work in the mornings after the post had brought no news from Tom. She worked in a hectic and ever more threatening atmosphere as Thorpley's plans for the take-over began to operate successfully in real life. In the evenings she cooked a meal and pecked at it, strode up and down her bed-sitter like a zoo-caged tiger or wandered desperately around places and haunts which they had frequented since the start of their affair. Tom did not phone. Twice she went into a call-box during the day and nearly dialled the offices of Speedy Homefinders. The second time, as part of the process of resisting the impulse, she stroked and wavered her finger point over the cool, metallic perforations both shielding and revealing the magic spelling of her desire.

Time after time she added up the factors of the problem and always arrived at the same answer. Whenever she tried to think about her own feelings in the matter everything became lost in an all-pervading fear of a still deeper loss, whose pos-sibility she would not accept. If she tried to think her way into her lover's head and heart the matter became plainly an emo-tional tug-of-war. Who would give way first? It seemed to her that it must be herself and against this answer to the sum all that was strongest in nature, reinforced and disguised as 'a matter of principle', protested and rebelled. Thus the forefinger of action hovered and paused over the indifferent dial of contact.

In the middle of it all Donald phoned her and there was nothing to be done but accept an invitation to lunch. He knew more of what was going on in the duel between Sir Henry and Thorpley than she did herself.

She had to hold herself in tightly all the time she was with him. If he noticed he might put it down to the way things were going with the firm.

Typical of Donald that he should take her to somewhere quite new for lunch. She had had the impression that the chophouse, with its ancient smell of dust and coffee going back to the days of Dr. Johnson, was a regular haunt of his, but he seemed equally well known at the rather brassy, loud and open place much further west to which he took her this time. The headwaiter bowed and scraped around him. An orchestra of six elderly former refugees scraped out sprightly tunes and craned grey necks over the rests of violins so that their white collars gaped and pointed like the prows of ships.

Catching her eye Donald said, "The point, or rather points, is, or rather are, that the food's not bad at all, it's out of the City here and no rumours will start as a result of 'that fellow Warwick's been seen lunching with that queer girl that old Harry trusts for some reason best known to himself.' The surroundings are not so congenial that one is tempted to linger over liqueurs, which neither of us happens at the moment to have time to do."

Carole smiled and said something about Donald always knowing the right places. They talked of films and plays and the careers and mishaps and successes of mutual friends, and then ate. An extraordinary tightness, which refused to go away, however much she analysed its cause and tried consciously to overcome it, settled coldly in Carole's inside these days and forced her to do no more than chase her food around her plate and tuck the meat under the vegetables and hope Donald wouldn't notice; which, being Donald, of course he did.

However, he made no comment on her lack of appetite and

over the coffee put his elbows on the table and started to lecture. "I think you should know what's going on and what's going to happen, my dear," he said. "After all we're old friends."

Carole nodded. For once she just could not be bothered to make up some words or compose an expression of the correctly friendly yet chilling kind. She looked brightly but quite blankly at Donald as if he were no more than a client of some kind calling with an enquiry in Sir Henry's absence at the office.

Donald paused to take in and swallow the full taste and quality of her gaze and then continued, "Your boss should've sold ages ago. I didn't think so at that time either, but then it didn't concern me so directly, and it was only one of many things I had to think about." Carole watched vanity and that deeper vanity which must always appear in the form of self-depreciating frankness battling in Donald's features. She knew which trend and tendency would win. "All the same I had rather under-estimated our friend Mr. Thorpley's realisable reserves, I must admit. "When," Donald went on, "Thorpley issued his first public offer saying that he would buy all shares in your firm at 35/-, after they'd sunk from 41/3 last year, your boss should've jumped in quickly and taken up all he could lay hands on himself, even if it meant selling up part of his plant, mortgaging the ancient pile still further and sacking Miss Brockett and all other highly paid employees. Instead of this, however, he issued his statement advising the public not to accept. Now the public are accepting, have accepted. Together with the chunk he bought from Illstone—think you know him —a long time ago, Thorpley now has a controlling interest and is going to move in. Now then, listen close—as our new hero has a habit of saying. He asked me to lunch yesterday and as good as told me his next move. Let me just add in parenthesis he's very shrewd. He said to me, 'I've got you weighed off, Mr. Warwick. Every man has two things that drive him, money and something else. With you it's being in the know. Well now, I'll put you in the know. And in return you can put old

Thorpley in the know about one or two things as is beyond *his*
ken.' " Donald, chameleon-like, imitated Thorpley's mannerisms and intonation so perfectly that Carole had to giggle.
For a second she even felt gratitude. Donald did things so well
that she had been momentarily quite lifted out of herself, even
the cold weight labelled 'Tom hasn't phoned' faded. Donald
made life seem brightly under control, all a great big joke. He
was good to be with when you were feeling low.

"Now," Donald went on. "You and I might think he'd set
about going bull and boosting his new holdings up as much as
he'd knocked 'em down. Not a bit of it! His plan is to knock
'em down so far that your Sir Henry has to sell his own holdings for whatever he can get before they are completely valueless.

"In return for 'certain services' rendered, I may say very
long ago—'old Thorpley never forgets a friend'—I am going
to be given first exclusive on all public statements. I can tell
you now that the next one is going to be on the lines that he has
uncovered 'grave mismanagement' at your concern and it will
be a long time before there is any dividend. He reckons that'll
just about knock the bottom out of any remaining value. Then
Sir Henry'll have to sell quickly before all his own holdings
become quite valueless. After that Mr. Thorpley plans to re-
form the company and merge it with his own property concern
and launch out into building, building components, part
backing of big contracts with others in the top twenty and so
on. He's got Illstone lined up as a kind of tame stag to take up
the new issue, and of course there'll be 'considerable interest
aroused' and all that. That's where I'll come in."

Carole had now additional call for gratitude. At least one
fear was lessened. She now knew the worst as far as her job and
her professional future were concerned. She was not going to
work under Mr. Thorpley.

Donald went on, "I'll now sport a bit of cash as a bear. It's
ten days off account day. You could do the same, Miss
Brockett, if your scruples would let you."   P

Carole said, "No, I couldn't. I wish I could help Sir Henry somehow."

"No," said Donald, "you don't at all. What you really wish is that everything could go on the same with no threat to him from Thorpley and no need to think for yourself nor to take any decisions."

The orchestra scraped and nodded and jerked its way through a Viennese waltz. Donald had landed a blow on her and she was in no fit state to parry. With a vision not comforting but frightening in its clarity, she saw that there was absolutely nothing she could do about things. If she went and told every word of what she knew to Sir Henry he would only either dismiss it as City gossip put about by his enemy or dig his heels in still more. Only now did she begin to understand *Jurgen*, the story of a man who has a second chance in life and makes exactly the same mistakes.

She thought of her own rôle in all this. Tom was right not to want her. This pulled at her sharply indeed and, to the surprise of both, she snapped out at Donald, "I didn't ask you for one of your brilliant analyses of my state of mind, thank you. The trouble with you, Donald, is that you always think you can have your cake and eat it. If people were pastry you might be able to. You brought me here to pretend to help me but really to show off how clever you are. Then you switch it round so that you try to get under my skin. You blasted men are all the same."

"Men," said Donald, outwardly quite unmoved by her outburst. "Men. Why should you be generalising about men? Are you in some kind of a jam, Carole, apart from your job and so on?"

In the most shameful fashion, aware of what she was doing and certain that she would soon regret it, Carole found herself, first hesitatingly and cryptically, with bitter generalisations and mysterious references, and then in a rush of detail, telling Donald all about it.

Donald listened and put his elbows on the table with his shoulders hunched and looked at her with his deep, sad and luminous eyes, for the moment unshuttered by shrewdness, and nodded from time to time. He did not speak until she had stumbled to a finish and then he said, "Either he packs you up or he doesn't. Now we'll just consider these alternative possibilities if you'll bear with me." Carole had started to blush—and with Donald, too, of all people! What on earth had possessed her to let go and tell him?

"If he doesn't," Donald went on, "there is nothing to be said by me. If he does, then you are going to find yourself, in a modern setting, with a very old-fashioned object known as a broken heart." Carole smiled, trying to put a brave and gay front on it. Donald took one swift look at her face and she knew he had her state of mind as accurately measured as a balance-sheet. "Now," he continued, "the technique for dealing with a broken heart is simple. First, ignore all the Cheerful Charlies of every age and clime—'This heartily know, when half-gods go the gods arrive'—and all that bunkum. It's hell and it takes more than the Spirit of the Age of Progress to prove that it isn't. Next—and this is peculiarly a modern problem—don't dream of patronising the couch trade or think that re-reading Adler or Jung is going to help. If he didn't want you before you told the psychologist all about it, is he going to want you after? '. . . Prithee why so pale? Think'st if looking well won't win her, looking ill will do it?' Then, you should not try and fight against all the self-indulgence and self-pity. Go and mope around all the places you have ever been together." Carole winced slightly and Donald tactfully failed to notice.

"Go over and over everything you ever said and did together until your state is indistinguishable from that of total obsession. Here is where the Warwick system differs so from all traditional methods. Don't 'try to put it all out of your mind'—it isn't really your mind any more, it's partly his. That's what the priest-craft and the couch trade boys can't understand. I shouldn't really tell you why I give this advice. It might not work now, but with someone like you, Carole, I know you'll only ask anyway or else work it out for yourself as soon as I've stopped speaking, so I'll tell you the theory. You keep on doing these things over and over with all the self-pity and self-dramatisation you can muster and, sooner or later, you'll begin to feel just a teeny-weeny bit foolish. After that it all starts to heal. Of course there'll always be a scar and it'll open slightly and suppurate every spring. Meeting 'after long years' isn't always such fun either, but there it is. There's just one thing more, the most important thing of all. Habit and the body will pull you through but you must give them a chance and eat and sleep, calling, if need be, modern chemistry to your aid. The good old body will go on doing its bit and each day making you a tiny bit better than the day before. The body doesn't ask a lot, just a chance to function. Now we come to the important bit. It can't function if you fill your lungs with coal-gas from the oven or have your trunk chopped up by train wheels. If need be, throw out an anchor ahead on to the mud-flats and drag yourself hand over hand towards it. Say, 'I'll do it in three months if I'm no better' and when the three months is up say, 'I'll give it six months more just to prove Donald wrong.' There, that's all there is to it. Of course if you meet by chance, or in the course of business, just be bright and witty and charming to show him what he's lost."

Carole had been looking down at the tablecloth and Donald delivering his lecture to an imaginary audience above her left shoulder. Partly to conceal how near the mark his words had gone but mainly to keep the conversation going and thrust out of her mind the thought of the possibility that Donald's advice might be needed, she looked at him. He really was clever and very human. Thinking to please him she said, "Good heavens, Donald. How do you know all these things?"

CHAPTER 16

London Bridge is Falling Down . . .

DONALD's information proved true. In a short time the City was full of rumours of Sir Henry's difficulties. There was a further drop in his shares. A stormy meeting of shareholders, of whom Mr. Thorpley was now the largest, elected him to the board. An 'independent committee' of shareholders was set up. This was dominated by Thorpley, who enjoyed himself dazzling, cajoling and bullying his fellow members consisting of a retired army officer with various small investments, elected for his moustache and accent, a clergyman who was the administrator of the estate of some old acquaintance of Sir Henry's, and the junior solicitor employed by one of the smaller trust companies.

The committee met and issued a statement saying that there had been serious lack of firm management and over-investment in ambitious expansion schemes at a time of growing credit restriction and economic uncertainty. Thorpley had turned up at a meeting with the draft ready in his pocket. It had been surprisingly well put together. The committee wondered who could have done it for him.

The shares fell still further. It was time to move in for the kill. Thorpley invited Sir Henry to lunch.

Sir Henry started out to walk to the Royal Consort Hotel as he had done so many times over the years. There was the hint and threat of an early autumn fog in the air. He thought of other lunches and past crises surmounted in years gone by.

He was still here and so was the City. The lobby felt a bit cold and damp, as if it were losing its battle with the drizzly, smoke-heavy air outside. A few yards in, over the worn carpet, however, and the familiar smell from the grill-room won the day.

Symbolically there was no arrangement to have a drink first. He paused in the lobby for a moment and Thorpley came bustling up to him. He'd brought one of his tame committee men along for some reason. Most likely so that he could have a witness to his triumph. He'd chosen the clergyman.

They went in and ate. Sir Henry ordered a mixed grill and took a pint of bitter with it. There was no talk of golf and such matters on this occasion. The little stooge was obviously enjoying himself. There were always jokes about country clergymen among City sharks; well, here was one quite at home there.

When they had eaten Thorpley said, "I told you in this very place, Sir Henry, that one day you'd have to sell to me for a pound. No, that day hasn't come. You're going to sell to me now for ten bob."

Sir Henry had taken an exact review of his forces during the last few days. He had nothing much with which to fight but he now brought up such guns as he had.

"I know very well your plans for the company, Mr. Thorpley. What you forget is that it'll take some pulling up after all the knocks you yourself have given it. Now, I'm very well known in the City. My name still on the board would be a help and, as well as that, I know the whole production side of the business. You'll start off by making enemies if you squeeze me right out."

He was about to go on, but Thorpley cut him short, "You don't know the whole production side of what I'm going to produce, only what you used to produce. That's two different things. I've got it all fixed where I'm going to sell the stuff when it is produced, markets as you and your lot know nothing about."

Thorpley believed in hitting a man when he is down. "If you can raise any cash after the mess you've gone and got yourself into you could do a lot worse than buy in again, in a small way, in a few weeks' time. There'll be a new issue and a lot of ballyhoo. You could get in even before the stags if you liked to fix up with me."

Sir Henry thought, 'Heavens! what have I ever done to make such an enemy of this fellow? I suppose it's because I rather patronised him at our first meeting. I'll not knuckle under completely now for the sake of a few hundreds. It's not worth it.'

'Stags' are those speculators who take up new issues quickly and in small amounts and sell again as soon as the initial rise has taken place. They are regarded as partly a nuisance, keeping 'real' investors away, and partly as being useful in creating a stir and keeping a new issue afloat through its first difficult days. Sir Henry was being asked to help raise a monument to somebody else above his own grave.

"I expect I'll manage, thanks," said Sir Henry. Irony, however, is no weapon for use in Britain and least of all with Britons such as Mr. Thorpley. "Yes, yes," he said. "We all hope so, we do *reelly*, don't we, Reverend?" And that old idiot nodded like a mandarin and put on his helpful, parish-visiting face.

Over cigars and coffee they really got to grips and Sir Henry had to give way altogether. The clergyman bridged the terrible gap and made it end, on the surface at least, like any other business lunch.

They shook hands in the hall. Thorpley indicated that he was going back 'to the office' as he was now fully entitled to do. For some reason this made Sir Henry think of his staff. Dentham was staying on. Miss Brockett had resigned and asked him for a reference. It was rather touching to see how badly she was taking it. She seemed to be very strung up and tense these days. He went below to the washroom.

That night he'd have to tell Mary all about it. If he had been a younger man with another ten years of fight in him it might've been different. As it was, he could only kid himself for a time if he felt like it, and then in the end have to face Mary saying, "I don't understand, darling. If you say we have to move, then we have to move, but why does Olga have to go? The Home Office might cancel her permit if we sack her and it's just now, when she's settled in so well, that we ought to stand by her. . . ." The whole feel of his life came upon him as it had not done for a long time. Christ! What a mess! Saying this to himself in previous years had, after a few moments, always resulted in the upsurge of aggressiveness and courage necessary for survival. When your back is to the wall you suddenly find that not only must you fight but that you can as well. That is all to the point if you are a young man, but if you are old, then you wait, you pause, you expect the urge for an almost vindictive punching back to come tingling up from your toes, as if you had just downed a double rum on a cold night, but instead nothing comes to you, only a sense and sensation of your own old body in its clothes, with its ailments and its dryness. 'Damn it,' thought Sir Henry, 'I'm finished. I'll be lucky to keep out of Carey Street as it is and Mary and I will have to live on that tuppeny-ha'penny annuity I've been carrying.' Even in these thoughts there was an element of self-deception, for such imaginings carried him forward some weeks or months to the time when it would all be over. The immediate future did not mean licking his wounds in a wretched small house somewhere with a bewildered Mary fretting over him. Before that time came there must be weeks of walking about and working with the sense of failure, of cutting down on taxis and drinks and ignoring the whispers and glances of his City acquaintances.

He walked slowly back to the washroom. Harris was sitting

dozing in his cubby-hole and jerked up to his feet and fussed around him with a clean towel and a new bar of soap. Some automatic device set all the flushing system going at the row of slabs and the pipes clanked and grumbled.

This was often the nicest moment of the day. After a good lunch, when things were going well, he would freshen up and have Harris brush his coat and then stroll back to the office in time to check on the closing prices and sign some letters. Then he could get away to London Bridge before the rush. His life was rather like the plumbing in this place, old-fashioned perhaps, but solid and still in working order. He squared his shoulders, just as always, and washed his hands. Glancing up he saw a reflection in the enormous mirror over the basin. In the background Harris was salaaming his way around some-body who had just emerged from a cabinet, and the mirror on the far wall repeated the pantomime. He could see the back of his own head. He habitually shook himself out of day-dreams and did so now, looking himself square in the face and picking up the hair-brush. An old man looked back at him. He looked into his own eyes for perhaps the first time since his adolescence. Damn it, he'd had a good lunch. Whatever else may have happened there was no reason to feel queasy. 'Ought to com-plain to the headwaiter, damn silly thought. Nothing wrong with the food. It's my fault, not theirs. Grill was all right, bitter not off. God! it's my fault, all of it.' All at once he had to cross to the slabs and steady himself. The rounded top felt cold against his damp palm. His dizziness increased as the body concentrated itself to commence the first spasm of reversed peristalsis. There was time to lean his head forward and to think, 'Harris'll see,' and then down between the points of his neat, black shoes, into the stained drain trough, fell the slimy, part-digested grill, curdling in two pints of good English bitter beer.

Oh well, if it had happened, it had happened. He shook his head aggressively and had a sudden picture of himself wobbling about as if he were a very old man with the tremors.

"Took bad then, sir? Took bad, was you? Dear me, dear me!"

"Quite all right now, Harris, thanks. Can't think what it was. Never done that since I was a boy."

"Sure you're all right, sir?"

"Quite all right, Harris, thanks."

" 'Kew, sir. 'Kew very much."

Harris swung the heavy door open. The automatic flush switched itself on behind them. The old, one-legged magpie watched his back for a second. His face was set in an expression of venomous and total contempt.

Sir Henry held his head well up and walked through the dining-room with a vague plan of asking for a glass of water and a brandy. The waiter was just clearing up their table. The sight brought back the whole feeling of the disastrous lunch. He walked straight past the table. His face was the colour of the white cloth grinning through the cold cigar ash.

Outside, on the steps, he paused for a moment. The fog had held off but high smog, trapped under the clouds, shut all the sun's rays from the City, making it colder and darker except for an unreal, yellow luminosity. All the lights were on in the offices and the buses. He could see the people sitting inside. The newsboys were shouting the first early evening editions. One day soon they would be shouting the news of his own defeat. The air chilled his damp face. He walked down the spacious steps towards the darkened bustle of the cold and ruthless City.

CHAPTER 17

A Lonely Walk

Tom asked some of the fellows how you did it. At once it became plain to him, for the first time, just what it meant to be the manager. They all snatched at the chance to meet him on the old terms of equality and yet avoided offending him. He'd done it himself often enough to know the symptoms. It occurred to him that that was how old Thorpley must often have thought about him. All the same the boss'd never let it show. He'd better try not to either.

So there was nothing left for it but to ask Thorpley how to go about it. The boss'd only had one when he sprung it on him. This didn't seem to handicap him any. He started right in, "Going a bit wrong is it, son? Well now, what you've got to remember is this: a girl'll never pack up a bloke until she has something else either in mind or already lined up and in tow. Think about it a minute. A girl may have all the inde-bloody-pendence as she likes but she can't go round the boozers, nor even eat out regular, without a steady boy friend. Consequence is that she don't ever pack a man up until she has another one under her thumb. Mind you, this don't mean that either of them is fully aware of it yet, but all the same she's ready to start on her next attempt. How do you set about packin' her up? Well, boy, the words you use, and all that, is up to you. Just remember this: make it definite. Always remember a woman is cleverer than what you are. Don't leave her any loophole. Don't do it in any caff or pub or restaurant as is likely at all to make you feel bleedin' senti-mental. Choose a place as is new to both of you, and then do it. Just say it and don't let yourself enter into any arguments. Remember you're the man and she's the woman and you're telling her that you don't want her. That's all you have to remember, boy. The rest comes easy. There's only one other thing: you'd better get it stuck into another one quick or you'll start wantin' the first one bad, real bad. Now, I'll put my cards on the table, you know old Thorpley, he's like that. I don't mind giving you a few days, a long week-end, off if you need it to make some other rare piece. Just say the word and I'll understand. I won't ask questions. I'm trusting you, boy, to get yourself over it with a mini-bleedin'-mum of dis-bloody-ruption to all concerned, especially me. Just do it, that's all I ask. And then get yourself over it as best you can. Always remember, you're the man, after all's said and done. And, knowing you, I reckon you have done it, all right!" This set him chuckling and spluttering into his drink and over the bar, whilst Tom had thus time to think and wonder how the boss knew it all, and resent the fact that he did.

When he thought of Carole's gentleness towards him, ages ago at that dance, he knew for a certainty that he couldn't do it. Then when he thought of all the boss had told him and warned him against and of how she had put on airs, correcting his grammar and all that, he felt hardened enough to do it. Besides she only came from a crummy house round about 'The Poets' after all. He went on and on, busy screwing himself up to it.

She phoned him. This meant that he had won the game of seeing who could hold out longest, but the victory meant nothing now. Both seemed to sense that a bigger battle was coming. They fixed up to meet. For some silly reason Carole insisted on making it in 'her' restaurant. He was feeling pretty scared by the time he got there. Suppose she carried on at him or cried. One of the lads had even pulled his leg about finding himself sued for breach of promise. He thought, 'With all this work I've not had time to look for my own place; then she starts blaming me and running old Thorpley down all the time. What's she got against him anyway? You couldn't wish for a better boss than him. And look how he's got on!' He continued exaggerating her faults, working up a sense of injury from the recollection of old, forgotten tiffs. He asked himself, with a touch of pomposity, conscious that he was doing the right thing, dealing with a personal problem in the way the magazines told you to, 'What do you really want?' No doubt about the answer, it was to live like the boss, only now, while he was still young enough to enjoy life. Looking back, it seemed the reaction had started as soon as he'd proposed to her.

When he saw her sitting at the table he knew it was going to be tougher even than he'd feared. He sat down and ordered. She looked at him. No sense in putting it off, prolonging the agony. All his prepared speeches went out of his head.

Leaning across the café table with its dark-green tartan-check cloth, he said, "I've something to tell you, Carole. I've stopped loving you."

"I know," she said. She had gone very pale and looked suddenly and desperately round the room as if searching for rescue or escape.

"You go," she said. "I can't move just yet. Besides there's the order. Go and cancel yours and go."

"I don't think you'd better stay here," he said. "Why not go home? You'll feel much better when you've had your tea."

She seemed to have shrunk, become much smaller and gone away into herself. "I'm sorry," he began, "I . . ."

"You go," she said. So he did.

Outside he didn't feel relieved nor ashamed, just very tired and suddenly hungry. He drove away quickly and stopped at the first pub he came to. The bar was nearly empty. He caught a glimpse of himself in the mirror behind the bottles of fancy stuff on the shelves. He didn't seem to look a bit different.

"Yes, sir?" asked the barmaid.

He was about to order his customary glass of beer and some sandwiches when he felt a terrible pang of pity for the girl he had just left. Oh well, it was too late for all that now. He'd try something a bit stronger.

"A double gin-and-tonic, please, miss," he said. It always seemed to make the boss feel more cheerful.

Carole seemed to be witnessing her rejection from some high vantage point in a gallery permanently fixed above any street or room in which she found herself. From this observatory she watched an act of sickening brutality. "You'll feel much better when you've had your tea," affected her in much the same manner as the reading of the account of some act of bestial cruelty towards a dog or horse might have done. It seemed almost unbelievable that Carole Brockett should have been treated in such a fashion.

All this nonsense only lasted two days. 'One might,' thought Carole, 'have supposed that such externalisation and objectivity would have brought its own reward in the form of relief.' This generalisation, occurring some time during the fourth day, was intended to lessen the blow. Alas! It served only to underline the fact that the initial state of shock had worn off and the real suffering was about to begin.

Not many of Donald's tricks seemed to help very much. She had seen him once since the break with Tom, to ask his advice about another job. As if life wasn't difficult enough, she had to start on all the business of writing letters and attending for interviews, filling in forms and checking on dates of forgotten exams.

In the meantime life went on. All over London there was the pig poster which had so irritated her during her journey to meet Tom some weeks before. Sometimes it was stuck next to one of those sharply grey, brown and black ads showing leafless trees, an autumn sky and a ploughed field and telling you how nice it would be to go and walk in the country and how to get there. At other times it was next to the head and shoulders of Victor Mature, wearing a tropical shirt, with a background of palm trees and somebody's bosom and jagged, scarlet lettering underneath.

Pursued by the pig doing its jig, she went to work and back to her room. Something Donald had said about being bright and charming put her on to a clue in the search for fresh detail to fill in her memories—these had become her main pre-occupation and obsessive hobby, to which the cares of the present provided a tiresome distraction. In some fashion, she had known as long ago as the evening of that drive out to the café with the pin-table that it was going wrong. Perhaps the jilted always knew first. The other person had already stopped loving, so he lost that little bit of extra awareness, but the about-to-be-jilted, still fully in tune, knows but refuses to admit the truth. That was why she had made herself especially, desperately responsive and charming and bright the last few weeks before the end; pretending that there was not an icicle in her tummy growing slowly upwards, like a stalagmite, later to jab and tear at her heart and chest.

In the endless weeks following her dismissal, all this and many other aspects of the matter had been turned over and over in her mind, a dreadful personal prayer-wheel which only the pressure of work could stop spinning in rasping rotation.

In between working, applying for jobs, and sleeping there didn't seem to be much choice: either spinning the prayer-wheel and helping the icicle to grow by ". . . you'll feel much better when you've had your tea . . ." or else THE PIG IN A WIG DID A JIG.

One Sunday she decided to nurse herself along a bit. Well, it was Donald's advice, wasn't it? And he was clever, wasn't he?

So she decided to have a hot bath and then either go to bed

and read or else get away right out somewhere, for a walk or a show or something. She asked Mrs. Lenton, sitting in her tattered armchair in her basement kitchen with the cat on her lap, if anyone had booked the bath. "Not at *this* time of day, Miss Brockett." So she put the pennies in the blackened geyser stuck like a scale-model traction-engine over one end of the high-legged, Victorian bath. It spurted its boiling jet on to the rust-streaked enamel. The high ceiling was criss-crossed with cracks and dark patches like a highway map. Men tenants and boarders had left flecks of shaving-soap around the wash-basin and hair-oil spattering the mirror like fly spottings.

Lying there in the warm, reading the name-plate on the geyser over and over in order to keep away ". . . you'll feel much better" and "THE PIG IN A WIG . . .", she suddenly became very consciously aware of her own body, as a physical object occupying time and space. She thought of it coldly, as if it were some clothes she was washing out instead of herself, looking down her steam-wet chin at the long, white legs under the soapy water and at the strange, dark triangle you didn't think about and the two nipples just clear of the surface, thinking only, 'He doesn't want it, so what use is it?'

When she had dried and re-dressed this unwanted body she knew it was impossible to stay in the room for four hours and then go to bed with something cosy to read like *Pickwick* or *Lorna Doone*. She had to get out of that room.

She put on a pair of low-heels and her olive-green coat with the high, coachman's collar, and walked out into the London afternoon, a dark, slight figure with the shoulders hunched unbecomingly as if she dared not relax for fear the pain of the icicle would push her chest apart and she might scream and be taken away, still screaming, to the loony-bin, or else fly apart into little bits, explode. That was being silly, of course, but that was how it felt.

She walked across the damp square and down the empty

Sunday-afternoon street towards the soapy, rain-cleaned white, blue and red of the Tube sign.

The tall, old buildings mouldered, peeled and flaked away under a high, yellow sky. Already a few lights were turned on and you could glimpse an orange lampshade with a fringe, two budgerigars in a cage or the flicker of firelight on a dusty, moulded ceiling. Every ten yards a juicy and hempen smell of coal sacks hung over little blackened iron port-holes as if there were, underneath, a rope factory with a canteen serving roast beef.

An empty bus swayed past the end of the road and she glimpsed a young clippie bending her knees inside the coarse, blue serge slacks, on the platform, like a skater taking a corner, and reading the *News of the World* as she stood. Two Indian students in stiff, new, grey gabs looked vaguely after it and then bent their heads over a street guide.

'London,' she said to herself. 'Just a Sunday afternoon in London and you live in a bed-sitter and have a broken heart. There's nothing to be afraid of in that.' Thus will a child scribble its name laboriously in the front of a story-book and add, 'Northern Hemisphere, World, Universe', in its first painful gropings for firm ground on which to stand between the no-man's-land of the childish subjective and the implacably hostile reality.

She huddled further into her high collar. 'This bit's all right,' she thought. For the first time in her life the incantation failed altogether. 'It' remained as it had been before, anything but all right.

The sight of the two students had reminded her of men, and that started off such a rage of hurt pride that she all but stood still and stamped her foot.

'If you are really as bad as all that,' she told herself, 'then it is silly to feel a fool.' Yet when she faced the ticket man in his little glass hutch, that was how she did feel as she said, "To the end of the line, please," and, meeting his bored eyebrows, raised by a supreme effort of the will, it seemed, as if he owed it to himself to seem surprised and impolite, "As far as it goes, then, please."

There was a pig poster facing her and she had to stare at it for a very long time, and then the black and red worm of the Tube train hissed up, rolling back its jaws.

She sat, thinking of nothing, with her knees pressed tightly together for a long time while the train rattled and roared and the doors slid open and shut. Then it didn't go any further. "All change, all change," a West Indian girl shouted. She came out on to a platform and climbed some fresh cement steps into a clean, tiled entrance-hall smelling of disinfectant and fresh air. A shuttered fruit shop and a cigarette kiosk faced her, looking as if they would never open again. It was all very different from the feel of a Tube station in central London. 'This bit's all right,' she told herself, but with even less hope than before.

Outside, it was already dark, and the lights, hanging from high, concrete posts, set shadows jerking across the roadway as the leafless trees moved their branches.

You had to climb a lot of steps to get away from the station and then there was a big hill. Everything was dark and strange and it would have been easy to get lost. Once, in a magazine which she had read as a girl, there had been an article about loss of memory cases. The well-documented stories were full of things which no imaginative writer would dare to write, for nobody would believe him. But life does not ask to be believed and so the article told of the overworked business-man on his way to Perth in Scotland who 'came-to' twenty years later running a shop in Perth, Australia.

The point was, she thought, that all these people seemed to have been on the way to somewhere. 'To get away, to get away,' they must all have been thinking. Then something had gone 'click' and there they were with no memory or with a brand-new fantasy to take the place of recollection. Where there is no recall, then there can be no shame and humiliation, nor any fear. 'I am going mad,' she thought. But this really only meant, 'I wish I could, so that whatever happens would not be my fault.'

She turned down a side road. A lumpy bank of earth and clay ran along the edge of a newly-dug trench. Broken bricks and builders' rubble littered the waste ground, from which mounted the trunks of twisted trees. It was as if the land had not yet submitted to being built upon and resented becoming a suburb. So it tried to make things difficult by tripping you up with lumps of clay stuck with pebbles and thrusting coarse grass up between the new paving stones; whilst the old oaks stood their ground and shook their arms angrily.

Why was the weather always so different as soon as you got outside London? In town she had hardly noticed the wind, but here it ballooned her skirt and coat, making her shiver, and stung her face with a fine, cold rain smelling of dead leaves and wet cement.

Side by side the little houses climbed the hill each as identical as the steps in a stairway, and yet each having a different viewpoint and relation to all the rest. Then the road turned to an unmade stretch of pebbles and gravel full of puddles and motor-cycle ruts and it became even darker, with new, fluted-iron lamp-posts showing their rusty roots but not giving any light yet. And then, all at once, the road led into a part of the old town. There was the vicarage with high walls and dark, damp grounds and big houses made into flats and their gardens left to go wild and ragged, as if there were now not enough people living in the district to tend these, instead of too many. In the High Street tall sodium lamps glowed orange in the haze. You would think that they ought to have made everything shine with a lovely golden light, but instead they sucked the colour from the shop-fronts and turned the scarlet sides of passing buses to a muddy brown. Heavy trucks and coaches, cars full of family parties on their way back from visiting relations, swished and roared along the wet road. One half of the world was upstairs listening to the wireless or watching the telly in cosy flats above the shops and the other half on their way home by car and coach. She was neither.

At the top of the hill the road forked and she chose the darker and quieter of the two ways. She had not realised how high it all was. Looking out through a gap she saw a whole valley of houses dropping, step by step, away from her, all with their lights on and drawn curtains. Although it felt as if she had been wandering about for hours it must only be about eight o'clock. Bedtime! The tea things washed-up in every little brick box of all those hundreds, children were watching the telly with bright eyes and the firelight falling on their red cheeks. She thought, 'Never for me. Never for me, now.'

She allowed self-pity to douse and drench over her, that soothing balm which leaves the sore worse than before. But a hard corner of her mind said, 'It's too stupid. It's like "The Little Match Girl".' She turned, crossed the road, and walked on.

Now genuinely lost, she wandered around corners and down unlit turnings, finishing in a muddy path leading into some kind of park. The moon rose, high and pale, and black clouds streamed across it looking like the smoke from tugs on the river pulling out one of those great silver and white liners, so large that it seems not to move at all but to be fixed against a gliding background of cranes and buildings. Was the earth racing past the moon or the moon around the earth? 'That's just being silly,' she told herself. 'The moon goes round the earth and the earth goes round the sun and . . .' A gust of the late autumnal gale rushed up, pulling at the limbs of the old oak trees so that they groaned and screamed in rage. She hurried back to the street. This part of the town was lit with old-fashioned gas-lamps flickering slightly, the panes of clear glass rattling in the wind.

She came to a small cinema with an unusual name, not one

of the London circuit sort. It all added to the feeling of being
out in the country. The rain set in harder, bouncing and
splintering in the car headlights and that made a good excuse.
So she crossed the road and went in.

The fug inside was stifling and the grey flicker of the screen
seemed to melt out into a haze of cigarette smoke. Down in the
cheaper seats at the front a gang of the local lads whistled and
catcalled at every clinch. Their rough, newly-broken laughs
were not quite cockney and not quite Home-Counties burr
either. She thought, 'I suppose if you brought Professor
Higgins here to listen he could tell you straight away what part
of London you were in.' This would have been something to
explain to Tom, a joke to be shared, if he had been there, but
he was not. Probably having his tea and feeling much better
by this time. "Got rid of Carole at last. It was getting too
much. Pity, but just one of those things. She took it very well,
really. . . ." 'Curse him! May he rot in hell! Oh no, I didn't
mean it, Tom. I'd die for you!' But what to do if the person
you would die for doesn't care if you live or die, except in so far
as he may be said to have a general philosophical bias in
favour of life for human beings?

The goodies on white horses were chasing the baddies on
black horses. There weren't even any of those interesting flat-
topped mountains to look at. It seemed a very complicated
plot to do with forged bonds and railroad land and the Wells
Fargo stage being late. When the aged star got his girl in the
end and kissed her, there were more whistles from the front
rows and grunts and a shout of "Get in there". Then there
were slides of the shop-fronts of local tradesmen and for a car-
hire firm, very black and white with tasteless lettering and
fancy puns, with a bride in a white dress stepping into a huge
black car. More whistles and catcalls from the front.

She gave herself up to what she had really wanted to do,
going over every incident and fragment of their love affair,
each separate day and conversation and gesture, searching for

a clue to the puzzle of what went wrong, like an impassioned archæologist turning and examining the fragments of a mosaic scooped up and dumped down by an indifferent shovel, finding every now and then some faint indications of a pattern to the puzzle. But each sharp chip to this pavement was a piece of her heart.

JEFF THE JIFF MAN jumped out on to the screen and painted the room 'in a jiff' with his tin of JIFF enamel. "Dries fastest, lasts longest," squeaked out JEFF. "Your home too can be a brighter place . . ."

'I can't stand it,' she thought, stood up and pushed past the knees of the people in her row. Two sprawled lovers, the boy with his shirt open and tie-knot slipped down his chest, looked up at her in a dazed and appealing manner, sorry they couldn't move their legs in time, sure she would understand. She forced her way through, all but kicking at them. "Blimey! Where's the fire, dear?" said the boy. He wasn't shy of women any more.

The fresh, gusty night was a pleasure even though it made her shiver. It had all been a silly idea. Bed straight after that bath would have been better after all. Unexpectedly at the end of the street there appeared the Tube station, seen from quite a new angle, and she ran towards it, making the rain an excuse to any passers-by.

On the platform she had to make up her mind. Facing her was one of the big sort of pig posters on the curved wall of the Tube, next to a brewery series on the Four Seasons. ' "Season of mists and mellow fruitfulness," wrote the poet John Keats . . . even in his day the House of . . . and what, after all, more mellow than a glass of . . .' and so on. And that damned, soppy pig next to it with its full-bottomed judge's wig falling to midway down a fat, pink belly dented by a human navel, the trotters skipping out the steps on a lizard-green field so that you would know that it was an *Irish* jig. The dust had settled in a fold, almost a bulge, of age running right across this particular reproduction of the accursed poster, fawn and grey so that the light cast a sharp, black shadow just in line with the bow with which the pig scraped out its jig, elongating it unrealistically. Oh, well! it made a change. THE PIG IN A WIG DID A JIG AND . . . ". . . And now go home, you'll feel much better when you've had your tea." Who but a man could be so smug and cruel and pompous all at once? "THE PIG IN A WIG . . ." Stop it! Stop it!

Coming down shivering out of the rain there had been the West Indian mind-the-doors girl opening a dark wood door with a shiny brass knob. Carole had caught a glimpse of a tiny room, hung with a time-table and with grey-painted pipes running up the walls and across the low ceiling. There had been a tin kettle on a dangerous-looking glowing ring. One of the perks of working with electricity, she had supposed.

If she did it now, flung herself forward so that sparks came out of her ears, or whatever it was that happened, then it would seem like having given in to the pig, as if it had won. She really couldn't do it with that for a tombstone above. Next morning people would come and stare and wonder if this was the exact spot or not. Later other people would not even wonder and you would be forgotten.

Besides, look at the trouble it would cause! It wouldn't be fair when you came to think of it. Others had their lives to live even if you didn't want to live your own. That West Indian would come running up and the guard go to an emergency phone in some mysterious metal box at the end of the plat-form. And then all the form-filling for everyone. When it was over they would sit in that cubby-hole, under the grey pipes, and the driver would stare at the *Daily Mirror* without really seeing it. ("We two old codgers say that lace-panties are a girl's own concern . . .") and say, "Proper puts you off your supper, a thing like that, don't it? Looked quite a pretty girl, too, I mean, before, I mean . . ."

Faintly in the distance there came the rumble of an

approaching train. Now or never. She swayed slightly and then stepped back. When you reach the end of the line you either stay there or go back again.

The escalator rumbled and creaked upwards. It didn't seem to want to work on Sundays nor so late. At night they always made this complaining noise and at other times you barely noticed it. Outside, the empty, Sunday feeling had gone. It was like any other evening very late in London. Couples with nowhere to go now that the last cinema had shut waited at the bus-stop. The high wind seemed to have failed to penetrate to the centre of the city and the air was full of a fine drizzle, like cold steam, which muffled the traffic noises and wrapped the city in a damp flannel blanket smelling as if it had been hung too long on a high clothes-line catching the smoke from a sooty chimney.

Back in her room she washed out some stockings and hung them on the back of a chair to drip on to a newspaper. She undressed and got quickly between the cold sheets. Although her feet felt frozen she did not push her hot water-bottle down but hugged it like a child to her chest, as if its bulk could fill the imaginery cavity under her left breast, somehow melt the icicle inside her. She had mistaken her element. This process was to be accomplished not by heat but by time.

London,
April 1957–December 1958.